Of BETTER BLOOD

Of BETTER BLOOD

SUSAN MOGER

Albert Whitman & Company
Chicago, Illinois

Library of Congress Cataloging-in-Publication
data is on file with the publisher.

Text copyright © 2016 by Susan Moger
Published in 2016 by Albert Whitman & Company
ISBN 978-0-8075-4774-8

Printed in the United States of America
10 9 8 7 6 5 4 3 2 1 BP 24 23 22 21 20 19 18 17 16 15

Cover and interior illustrations by Kyle Letendre
Design by Jordan Kost

For more information about Albert Whitman & Company,
visit our web site at www.albertwhitman.com.

For Trudy and Charlotte

The laws of nature require the obliteration of the unfit.
—Morgan Grant, *The Passing of the Great Race*

The science of improving stock...means [giving] to the more
suitable races or strains of blood a better chance
of prevailing speedily over the less suitable.
—Sir Francis Galton, *Inquiries into Human Faculty
and its Development*

PART 1
UNFIT

CHAPTER 1

New England States Exposition,
August 1922

Four times a day I drop the baby.

It's not a real baby, but for a stunned heartbeat the audience believes it is. That's enough to get some of them on their feet, screaming, *Stupid, clumsy, gimp.* The words slide into my skin and stay there.

When I ask Mr. Ogilvie, the director, if just once I can catch the baby before it hits the stage, he frowns and puts his hands on my shoulders. I squirm away, but he holds on. "I love your sensitivity, Ruthie," he says, showing corn-yellow teeth. "But sadly a cripple like you can't be a hero."

Mr. Ogilvie isn't the only thing I hate about the Unfit Family show. I hate the name of my character, "Ruthie," who limps like I do but has no backbone. No one ever calls me my real name, Rowan. I hate the ragged clothes and the idiotic things Mr. Ogilvie tells me to do. And I hate the people in the audience who think they're not only better off than we are, but better in every way.

Today when Mr. Ogilvie calls, "Places," I follow the script. Lie on my stomach, breathing in dust, legs toward the curtain, arms stretched out upstage. I look like what I'm supposed to be, a help-less quitter who fell and can't reach her crutch.

The late August afternoon sun turns the tent into an oven, bak-ing all of us, actors and audience, in the smells of fried onions, tobacco, hair pomade, and sweat. The other actors mutter as they take their places for our opening scene. I can see their feet—Jimmy's clodhopper farm boots, Minnie's worn moccasins, Gar's dirty spats over scuffed black shoes. I'm barefoot.

The head of a nail pokes my thigh, and I shift position.

Mr. Ogilvie's voice sounds from the other side of the curtain, high-pitched and irritating. "Welcome to our show, *The Unfit Family: A Blight on America*, created by Miss Fanny Ogilvie espe-cially for the New England States Exposition of 1922."

The last statement is a lie. We have performed the same show at county fairs all over Massachusetts for the past month. But these shows at the Exposition in Springfield are worse. There are four shows a day and more people in the audience for each one.

"The actors will act out the story as I narrate it," Mr. Ogilvie goes on. "And now allow me to introduce the Unfit Family." The pulley squeaks as he tugs open the curtain.

Sharp gasps from the crowd make my stomach clench.

Mr. Ogilvie points me out first. "Lying before you where she fell is Ruthie, the crippled daughter, thirteen years old." Like crows, the audience's curiosity and pity land on me, peering and pecking at my leg, back, and head.

Mr. Ogilvie didn't just change my name; he shaved three years off my age for the good of the show. He told us, "Your job is to portray the worst family imaginable. But don't take anything I say to heart. I'm talking about the characters, not *you*." On the other hand, he tells us, "Don't act. Just be yourselves."

"Over there by the table," Mr. Ogilvie goes on, "epileptic son, Jimmy, fourteen, is in the throes of a seizure, unable to speak. In the laundry basket is Baby Polly, nine months old and already neglected. And at the stove, feebleminded Minnie, their mother, watches a pot of boiling water. Minnie's shiftless husband, Gar, father of the children, is seated over there with a whiskey bottle, his constant companion." Gar always gets a few nervous snickers from the men in the audience. Today someone whistles.

The stage creaks as Mr. Ogilvie paces, drawing in the crowd with his confiding voice. "Some may find this portrayal unbelievable. I assure you it is no exaggeration. Many, many families are destined by their heredity to live like this unfit family."

The word "family" is my cue to get up on my knees and crawl with difficulty to my crutch. Crawling isn't easy with my weak left leg, but I play it up to please the crowd. Once I have the crutch, I struggle upright and turn to face the audience.

The wooden benches are full, and it's standing room only in the back. Men in suits and women in Sunday-best dresses snap their paper fans back and forth, wafting sweat and rosewater into the hot air.

I pick up the basket with Baby Polly in it. As usual, Jimmy, in the grip of a fake seizure, bumps against me. As usual, I let go of one basket handle. Baby Polly falls out.

A gasp flutters through the audience like a gust of wind. One woman calls out, "For shame!"

"Ruthie tries," Mr. Ogilvie says, "but as you can see, when it comes to caring for a baby, she is unfit."

Ruthie isn't "unfit" and neither am I, Rowan Collier. As the daughter of Dr. Franklin Collier, scientist, inventor, and historian of our family heritage, I grew up knowing we are the fittest of the fit. Family has always been important to us. I'm named for Father's great-grandmother, Opportunity Rowan Collier. Father decided that Opportunity sounded too old-fashioned, so I am plain Rowan.

CHAPTER 2

Gramercy Park,
New York City, 1914

I was eight years old and on an important mission. It was so important that I had to disturb Father while he was working. Softly, I knocked on the open door of his study. The shutters were barely open on this hot afternoon, and it was dim inside except for the golden pool of electric light from Father's crookneck desk lamp. Familiar smells of cherry pipe tobacco and oiled leather welcomed me. Father looked up and smiled. "Come in, Rowan. Sit down."

A rotating electric fan on the desk fluttered Father's papers, so he weighed them down with his paperweight, a miniature sailing ship.

"Julia is published again." He handed me a folded newspaper. "The latest *Betterment News* has her article arguing that the best people, people like our family, need to marry and have large families for the good of our country."

When I was little, my older sister Julia was my chief playmate. Nanny, who lived with us and took care of us, was kind but too old and creaky to get down on the floor and play. But once Julia started working for the Betterment Society she became too busy to spend time with me. She even brought her work to the breakfast table. Just this morning after Molly, our cook, served the omelets and left the dining room, Julia said, "Molly really shouldn't have any more children. She has *eight* already. She is Irish after all." She waggled her butter knife at Father. "Please speak to her."

Father had taken a bite of his omelet and sighed. "I will speak to her of *this* with pleasure," he said. "A perfectly made omelet is a gift fit for the gods. Molly manages perfection every time she cracks an egg."

Julia frowned.

"You know, Julia." Father cut another piece of omelet. "A wise man knows when to hold his tongue."

Now in his office, Father struck a safety match and held it to the bowl of his pipe as he sucked noisily on the stem. "Julia collects valuable information and writes about it," he said. "She is a foot soldier in the Betterment cause."

"Are you a *general* then?"

Father laughed. "Not a general. But as an engineering consultant to the U.S. Navy, you could call me a captain in the Betterment fight."

He pulled a typed page from under the paperweight. "Now," he said, "I've been working on our family history. Would you like me to read some of it to you?"

I nodded yes. This was a detour from my mission, but Father's book was important too.

"Very well." He read aloud in his deep voice, "'The soundness of my own family, Dutch-English-French, through fourteen generations is unquestioned. My wife's family made their fortune in the stony fields of New England and the gold fields of California. They married well for generations before we joined our heredities. Our daughters represent the finest qualities of both bloodlines.'"

He looked at me. "Do you know what that means, Rowan?"

I squirmed on the chair, my sweaty bare legs sticking to the leather. All I could think of was the question I had come here to ask. "Um," I said and then found an answer. "Is it like the time when you said I got over the measles so fast because I'm a Collier?"

"Exactly right." Father beamed at me. "When we Colliers are tested by a catastrophe or an illness, we draw on the strength of our family heritage." He sucked on his pipe. "Well done. Never forget that, my dear."

His praise gave me courage. "Father, please tell me about Mother," I said in a rush. "I would really like to know more than I do." I'd memorized this opening and had no idea what would happen next. Whenever I asked Julia about Mother, she said, "I loved her very much." Which wasn't very informative.

While I waited for Father's reaction, I studied the portrait of Mother hanging over the fireplace. Sir John Lavery painted her in 1891. In the portrait Mother wears a high-necked white dress. Her auburn hair is piled high, but a few strands hang down by her face. She looks straight out of the frame with a slight smile; her brown eyes gleam.

Father cleared his throat. "That portrait captures her perfectly. That light in her eyes." His voice shook. "I always feel her presence in this room."

He dabbed at his eyes.

"Tell me one thing about her." I lean closer to him. "Please. I won't ask again."

I expected him to say, "She was a good mother," or "Everyone loved her," so I almost fell off the chair when he said, "She was a photographer."

He pulled open a desk drawer and handed me a red leather photograph album. Here were photographs of Julia as a little girl, posing with her toys and dolls and squinting at the sun. Father, in a one-piece, knee-length bathing suit, stood in the surf holding Julia on his shoulders. Julia, who hates the ocean, smiled at Mother, the photographer. All the photographs were labeled *Paradise-by-the-Sea*, the island community off Long Island's south shore that has been our summer home for years.

On page after page, Julia smiled out at me. In the last photograph in the album, she sat in a white party dress with a big white bow in her hair behind a cake blazing with candles.

Mother wrote under the photograph in white ink, "Julia's 10th birthday party, April 3, 1906." Two months later I was born. Mother died the same day.

The photographs of happy Julia made me feel lonely. "Why did Mother die?" I blurted out. "She had strong heredity. You say so in your history." The words rang in my ears like hammer blows.

Father cleared his throat. In his lecturing voice, he said, "Sometimes a family weakness goes unnoticed until it strikes someone in perfect health. *But...*" He slapped his hand on his blotter and I jumped. "You and Julia did *not* inherit this weakness from your mother. You both take after me, and we Colliers are strong stock."

He took the album back. "These are not her only photographs," he said.

"Where are the others?"

"Look around."

The framed photographs on the walls of the study were as

familiar as the smells of pipe tobacco and leather. I jumped up to look closely. Flowers and shells, the front stairs in a shaft of morning sunlight, a seagull perched on a sand dune, and my favorite, bird tracks crisscrossing in the sand. One lip curl of foam nudges the edge of the picture.

"You always said these were Mother's," I said, "but I thought you meant they belonged to her."

"They do," he said proudly. "She had a very special way of seeing beauty and bringing it to the attention of others."

That night Father brought Mother's camera to my room. A small, black box with a knob on one side and two little windows. A silver lever that made a satisfying click when pressed down. A round eye in front and a celluloid orange circle in back. I looked up at him. "Thank you for showing it to me, Father."

"It belongs to you now, my dear. You have an eye for the interesting that is so like your mother's. Julia has no visual sense at all."

The next week I was allowed to take the camera with me to Long Island. Father put in film and explained how to wind it. Then he helped me look through the viewfinder and press the shutter release.

"Good luck with that old thing," Julia said the first time I took her picture. "These days everyone prefers the latest Brownie."

Father had my film developed in Freeport and bought me an album of my own—blue leather with black pages. We discussed photography the way he and Julia discussed the Betterment Society. I photographed her at the table in bright sunlight surrounded by note cards. "What are you doing?" I asked as I clicked the shutter.

"Researching ways to keep our country strong."

"Julia, a Patriot," I later wrote in white ink on the black page under the slightly blurry photograph.

"Father, an Architect," was the label for a photograph of him standing on the beach next to his sand sculpture of the Parthenon.

For three years that camera connected me with both Mother and Father. I felt Mother with me when I photographed the beach she loved. I learned from Father about turning film images into photographs in the darkroom. Then, like a print left too long in the developer, everything in my life went black.

CHAPTER 3

New England States Exposition,
August 1922

Onstage, I pick up Baby Polly and put her back in the clothes basket. Jimmy, no longer in the grip of his fake seizure, piles firewood dangerously high. I struggle to sweep, holding a broom with my free hand.

Now Minnie, her round face beaded with sweat, drops the pot overflowing with cotton batting "steam," "scalding" herself and Jimmy. She sinks to the floor and curls into a ball while he hops from foot to foot cradling his hand.

A murmur of concern rises from the audience.

"Save your sympathy for the neighbors of this family," Mr. Ogilvie says. "Like you, they are kind, upstanding folk who, time and time again, have helped Gar and Minnie. But ask yourself this question: why should they have to?"

Gar drains the whiskey bottle (full of weak tea), drops it, and staggers to the table for another. As he passes Minnie, he pulls her to her feet and mimes a backhand slap across her face. She stumbles against the stove, a crate painted black.

Minnie shakes her fist at Gar and then whacks a rolling pin on the table sending up a cloud of white flour. The fist, the whack, and the flour cloud bring a gust of relieved laughter from the crowd.

Mr. Ogilvie points out our individual weaknesses like tasty menu items. "Ruthie was born with a withered left leg. Jimmy's seizures will be lifelong. These defects were prevalent in their parents' families. That's why you must know your family history before you plan to marry and have children. After the show, visit our exhibit next door to learn what a fit family looks like."

In real life Jimmy is an epileptic. They chose him so they can blame his illness on his parents. He also makes the fake seizures look realistic. But Mr. Ogilvie lies about the rest of us. I wasn't born crippled. I had polio when I was eleven. Minnie isn't feeble-minded; she has only a fourth-grade education and sometimes gets confused. Gar isn't a drinker, but he admits being at loose ends since the war ended.

"With her intelligence, Ruthie could have a better life," Mr. Ogilvie says in a fake concerned voice as I act out reading a newspaper to Minnie. "Yet, sadly, she is trapped in this family and in her broken body."

I'm also trapped with him and Aunt Fan for seven more days.

At the end of the show, I drop my crutch and lie sprawled on the floor, arms outstretched. Jimmy twists his body in a fake seizure. Minnie stands at the stove, looking at the pot boiling over. Gar sits in the chair with a whiskey bottle.

"As you see, nothing changes for this unfit family," Mr. Ogilvie says in a mournful voice. "Nothing will ever change. Left to themselves, they will continue to reproduce and bring more suffering children into this world."

My leg is cramping so I ease it into a new position, careful to avoid the nail.

Mr. Ogilvie ends with his worst line of all, "What farmer would allow unfit livestock to breed year after year?" The words *livestock* and *breed* make me want to gag.

A man in the audience shouts, "These unfit folks are still God's children, not animals." A ripple of applause spreads through the tent.

Mr. Ogilvie raises his voice. "It is for us, the fit, to take the necessary steps to prune the unfit from the American family tree. We have the tools. Do we have the will?"

It's over. I scramble up and move downstage with the others to line up in the glare of the stage lights. We bow to more applause, whistles, and foot stomps.

Now Aunt Fan tip-taps across the stage in high-heeled pumps, a yellow linen suit, and a white hat. A scent of gardenias follows in her wake. Mr. Ogilvie bows to her. He and Aunt Fan are brother and sister. According to Dorchy, their assistant, they live together here in Springfield. Both are high school teachers the rest of the year, but they spend their summers promoting fitter families.

Speaking to the audience, Aunt Fan sounds sweetly persuasive. "I am Fanny Ogilvie, a hygiene teacher here in Springfield and a volunteer with the New England Betterment Council. Thank you for coming. Now, please follow Mr. Ogilvie to the cottage next door to take our Fitter Families test and validate your family's heritage." She makes it sound like an honor. "We are a nonprofit organization, so donations are appreciated."

We remain onstage while Aunt Fan directs the audience out of the tent. Being onstage means we get pitying looks from people shuffling past. We also get money. People place pennies, nickels, dimes, even quarters—and once a silver dollar—on the stage in front of us. Maybe they're making donations as Aunt Fan suggests, or maybe the stage is like a wishing well. *Give the unfit money, and your wish will come true.* I don't care why they do it; I concentrate on moving my right foot fast enough to cover the coins before any of the others do.

Today Dorchy, the assistant, waves at me from the back of the tent. I scowl at her. We don't trust her because she works for the Ogilvies and could be spying on us, though we have no proof of that. She's about my age, ramrod straight. Dark hair, green eyes, always dressed in a blue gingham dress and white apron with "New England Betterment Council" embroidered on it in red. Minnie and I have uniforms exactly like it to wear when we're not onstage. Dorchy's face isn't exactly pretty except for those emerald eyes. The eyes of the witch in my book of fairy tales back home.

It's Dorchy's job to pick up anything the audience drops during our shows. Today when she finishes going up and down the rows, she comes over to the stage, a book in one hand.

She holds it up to me. "If you can read, you can have this. Say, how old *are* you? You don't look thirteen like he says in the show."

"I'm sixteen." I study her face and make a guess. "The same as you?"

She nods.

"Dorchy! Back to work." Aunt Fan trots across the stage, clapping her hands in front of her as if she's shooing a chicken.

"Sorry, ma'am." Dorchy gazes up at Aunt Fan and rests the book on the edge of the stage. "I just wanted to tell Ruthie how much her acting has improved."

I drop my ragged costume apron over the book.

"It's not your place to tell her *that*," Aunt Fan snaps. "Run along. Mr. Ogilvie needs you in the cottage."

Dorchy winks at me over her shoulder as she walks away. She moves like someone who knows where she's going and could get there blindfolded.

"Now off the stage, all of you," Aunt Fan says. "Be quick about it." She rubs her mouth. Her false teeth must be hurting.

As Jimmy, Minnie, and Gar leave the stage, I bend over and scoop up my apron and the book.

Backstage I suck in a breath when I see the title *Little Women* in gold letters on the faded red cover. This is the twin of my own copy of *Little Women*, left behind in New York, and as familiar as the palm of my hand.

Later, in the room I share with Minnie, I open the book. The first sentence greets me like an old friend. "'Christmas won't be Christmas without any presents,' grumbled Jo." The wall I've built between my life *before* and my life *now* splits open. I was reading this book on the day I got polio, the first and last day I rode a wave.

CHAPTER 4

Paradise-by-the-Sea,
New York, 1917

Julia gave me *Little Women* for my eleventh birthday, the day before
we left to spend the summer on Long Island. Polio was stalking the
city that summer of 1917 as it had done the summer before when
thousands of New York children got sick. Three of those children
were our neighbors at the beach.

Still Father believed our spit of sand, Paradise-by-the-Sea, a ferry
ride from Freeport, would keep me safe this summer. He also believed in the protection of the horrible flaxseed porridge we all ate
for breakfast. And, of course, my Collier heritage. At my birthday
dinner that night, I blew out my candles in one breath and made
a wish that Marjorie Powell would be friends with me at school. I
should have wished for good health.

* * *

"Remember, the trick is picking the right moment," Julia yelled
from shore as I waded into the surf. "Start off just before the wave
starts to fall. If you start too soon, it will fall on you; too late, and

you'll be watching it roll in without you." She never went in the ocean, had never ridden a wave in her life, but she had decided to teach me.

I stood in the sparkling Atlantic Ocean in a one-piece red wool bathing suit. The wind was light; the waves were chest high. Julia's dark hair, usually raked back in a bun, had come loose. This first wave-riding lesson had already lasted too long. I was sick of being knocked over, pushed under, and tumbled around by waves. I wanted to give up, but a Collier never does.

I chose a wave, flung myself in front of it—hands outstretched, head down—and kicked hard. For the first time, I felt a leap of joy as the wave thrust me forward. I rode it all the way up on the shore.

Julia clapped her hands and shouted, "Bravo!"

I said, "I'm going to do it again, but first I have to tell Father."

I ran down the beach to where he was putting the final touches on his annual sand sculpture. That year it was the Pharos lighthouse of Alexandria, one of the seven wonders of the ancient world.

It was already three feet high, and Father was shaping the dome. An incoming wave surged up the beach and stopped short. The breeze carried the hot, salty smell of seaweed.

"Father." I twirled around, arms outstretched. "I rode a wave today. Would you like to watch me replicate the experiment?"

He laughed as I knew he would if I quoted something he would say. We walked together down to the water's edge. I handed him Mother's camera, so he could record my achievement, and headed out into the surf.

Another perfect ride unfolded, and I felt like a sleek animal—an otter or a dolphin—part of the salt water, sun, and fresh sea air.

"Well done." Father smiled and bent over Mother's camera. He took my picture standing up as the receding wave rushed past my feet so fast it carved channels in the sand. I wanted to run back in and ride another wave.

But Julia said it was time for lunch.

After lunch on the screened porch, my stomach hurt and Julia ordered me inside for a nap. I lay on the sofa reading *Little Women* until I fell asleep.

When I woke up, rain pattered on the porch roof. Reasoning that I could ride waves in the rain, I started to get up.

And couldn't move my legs.

I screamed for Julia, who ran to get Father. Lying back I told myself, *Everything will be fine once Father's here.*

After a long time the door clattered open. Father wiped his feet on the mat and rubbed his hands together, saying, "A storm is coming in. I had to build a dike around the lighthouse."

"It might not be polio," Julia said as Father stared down at my immoveable legs.

He nodded. I wished he would hold my hand and tell me everything was fine. Instead he examined the bowl and stem of his pipe thoughtfully before taking out his matchbox. His face showed me nothing.

"After all, the epidemic was last summer." Julia didn't look at me either. "The newspaper says the cases aren't as bad this year," she went on. "Statistically speaking—"

"Who cares about statistics?" I wailed.

"Rowan is right." Father sucked energetically on his pipe. "We will deal with the crisis before us. First, we must keep her warm." Smoke curled from the pipe clenched in his teeth as he clumsily wrapped an afghan around my legs.

I couldn't feel his hands or the scratchy warmth of the afghan. Terror coiled around me, making it hard to breathe. I was inside a cold bubble looking out. *Cut in half. Below my waist I did not exist.*

* * *

We took the ferry to Freeport. Father wrapped me in a sticky yellow sou'wester jacket and pulled me in a big wagon to the ferry dock on the bay. Julia pulled another wagon with our luggage. I left *Little Women* behind. It belonged to the world outside my bubble.

The bay was rough with whitecaps, and the rain came in gusts. I lay on a wet bench on deck while Julia held a mackintosh over our heads. Father stood next to the ferry captain smoking his pipe. The trip took longer than usual because the wind and tide were against us.

"A terrible tragedy," the ferryman said as he helped Father carry me onto the dock. I assumed he meant me.

"Yes," Father said. "I worked on it for the better part of a week, and it was a fine replica. Very fine."

At the doctor's office, a nurse dressed me in a short gown and laid me on a metal examining table. I shivered under a thin white blanket. Inside my bubble I felt fine except for a sore throat and my unworkable legs. *They* will *come back to life. They have to. I'm a Collier.*

The doctor loomed over me. "Unwrap her," he told Julia.

May I have a cup of hot cocoa? I formed the words in my mind, but I knew no one would hear me if I spoke out loud. Julia pulled the blanket off, and I watched the doctor squeeze and prod my legs.

Before he spoke I hung in the air like a seagull in an updraft. Then he said "Polio," and I dropped like a stone.

"I rode a wave today," I said into the silence. Nothing—not the bubble, not the doctor, not even polio—could take that away.

"You'll need to quarantine her at home," the doctor said to Father. "I will arrange for..."

"No," Father broke in. "Take her to Bellevue." Without looking at me, he said, "You're going to the hospital. The doctors there will know what to do. You must be as brave as I am."

He came to see me the next day at Bellevue. Even though I was quarantined, they let him come into my room. He stood over me and said in a hushed voice, "I won't be able to see you for a while. The navy wants me, so I'm off to the war in France."

I struggled to speak but couldn't get the words out. He looked down at me and quickly looked away.

"Julia will come to see you when she can," he said. And then he was gone.

I haven't seen or spoken to him since. I remember sometimes, as if it's a dream, how he smelled of cherry tobacco and bourbon and called my red-gold curls Botticelli hair. How, before he went out for the evening, he paused at the long mirror in the parlor. He called it a pier glass. He called me his pride and joy.

But that was before.

CHAPTER 5

At four thirty, after our last show, one of the ladies from the Council comes to stay with us in the tent. This Exposition is like a state fair but we never get to see it. Occasionally we hear sounds of hurdy-gurdy music or cheers from the racetrack. People carry food into the tent to eat during our show. The smells of popcorn and fried meat make our mouths water, but we never get to taste any. Today I fold brochures and stuff them in envelopes. At six o'clock other ladies bring us dinner. Tonight is a good one, ham sandwiches and lemonade.

At seven, the Ogilvies escort us to the one-story cottage next to the tent. Under the American flag on the roof, a sign proclaims, "Fitter Families Protect America's Future." The cottage contains several small rooms that open off a wide, straw-carpeted center hall. Tables are set up in the hall under posters reminding people what a burden the unfit are.

During the day, families come into the cottage to fill out

questionnaires and have their mental and physical traits measured. Points are subtracted for any family history of crime, insanity, feeblemindedness, alcoholism, shiftlessness, poverty, disease, or deformity. At the end, family members discover if they qualify as a "Fitter Family."

Before we enter the cottage, everything valuable is locked away and our cots are set up in two small rooms. Jimmy and Gar sleep in a room next to the front door, while Minnie and I are by the back door. In each room is a bucket we use at night and empty in the outhouse every morning.

For the first time all summer, we sleep under a roof in actual beds. At the county fairs, we all slept on folding cots in the tent where we put on the show. Here the Ogilvies lock us in our rooms and, for good measure, lock the front and back doors from the outside. They say the Council added the locks to protect us, the unfit, from prying eyes and bullies. Gar says it's because the Council doesn't trust us in their cottage or out on the fairgrounds. Both he and Minnie were hired for the Unfit Family show by Mr. Ogilvie when he met them at a church soup kitchen in Springfield. "They send the money to our kinfolk," Gar says. "It's pretty good pay, but not good enough for me to put up with being treated like an imbecile."

Locks can't hold Gar. On the first night, he picked the lock on the front bedroom door and showed me how to pick ours. He also fixed the back door so it doesn't lock completely. At night he disappears for a few hours. When I asked where he goes, he said, "The bright lights are calling me, kid. It's a risk I'm willing to take."

At the county fairs, Mr. Ogilvie never spoke to me except about the show, and his camera was out of sight. But here at the Expo, I've caught him taking my picture in the cottage and backstage.

Father told me that some people won't allow themselves to be photographed because they believe a camera can steal their souls. I feel the same way about being photographed by Mr. Ogilvie. It's as if he's keeping something of mine inside his camera. I want it back.

Last night he left a red rose under my pillow. I threw it in our bucket.

Tonight after he locks us in our rooms, I pick the lock, prop the door open, and sit on my cot reading *Little Women*. We aren't allowed to use candles or the electric lamp, so the only light comes from a small window near the ceiling and the glow from Minnie's cigarettes. Sometimes at night I stand on my cot and watch the spinning lights of the Ferris wheel. I imagine Gar taking me with him one night so I can take a ride on it. But that won't happen. Our unspoken agreement is that one of us has to stay in the cottage with Jimmy and Minnie.

Minnie throws her cigarette in the bucket and leans over to stroke the book's cover with nail-bitten fingers. "Can I hold it?"

I hand her the book, and she opens it to the title page where I've written my name. It is my book now. She traces a finger over the letters. "What does it say? I don't read so good, but I like a good story."

"That's my name, Rowan Collier."

Minnie shakes her head. "Your name is Ruthie."

CHAPTER 6

The Boston Home for
Crippled Children, 1922

It's been five weeks since Rowan Collier became Ruthie the cripple. Five weeks ago, but it seems much longer, Dr. Pynchon, black boots tapping and starched white coat rustling, called me out of the dining room at the Boston Home for Crippled Children with no explanation. I braced myself for another punishment as I followed her down the hall.

I came to the Home when I was twelve, exactly one year after I was admitted to the Bellevue Hospital polio ward. At Bellevue, the paralysis in my right leg went away on its own and Dr. Friedlander brought back some feeling and movement in my left leg. When Julia came to take me to Boston, he'd told her that with six more months of treatment I would walk without braces or crutches.

"If you put her in a home now," he told Julia, "she could be a cripple for life."

"My father believes Dr. Pynchon offers the best chance for Rowan." Julia paced back and forth in Dr. Friedlander's office. I sat in a chair, waiting for Julia to leave so I could get on with my treatment.

"My success speaks for itself," Dr. Friedlander said. "If your father came by for a demonstration, I think he would change his mind."

"He's still in France." She twisted the strap on her purse until it broke. "He instructed me to take her to Dr. Pynchon. A recent article featuring her ideas about crippled children impressed him."

Once Father's instructions were invoked, I knew I'd be leaving Bellevue. I choked back tears.

"I know Dr. Pynchon's work." Dr. Friedlander's voice was toneless. "I don't deny she cares adequately for some patients, but I am interested only in whether or not she can help *my* patient. The answer is absolutely not."

"Well, my father wishes it." Julia's voice shook. "Believe me, I wish he were standing here instead of me." She tucked the broken purse under her arm, still not looking at me. "I'll ask the nurse to pack her things. We leave today."

Father had won. Before we left, Dr. Friedlander handed Julia my records to give Dr. Pynchon. At the Boston Home no one ever mentioned my miraculous recovery in Dr. Friedlander's care.

* * *

"Here is Rowan," Dr. Pynchon said to the man seated on a chair in her parlor, legs stretched out in front of him. He had thinning blond hair, a long nose, and a clean-shaven chin. His blue eyes widened and his lips twitched into a smile when he saw me. A leather camera case hung on a strap around his neck. "You said 'intelligent and crippled,'" Dr. Pynchon went on. "She is both."

Intelligent. The only positive word I ever heard her use about me. My mouth dropped open.

Maybe he's Father's lawyer, come to take me home. Julia promised me that when I turned sixteen, I could come back to live with her and Father in New York. My birthday was two weeks ago, but no word from Julia. Besides, what would "intelligent and crippled" have to do with that? If he was from the Massachusetts Department of Health, I could tell him things about the Home that would curl what's left of his hair.

Dr. Pynchon opened the drapes, and the bright morning sun made me blink. "Pull up your skirt so Mr. Ogilvie can see your leg," she said.

I pressed my crutches closer to my body. "Is he a doctor?"

She fingered the braided strap that hung from her belt. "Now."

Face burning, I inched up the skirt of my uniform and showed him my black-stockinged left leg.

Mr. Ogilvie shook his head. "No, no, no, Dr. Pynchon," he said, wagging his finger at her. "No boots, no stockings, no crutches." He stood up, and I wondered if he planned to remove my shoes and stockings himself. "I want the bare leg visible, and her movements as restricted as possible." He sounded like a customer lecturing a shopkeeper.

"But I need the crutches to walk," I said politely.

Dr. Pynchon darted at me and slapped my face as if she were swatting a fly. "Sit down and take off your shoes and stockings."

I sucked in a breath of surprise and pain, but did not cry. Everyone at the Home knew that tears fueled her anger.

"From now on, you'll do as Mr. Ogilvie says," Dr. Pynchon went on, "and make the Boston Home proud. If you don't, I won't have you back. We have a long connection with the good people of the New England Betterment Council."

My face burned as I bent to untie my shoes and pull off my high black stockings.

Mr. Ogilvie studied my thin, pale left leg as if it were a lamb chop in the butcher's window. Then he stood and opened his camera case, extending the camera's accordion folds. The round headlight-like lens made it look like a steam engine. He adjusted the dials and peered into it. The clack of the shutter made me jump.

"Beautiful," he said. "But you'll have to braid your hair so you look younger."

I touched my hair, pulled back in the tight bun required by Dr. Pynchon.

She handed me a wrinkled flour-sack dress printed with tiny blue flowers. "Change in my office," she said. "Leave your uniform there. You may wear your stockings and shoes." Biting back questions, I took the dress and went into her office.

When I came back to the parlor, Dr. Pynchon snatched one of my crutches and I almost fell. "Mr. Ogilvie will only allow you to keep one crutch," she said. "Now pick up your bag." She pointed to a small carpetbag. "I packed your essentials. Enough for the six weeks you'll be traveling with the Ogilvies."

There's more than one of them? I thought.

"Did you pack my book?" I was halfway through Lamb's *Tales from Shakespeare* for the third time. Only books approved by the Home's Board of Visitors were allowed.

"Oh, you'll be much too busy for *books*," Mr. Ogilvie said. His high-pitched voice was as annoying as squeaking chalk. "Jimmy, a friend of yours, is coming too. You can talk to him."

I knew one boy named Jimmy at the Home, but I couldn't imagine any situation where talking to him would be a substitute for reading.

One last hope. "Has my father given me permission to travel for six weeks?"

Dr. Pynchon sniffed. "Not your *father*. Your sister, Julia." She pulled a folded sheet of paper out of her skirt pocket and waved it at me. "See?" A typewritten letter. Julia's signature. *Judas.* Her betrayal swelled inside me. *How could she promise to bring me home, the one thing I've wanted for five years, and instead deliver me to* this?

"There's no need for you to read it." Dr. Pynchon put the letter back in her pocket. "It says that your sister and father are traveling in Europe until the end of the summer, and they agree with me that you should spend six weeks doing educational work for the New England Betterment Council."

"What kind of educational work?" I asked.

Mr. Ogilvie and Dr. Pynchon exchanged a glance, and he touched my shoulder with a long finger. "Come along," he said, and picked up the carpet bag. "You'll find out soon enough."

I struggled with one crutch but managed to keep up with him, out of the house and down the steps to the driveway. He helped me into the backseat of his black Buick touring car.

"This is Jimmy, your epileptic 'brother.'" Mr. Ogilvie nodded at the boy sitting in the passenger seat, knees drawn up. "He'll keep his name in the show." He wedged the carpet bag under my feet. "But you're not highfalutin *Rowan* from New York City anymore." He paused. "From now on, you're Ruthie, the cripple."

And for five weeks and three days that's who I've been.

It's too dark to read now. I close my book and whisper a vow: "Tomorrow will be different."

CHAPTER 7

In the first show today, I catch the baby. Someone in the back of the tent applauds. Jimmy raises his eyebrows at me. I want to twirl around, shouting, "Look, I did it!" I imagine telling Mr. Ogilvie. *You told me to be myself.*

Mr. Ogilvie doesn't notice. He says the same ugly words, "unfit to care for a baby," all day, in all four shows. But in each one, I prove him wrong and catch Polly. After the first show, no one in the audience applauds, but no one yells at me either.

"You caught the baby." Dorchy sounds interested, not accusing, when she comes over to the stage after the last show. "The Ogress caught me clapping for you."

She clapped for me. I lean down and whisper, "Who's the Ogress?"

"Aunt Fan Ogilvie, of course," Dorchy says, "and he's the Ogre. I believe in calling people by their true names." She gives me a sizing-up look. "You're in trouble now. She saw you do it."

"I don't care." I tighten my grip on the crutch and glare at her. "It was the right thing to do."

"I'm in trouble too." Her grin lights up her whole face. "I clapped."

As the audience leaves with Aunt Fan, Mr. Ogilvie comes on-stage and calls Dorchy over. We actors gather round; this time we're the audience.

He grabs Dorchy's arm above the elbow. "It was your idea, wasn't it?" he shouts. "I know what you're up to, you *succubus*."

I've never heard that word before. It sounds horrible.

"You're the instigator," Mr. Ogilvie rages on. "Taking advantage of a poor cripple." He shakes Dorchy's arm. Her face is blank, except for those blazing green eyes. "Look at Ruthie!" His voice rises, and he yanks Dorchy around so she's facing me. "Not one defiant bone in her poor little body."

Minnie grabs my hand, but I shake free.

Mr. Ogilvie pulls Dorchy's arm up behind her. She squirms and tries to get away, giving me a furious look.

I find my voice. "She didn't tell me to do it." The words trickle out, weak and useless. Unheard.

"I should send you back to the orphanage for this," Mr. Ogilvie says to Dorchy. "You have undermined the message of the Unfit Family show. I cannot allow that."

"*I* undermined your message," I shout, "not Dorchy."

He drops her arm and stares at me.

The sound of my voice gives me courage. "It was *my* idea to catch the baby, not hers. I wish I'd done it sooner."

Dorchy smiles her approval.

Mr. Ogilvie walks off the stage and out of the tent.

Whatever happens now, at least I told the truth. I like the way my voice cut across his anger and filled the stage. I take a deep breath of the hot, dusty air, sucking in the last echoes of my words.

As I leave the stage, Dorchy walks over to me. Her curly black hair is pulled back with a red hair ribbon. She's wearing gold earrings with her usual uniform. A purple bruise blooms over her left eye.

"This is your lucky day." Her green eyes sparkle as she rubs her arm where Mr. Ogilvie's fingers left red marks. "We're going out."

"Out where?" *How did she get that black eye?*

"There's more to the Exposition than this tent, you know." She puts her hand on my arm. "We're going out on the midway, Ruthie!"

"Don't call me that," I say. "My name is Rowan."

"Come on, don't stand there. We have to go *now.*"

I touch the coins in my dress pocket, two nickels, two pennies, and dime. "I can't."

"Yes, you *can.*" Dorchy's eyes flash. "You've got moxie. I like that. Besides I need to talk to you." She looks ready to drag me out of the tent. "Mrs. Kohler, your babysitter over there, won't notice. She's as blind as a one-eyed cat."

I don't know what it means to have *moxie*, but I like the admiring look in her eyes when she says it. "What about the 'Ogres'?"

"Don't worry about them. He's taking her to the dentist. It's an emergency."

"All right. But I have to change and tell Gar."

"I'll be outside."

I tell Gar and go behind the curtain to change into my offstage uniform. I unbraid my hair and brush it hard. Curls spring out around my head, and a spark of excitement, damped down for so long, flickers inside me.

But as I leave the tent, choosing a moment when Mrs. Kohler

is talking to Minnie, Gar says, "Remember, be careful what you tell her."

Dorchy the spy or Dorchy the friend? I've made my decision.

"Turn your apron inside out like mine," Dorchy says. "I don't care to be a walking advertisement for the Council." I reverse my apron, and we head off down a wide gravel path. Instantly my senses are flooded—popcorn, fried chicken, shouts, and the distant throb of a brass band. Red, white, and blue bunting flutters from side-by-side Republican and Democratic Party booths.

Two women in white straw hats trot by, their white lace-up shoes kicking up swirls of dust. A wave of dance music washes out of a big pavilion. We're swept along in a river of people, more than I've seen in one place in five years.

It's too much. I stop moving forward. *I have to get back to the tent.* People flow around me. Dorchy keeps going. A man bumps into me and shouts, "Watch where you're going!" *I'm not going anywhere. I can't move.*

Dorchy comes back to see what's wrong. I whisper, "I want to go back."

She pulls a cigarette and a long match out of her pocket. "Come on, buck up. Where's that spitfire who broke the Ogres' rule and caught the baby doll?"

The fierce ache in my throat expands. I can't speak. Five years ago, when I was lying paralyzed in my hospital bed, Dr. Friedlander told me to never define myself by what I *can't* do. But that's exactly what I'm doing.

Dorchy strikes the match on the sole of her shoe. She lights her cigarette and gestures at the people shoving past us. "Don't mind them. They're rubes. We're carnies." She blows a smoke ring. "Remember that."

When I find my voice, it comes out as a squeak. "What are *rubes* and *carnies?*"

"Don't you know anything?" She blows a smoke ring. "Rubes are ignoramuses; carnies know everything. Rubes come to the fair with their eyes starry and their pockets full; carnies take them for all they're worth."

"That sounds...illegal." The word makes me wince. I sound like Julia.

"Come on, let's walk," Dorchy says. "Carnies run the concessions and games and sideshows. We take the rubes' hard-earned money. But they ask for it." She stops to point at a man in a booth selling tickets to Fred Fatherly's Fantastical Flea Circus. "Your Unfit Family show does the same thing. You trick rubes into paying money under false pretenses."

"We're not a flea circus."

A boy in a straw hat and farmer overalls reaches into his pocket, but his well-dressed friend—white shirt, corduroy pants, bowler hat—says something and they both turn around to stare at us.

Dorchy ignores them. "I'm not saying you don't give value," she says, "but you're not a family. Or unfit. At least the flea circus has real fleas."

"Afternoon, miss," the well-dressed boy says, tipping his hat to Dorchy. "Come on now. Give a fellow a smile."

As we walk past them, I think about what Dorchy said. It has never occurred to me that I've been in a sideshow for five weeks.

The boys follow us. "What about your gimp girlfriend?" This has to be the farm boy. He sounds younger, almost scared. "I bet she'd say yes to a spin on the Ferris wheel."

"Don't turn around," Dorchy says. "My parents were carnies before they died. I was born in a tent at the Ohio State Fair. Mama was a snake handler and Daddy was a talker." She touches her earrings. "Real gold. Mama put the holes in my ears herself."

That can't be true. She's making up a story to distract me from the boys.

She starts walking faster.

"Gimp girl, what's that crutch for?" Farm Boy yells.

"What's a talker?" I ask Dorchy.

"It's the other one who's got *it*, you numskull," says Townie. "We can have some fun with Miss Gold Earrings."

Dorchy says, "The talker stands outside the tent and gets the rubes excited about the show so they'll pay to go inside. I'm a pretty good talker myself."

"You?"

She grins at me. "I got you to come out here with me, didn't I? Those stupid boys are trying, but they couldn't get a hungry squirrel to eat a nut."

We walk past the carousel with its painted horses bounding in place to calliope music. I take a deep breath of roasting peanuts and fried sausages, then dig my crutch into the dust and swing along faster. After five years of being observed, criticized, and told what to do and when to do it, I'm free. The last time I felt this way was at Bellevue when I met Dr. Friedlander.

CHAPTER 8

Bellevue Hospital,
New York, 1917

For the eight weeks I lay in quarantine in Bellevue Hospital, my world was a white bed with barred sides. It looked like a crib, and in it I felt as helpless as a baby. Nurses banged the rails down to tend to me and banged them up when they were done. "We have so many children to care for," a nurse said, accusing me of—what? Not being cared for at home, I guess. Only six blocks away, "home" might as well have been on the moon.

A long, meandering crack in the ceiling was my escape. I imagined it was a road, and I followed it—away from the ugly smells and loud sounds of the hospital, away from my body that ached and could no longer move, away from Father who had left me here and Julia who wasn't allowed to visit.

No one spoke my name—not the nurses, not the aides, certainly not the doctor, an impatient man with icy hands. While he poked and lifted and twisted my arms and legs, he talked *about* me, never *to* me.

Everything changed one morning when a tall, white-coated doctor with smiling eyes came into my curtained cubicle holding an orange. "Hello, Rowan," he said, and sat down next to my bed. "I'm Dr. Friedlander, your 'knight in shining orange.'" He peeled the orange, and the sharp scent filled my nose and drove away the overcooked food and medicine smells. "Have a piece," he said, offering me one.

At the first bite, my heart expanded from walnut-size.

He had sandy hair and kind gray eyes. Not movie-star handsome, but by far the most interesting person I'd met at Bellevue—and he knew my name. "Now let's get some light in here and sit you up," he said, wiping his hands on his coat. "You've been flat as a flounder long enough." He went to the window and snapped up the shade. In the shaft of sunlight, I saw galaxies of dust motes. Then he cranked the handle at the foot of the bed, raising me to a sitting position. "Reminds me of starting a car," he said. "Now don't drive off anywhere, OK?"

Sitting up, I felt liberated, no longer a baby in a crib.

"Rowan," he said, lowering the bars on the bed. "I want to talk to you about your illness—*polio*. I used to call it infantile paralysis, and some doctors still do, but between you and me, I prefer the shorter name. All right? Or are you a traditionalist?" He grinned.

I shook my head no. Everyone else acted as if "my illness" was a tragedy too awful to mention, let alone give a name to.

"Polio," I said and smiled.

"Good, that's settled." He rubbed his hands together. "Now let's see if your right leg has improved a bit. No problem if it hasn't."

He lifted the sheet off my right leg. As he bent my ankle and knee, I felt a surge of relief. His hands were warm, not icy.

"Very good, very good," he said. "Now the left leg. I'll be taking over your care from the Frozen Herring as soon as you're out of quarantine."

"*Dr.* Frozen Herring?"

"You know him! I call him that because I heard through the grapevine that his hands are always cold. I'm glad you can confirm it." He winked at me.

"When will I be out of quarantine?" My voice trembled. I wanted him to be my doctor *now*.

He looked at his watch. "Fifteen minutes ago," he said. "Your sister will be allowed to come tomorrow. Let a nurse know what you would like her to bring you."

My relief turned to confusion. "But I thought she could take me home after quarantine."

He patted my hand. "We have a lot of work to do before that, if you want to walk again." His eyes bored into mine. "You do want to walk, don't you?"

"Yes."

"Well, here in the hospital you will learn how to do that. Not in this *cell*, of course, but in the ward. Starting tomorrow. Now, do you have any more questions?"

They whirled in my head like blowing leaves. "May I read? Do you have any books for someone my age?"

"You may read. And you may read aloud to others. Ask your sister to buy new books that you can leave here when you go home. We always need books. I'll telephone her myself, so she can come with books tomorrow. What would you most like to read?"

"*Little Women*," I said immediately, my heart racing. *I could read.*

"Now I'll answer the questions you didn't ask," he said. "The paralysis has worn off in your right leg. Now we'll put it to work helping Lefty do the same." He patted my left leg. "And when I say *we*, I mean you and me."

* * *

The next morning he came back after breakfast.

"Rise and shine, Rowan."

My heart raced. I closed my eyes. As long as I sat perfectly still, anything was possible.

"We start today, remember?"

The nurse swung me around so my legs dangled over the side of the bed.

"That's right," Dr. Friedlander said. "Now on the count of three, lower your right leg to the floor."

He waited. The nurse waited. I sat still. One heartbeat, two heartbeats, three…

Do as they say, Rowan. I heard Father's voice as clearly as if he were standing next to me. *A Collier fears nothing.*

I lowered my right leg toward the floor.

"Excellent," said Dr. Friedlander. "Now slide your foot, toes first, into this shoe." He pushed a black shoe, its laces loosened, under my foot. I slid my right foot into it. My left leg hung limp as a hank of seaweed.

Dr. Friedlander bent and slid my left foot into its shoe. Deftly he pulled the laces of both shoes tight and tied them.

"Take care of the feet, and the rest will follow," he said to the nurse who looked disapproving.

"It's my job to tie their shoes, Doctor," she said.

"Of course, it is." Dr. Friedlander beamed at her. "But I find the element of surprise to be therapeutic."

He offered me his arm. "Now, Rowan, lean on me for two steps over to the wheelchair and we're off to the chamber of miracles."

Safely in the wheelchair, I leaned against its high wicker back.

"Sit up straight," said Dr. Friedlander. "Nothing wrong with your back muscles."

The nurse bent down and arranged my feet on the broad footrests.

As Dr. Friedlander pushed me through the ward, whistling "Daisy, Daisy," children called from their beds, "Dr. Freedom! Dr. Freedom!" He waved and kept moving.

In a long, sunny room, boys and girls in braces and on crutches followed directions from white-coated men and women. Dr. Friedlander pushed me past them and parked the wheelchair behind a flowered curtain. Honey-colored sunlight flooded through a tall window. He switched on the phonograph resting on a white metal table and positioned the needle on a record.

"I'm a Yankee Doodle Dandy," warbled the tenor voice. My heart leaped. Father and I used sing along with this record.

"Stand up, Rowan," Dr. Friedlander said.

"Yankee Doodle do or die." I leaned forward in the chair. "Did my father give you that?"

"No, it's one of my favorites." He lifted me up.

"A real live nephew of my Uncle Sam…"

"Stand on your right leg and put your hands on my shoulders. That's it."

"…born on the Fourth of July!"

"Now we'll encourage your left leg," said Dr. Friedlander. "Let's dance!"

"I've got a Yankee Doodle sweetheart…"

Hopping on my right foot, dragging the left. I stayed upright for a full minute, all the way to the final line, *"I am the Yankee Doodle Boy!"*

Dr. Friedlander settled me back in the wheelchair. "Day one is a terrific success. Now"—he lowered his voice—"I'll tell you a secret. My ideas are different from the ones popular out *there*." He jerked his thumb at the curtain. "Polio is a powerful opponent. We fight it on multiple fronts—music, laughter, exercise, and massage. For massage I yield to the nurses. They will massage your left leg and right leg in equal measure after every session with me." He put the record back in its paper cover. "Why *both* legs, do you suppose?"

I shook my head.

"Are your legs alike or different?"

"Different. Of course."

"Do they *look* different?"

I looked down at my black stockings and shoes. "Yes, the left one looks..."

"Alive and well," he interrupted. "Affected by polio, but capable of walking again. Believe that and we'll do wonders. You'll see."

He sounded so sure. Maybe I *wouldn't* be crippled forever.

"It will get stronger?"

"If you work at it." He held out his hand for me to shake. "You have my word on that."

I shook his hand. Father judged people by their handshakes. Dr. Friedlander was worthy.

CHAPTER 9

We stop to buy sausage rolls with a dime from a leather pouch Dorchy wears on a cord around her neck. She holds the pouch out to show me. "Rubes can't hang on to anything," she says. "They all have holes in their pockets."

Three giggling girls in pale linen dresses and wide hats pass us, followed closely by Farm Boy and Townie.

"Look," Dorchy says, handing me my sausage. "Those idiots are chasing bigger fish now. Good luck to 'em."

I forget the boys because with my first bite I'm back in New York having pancakes and sausages with Father. He whistles "You Are My Sunshine" as sunlight pours through the tall dining room window, turning the syrup in the glass pitcher to gold.

Homesickness is a physical ache so intense that I can't swallow. For five years I've kept my life *before* locked away. Now memories ambush me at every turn. I squeeze my free arm against my stomach, dropping the sausage roll in the dirt.

Dorchy picks it up, dusts it off, and stuffs it in her apron pocket. "Wait here," she says. The ache fades as I look around and disappears as I watch people strolling past.

The crowd slows and jostles around an obstacle. I crane my neck to see what's blocking the pathway and gasp.

Mr. Ogilvie and his camera.

He is photographing a little girl holding a teddy bear.

Fear roots me to the spot. *He'll send me back to Boston if he finds out I left the tent.*

I lower my head, wishing I had a hat to shadow my face.

Did he follow us? But how? And why isn't he with Aunt Fan at the dentist?

He still has his back to me when I spot Dorchy coming toward me, carrying two green bottles with straws. I wave and point to Mr. Ogilvie. She holds a bottle up to hide her face as she passes.

She hands me one, and bubbles tickle my nose as the first sip of lukewarm sugary liquid slides down my throat. We stand with our backs to the walkway, pretending to admire a booth selling fried clams.

My voice shakes. "You said he took Aunt Fan to the dentist."

"He did." She looks at me, her eyes narrow. "You think I *told* him we were coming out here? I wouldn't tell him the time of day, but if you don't trust me, we'll go back now."

I make up my mind. "No. I was just surprised to see him."

"Me too." She takes a long drink. "I have an idea," she says, her eyes sparkling. "Let's follow him. I want to see what he does when the Ogress isn't around. She tucks her top lip over her teeth. "The dentith ith thuppothed to take a couple of hourth." She goes on in her own voice, "He must have dumped her there and raced back here for some reason we are going to discover."

"But what if he sees us?" The thought makes my skin crawl.

"He won't recognize us with our hair down."

"And our aprons turned around."

Dorchy grabs my hand. "Hurry up, he's way ahead of us and I think he's going to the midway." Excitement makes her voice tremble.

So we follow him. Past animal barns reeking of manure, out onto the midway.

Dorchy stops in front of a tent hung with life-size colored posters: "Teddy the Dancing Bear," "Thirsty Thorsten the Sword Swallower," "Gilda, Half Snake, Half Woman, All Wild." On a platform in front stands a short man in a red jacket and blue-and-white-striped pants.

"The talker," Dorchy says with a flourish as if she conjured him up just for me.

The man shouts into a megaphone at people walking past. "Hurry-a, hurry-a, hurry-a!" he says. "Come-a one, come-a all to our electrifying, death-defying, high-flying show."

Dorchy snorts. "My dad was a lot better than him."

"Faint of heart? Move right on by," the man booms. "What's inside will chill you, thrill you, and nearly kill you!"

Some people in the surging crowd have stopped to listen.

"Dorchy, look!" Mr. Ogilvie stands on the outer fringe of listeners, looking hypnotized. "What if he goes inside?"

"We sneak in. But first I want to show you something." A man in a gray suit, standing in front of us, pushes his straw hat back and laughs at something the talker says. "Now watch," Dorchy says. Faster than a blink, she slides her hand up under the man's jacket and pulls out a wallet. The man goes on laughing; he doesn't know. If she hadn't told me to watch, I wouldn't either.

She sidles quickly away into the crowd. I follow and grab her arm. "Give that back!"

She pats her pocket. "Carny code: 'If you take a mark's money without him noticing, he's got no beef.'"

"Well, I noticed. Give it back. Do you want to get *arrested*?"

She grins. "I'm not going to keep it. I just wanted to show you how easy it is." She winks and moves back through the crowd. I follow and watch her slip the wallet into the man's pocket.

"You were so fast he didn't even know it was gone." Now that she's returned the wallet, I can compliment her.

"It's all part of my plan." She sucks in a breath. "Hey, there he is. Come *on*!"

Mr. Ogilvie is disappearing through the front entrance.

We walk over to the side of the tent, pretending to admire the posters flapping above us. Dorchy suddenly pushes me down next to an open space where the tent wall doesn't quite reach the ground. A heavy smell of sweat and hot canvas hits my face as I crawl inside. Dorchy follows, pushing my crutch ahead of her. The only light comes from electric spotlights shining on the stages. No one pays any attention to us as we stand up and brush off our clothes.

In the dim light I realize it will be almost impossible to see Mr. Ogilvie, and that means he won't see us either. I begin looking around as we weave through the crowd of men and a few women who shuffle along, stopping at each roped-off stage to gape and applaud. We pass a dusty-coated dancing bear who looks sleepy and hot. The smell of "Ferdinand the Formidable Fire Eater's" torch makes me feel sick.

But "Gilda, Half Woman, Half Snake, All Wild!" brings me to a halt. She rises slowly from behind fake boulders, waving her bare arms over her head while her body sways side to side. Her green and yellow scarf ripples, and the rubes shout and whistle. Gilda arches her back and smiles at her audience. In the spotlight I see specks of red lipstick on her crooked teeth. People in the crowd shout comments that she ignores. She doesn't speak.

Dorchy grabs my arm. "There's something we have to see," she says in a low voice. "I've heard people talking about it."

Without taking my eyes off Gilda, I whisper back, "Not before I see her tail."

"You can't stand here for long, or someone will notice and kick us out. You have to be twenty-one to get in."

The rubes start clapping and shouting, "Gil-da! Gil-da!"

Slowly Gilda pushes aside the boulders and reveals her narrow waist above a scaly green and yellow snake's tail, as wide as her hips at the top, tapering to a narrow point.

I let out the breath I didn't know I was holding.

Gilda bends to the side and comes up with a live brown and gold snake wrapped around her arms. The crowd cheers as the snake's head lashes back and forth, tongue flickering. Gilda raises the snake above her head and rocks faster as the recorded music switches to a thundering drumbeat—*ba-boom, ba-boom, ba-ba-ba-boom.*

Dorchy says, "My mother's snake act would leave her in the dust."

Gilda's upper body is in constant motion, but she's pinned to that spot behind the rocks. I'm pinned to my crutch. I'll never run again, climb rocks in Central Park, ride the waves. I forget that she's a performer who can move wherever she wants to. Tears for both of us sting my eyes.

I move closer to the stage. Too close. Gilda's eyes widen. "Shove off, missy," she hisses. "This is no place for little girls."

CHAPTER 10

I hurry after Dorchy, deeper into the dim tent. She stops in front of a curtained stage where a poster announces, "Narda, the Nearly Departed: Can your love bring her back from the Pearly Gates?" From a poster, Narda, a golden-haired angel, arms and wings outstretched, stares down at us with mournful eyes.

A crowd of mostly men surrounds us. I don't see Mr. Ogilvie. Maybe we lost him. *What if he goes back to the tent and finds out I'm gone?*

"I think we should go back now," I whisper. Dorchy shakes her head.

The curtain opens and in front of us gapes a white coffin. It's tilted up so we can see the chalky-faced blond girl dressed in white lying inside. Her hands are folded, eyes closed.

A chorus of gasps rises from the crowd. One man calls out, "If she ain't the image of my poor Pru."

I step back onto someone's foot. I can't stop looking. *Is she breathing? Her chest under the white lace doesn't move.* I grip Dorchy's wrist. "Is she dead?"

"Of course not," she says, but she sounds unsure.

The talker steps onstage. "Sad to say, ladies and gents, Narda has taken a turn for the worse," he says. "Maybe she'll rise from the coffin this afternoon and maybe she won't. It's up to you. If you call out words of love, she *might* come around. No promises, but it's worth a try."

A man shouts, "Narda, darling, I love you. Please wake up." He starts to laugh.

The talker shakes his finger at the man. "Death is a serious matter," he says. "Especially to one as close to it as Narda. A little respect, please, and we might get a song from her today."

Another man coaxes, "Narda, please, please, pretty please, wake up. I paid a dime to see you."

Laughter gusts through the crowd. The talker looks annoyed.

A woman calls out, "Narda, Mama loves you. Oren loves you. Jake loves you. Milly May forgives you. Now open your eyes!"

Narda puts her left hand on her forehead and starts to sit up.

The crowd claps and calls out encouragement.

Mr. Ogilvie pushes through the crowd in front of us, moving *away* from Narda. His face is wet with tears. He doesn't see us.

Dorchy's eyes shine in the light from the stage. "We can't follow him out the front. We have to crawl under the tent."

"Let's go then."

Back outside, with no sign of Mr. Ogilvie, we move slowly along the walkway, past food stalls and games of chance. Part of me is still back there with Narda.

"Why do you think Mr. Ogilvie was there?"

She shrugs, "No idea. But I guess sometimes he likes to get as far away from Aunt Fan as he can."

My right leg throbs, and my arm aches from the single crutch jammed in my armpit. I slow down, wanting to rest.

Dorchy says, "You poor kid, you look about to faint. Sit down here." She glares at a boy eating an ice cream cone on a wooden bench. "Scram. This lady is *sick.*"

He takes one look at me and runs.

I sit on the edge of the bench. *Where is Mr. Ogilvie going now? Did he see us?*

Dorchy seems distracted. "The Ogress has it in her head that I should work for them permanently, not just these ten days of the Exposition." She chews her thumbnail. "It makes me puke to think of it. I need to get back to the carny world, working on a midway like this. It was home to me until two years ago."

"What happened then?" *Stupid question. She already said her parents were dead.*

"My parents died of influenza just as we started working this Expo. I got sent to an orphanage. The people there said they couldn't reach my uncle in Coney Island. He's a carny too. I don't think they even tried. Last year I didn't get anywhere near the midway, but this year, here I am. And I want to stay. Travel south with them, hit the road."

I nod. "So why don't you run away?"

"I'm thinking about taking what I'm owed and doing just that."

For a while we sit in silence, watching people stroll past. I feast on the varieties of shapes and sizes and ages. A boy on crutches catches my eye. He's walking with two younger girls and a man and woman. A family. The man waits for him to catch up and puts his hand on the boy's head, smiling.

"Mr. Ogilvie takes pictures of me when he thinks I'm not looking," I say, trusting Dorchy with my secret. "And last night I found a rose from him when I changed backstage."

Dorchy leans forward. "Was there a card?"

"No, but he asked me about it this morning and said he wants to take me to his 'favorite place in all the world.' And he doesn't want anyone, especially Aunt Fan, to know. It's 'our secret.' It makes me sick." I shiver at the memory. "He didn't leave me another rose today, thanks to Aunt Fan's bad teeth."

Dorchy runs her hand through her hair. "Maybe,"—she looks down—"we could *both* go with him."

"No! Why would you even think such a thing? I hate him." I stand up. "I'm feeling better. I want to go."

She stands up too. "First we're going to ride the Ferris wheel."

"But he might be waiting for us back at our tent."

"Come on." She starts walking. "I guarantee he's not there. He has to pick up the Ogress at the dentist on the other side of Springfield. Then he has to take her home." She waits for me to catch up. "It will be quite a while before he comes back. I'm just glad she didn't drag me along to hold her hand at the dentist's."

"OK, then slow down."

We pass talkers and food stalls, "Test Your Strength" games, and the red-and-black tent of "The Great Zurena, Foreteller of Futures."

"Why do you hate the Ogilvies?"

"Because they—" She makes a face. "All their talk about sterilizing 'unfit' people makes me sick. When we were at Coney Island, before we came up here, some nosy people from someplace on Long Island came poking around the freak show asking about 'family histories.'"

"The investigators don't go to carnivals," I say, thinking of Julia and her note cards. "They go to prisons and insane asylums to interview inmates."

"Well, they asked a lot of questions about 'heredity.' Like when a woman in a blue suit with a notepad asked Flo, the bearded lady, if her mother, grandmother, and *great*-grandmother had beards. Flo was in tears afterward. 'How do I know if my mother had a beard? I never knew her. I'm an orphan.'"

"My sister, Julia, does research on the unfit."

"Stop saying that word. Do you even know what it means?"

I decide not to tell her that Father used to say, "The unfit are a burden that the fit must carry."

"I'm sorry but it stinks what those researchers and the Council do," Dorchy says. "They call anybody they want to 'unfit' and sterilize 'em. No warning. No idea they'll never be able to have children."

I don't tell Dorchy but Dr. Pynchon warned *me*. A year ago she called me into her office. "Rowan, you're fifteen now, and I no longer need your father's consent to send you to a hospital."

"Hospital?" For the polio operation?

"It is your civic responsibility to have a quick, painless operation to make sure you will never have a child." She rustled through some papers on her desk.

I shook my head, raging inside. But I forced myself to speak mildly. "I don't need an operation. I can't pass my weak leg on to anyone."

"Well, of course not," she said, "but some inherited weakness made you susceptible to a crippling disease. That weakness can be passed on to your children. Better to have the quick procedure and be done with the risk."

"Never." I stared into her cold gray eyes until she looked away. "My father won't allow it. He will come here and stop you from trying."

"And I am supposed to be afraid of this threat?" Dr. Pynchon puffed up like a pigeon.

"Only if you keep insisting I be sterilized."

I managed to walk out of her office, but broke down as soon as I found sanctuary in the empty common room. Father believed, as Dr. Pynchon did, that a weakness inherited from Mother caused me to get polio. But would he want me to be sterilized?

No. I wiped my nose and straightened my shoulders. I was still half Collier, and even half a Collier never gives up.

CHAPTER 11

The stream of people on the midway moves faster than we do, but now people smile at us as they pass and a few even step out of our way. Dorchy studies the faces of the carnies in every stall and booth. She must be looking for someone she knew when her parents worked here.

We turn a corner and there, ahead of us, the Ferris wheel spins like a mechanical toy for a giant child. Until now I've never seen one up close. I stop for the pleasure of watching it turn.

Dorchy grins at me. "You're going to love it. It's my favorite ride, bar none."

"It's so high."

"Don't worry. It's safe as houses."

The Ferris wheel slows and stops. People get off and on. I can make out the faces of the people in the swaying seats high above us. A little girl with a pinwheel waves to me. I wave back, and she hides her face in her mother's shoulder.

Dorchy says, "I'll buy the tickets." She pulls two nickels out of her leather pouch and steps past me up to the ticket seller. Then we join the slowly moving line.

Behind us a woman in a flowered dress holds the hand of a red-faced little boy in a sailor suit. He scuffs at the ground, raising puffs of dust. The woman ignores him and pats her damp face with a handkerchief. In front of us, Farm Boy and Townie are too busy counting their money to notice us.

The little boy kicks my crutch, and I stumble forward, bumping against Farm Boy.

He grabs my arm. "Whoa, Nellie."

"Don't fall for him without giving me a chance," Townie says. He tips his hat. "Howdy, Miss Goldy."

Dorchy nods to them. "Mind your manners and maybe we'll let you buy us an ice cream."

The boys move forward, hand over their tickets, and climb into a seat. The Ferris wheel lurches upward. Now it's our turn. A uniformed attendant helps us in and fastens a metal bar across our laps. I'm on the outside. The seat rocks every time we move. "Make it stop," I beg Dorchy. She laughs.

At first it's pure magic as we move slowly upward. At the top of the wheel we stop. The breeze cools our faces. In the west, the sun is well above the horizon. Spread out below us are the tents, booths, and buildings of the Exposition. Beyond the fairgrounds, the Connecticut River coils red-gold in the evening light; on the other side the windows of Springfield blaze.

"Look east," Father coaxes. "Tell me what you see."

I press my forehead against cool glass. We're at the top of the Woolworth Building, the highest building in New York, at sunset.

"The Brooklyn Bridge," says Julia.

My breath clouds the glass. "Diamonds," I say. "Diamonds on fire."
The Ferris wheel starts to move. We plunge down and down, picking up speed, once around, twice around. The third time we crest the top of the wheel, I've forgotten everything—my life before polio, Mr. Ogilvie, the show—in the breathtaking rise and fall of the ride. I squeal with excitement, not fear, when we abruptly jolt to a stop, halfway down. Above us a woman screams.

Dorchy and I crane around to see. Ten feet above us the little boy—red-faced, mouth open—is half out of his seat, one leg wedged between the side of the seat and a metal strut. His mother's screams drown out any sounds from him.

Now a chorus of excited voices joins in, yelling, "The boy, the boy."

Dorchy pulls off her apron and starts unbuttoning her dress. Our seat swings violently.

I grip the bar, stomach dropping. "What are you doing?"

She pulls her dress over her head and piles it on top of the apron on my lap. The seat rocks again. Any second now we'll be dumped out. The ground looks very far away.

"What are you *doing*?"

She pulls off her shoes and stockings, ties her hair back with the red ribbon. Barefoot and in her cotton slip, she looks much younger than sixteen.

"Hey, girls," yell the boys from their seat below ours. "You scared?"

"Dorchy." I put my hand on her arm. She shakes me off and climbs over the seat back. I pitch forward. The metal bar rams my stomach. I rock back. Someone on the ground yells, "Hey, look at that girl!"

I turn around. Dorchy is crawling along the metal spoke that connects our seat to the hub of the Ferris wheel. Our position on the wheel gives a level line to the center hub. She moves slowly and steadily. Other riders twist around or lean over the sides of their seats to watch her. On the ground a crowd gathers. The woman above is speaking calmly to the whimpering boy. Directly below us a man with a bullhorn shouts over and over, "Remain seated. The fire department is on its way." Dorchy reaches the hub and stands up. A cheer rises from people on and off the Ferris wheel.

"Go, Goldy, go!" yells Townie.

She climbs onto the steeply slanted spoke supporting the seat above ours. People on the ground gasp and point. I bite my thumbnail and taste blood.

"She's a monkey!" Farm Boy shouts. "Is that why she took off her clothes?"

I crane around to see her almost directly above me, lying flat on the spoke, talking gently to the little boy. Everything holds its breath. *Don't let them fall.* She tugs on his leg. He cries, "Mama."

Then Dorchy works his leg free and helps his mother get him back into the seat. Safe.

A prolonged cheer rises from the crowd. Even louder cheers erupt as Dorchy shinnies down the curve of the wheel and back into our seat.

I've twisted her stockings around my hand so many times they resemble a rope.

"Dorchy, that was..." I pause. I am in awe of her right now. "How did you learn to *do* that?"

She shrugs, but her eyes are shining. "My dad always said, 'If you want to work as a carny, you better know how to climb.'" She grins. "So he taught me on a Ferris wheel early in the morning before he went to work."

Our Ferris wheel still isn't moving. Dorchy pulls on her dress, stockings, and shoes. "If anyone asks you my name or where I live, keep quiet. The Ogres won't like it." She loosens her hair and reties the ribbon on top of her head. "Get away from here as fast as you can. I'll meet you by the carousel. They'll be looking for a barefoot girl in a slip."

Finally the wheel starts turning, delivering us to the ground. The attendant salutes Dorchy as we get off. And then she disappears into the crowd without a glance back.

Townie and Farm Boy chase after her. I can't move. First the little boy's mother hugs me and presses a dollar into my hand, "For your brave friend." Then the man with the bullhorn asks me to follow him to answer some questions.

Instead, I head off in the direction of the carousel as fast as I can go. Today has been one adventure after another, whirling me faster than the Ferris wheel. First I shouted out the truth to Mr. Ogilvie, then ran away with Dorchy and was shocked by the crowds and the memories that came back. Then we followed Mr. Ogilvie and sneaked into the sideshow, where I saw the unforgettable Gilda. Best of all was riding the Ferris wheel and Dorchy's climb.

I know I'll have to face Mr. Ogilvie when I get back to our tent. But I'm not afraid. Maybe I will be again someday, but right now I'm fearless.

CHAPTER 12

"Where have you been?" Mr. Ogilvie asks with real pain in his voice when I come into the tent. He was worried about me.

Minnie's fork clatters on her tin plate of fried chicken and mashed potatoes. The Council ladies have served our dinner and left.

"Out back," I mumble, looking down. "Stomachache."

"You were *not* out back," he says. "I sent Minnie to look for you."

Behind his back, Gar shakes his head. I concentrate on looking sick.

"Stomachache?" Mr. Ogilvie reaches for the one untouched plate of food. My plate. "You won't be wanting this then."

* * *

The next two days feel different now that Dorchy and I are friends. Between shows, when she's not running errands for the Ogilvies and the Council, we talk in the tent or at the picnic table behind it.

"I wish I could sleep in the cottage," she says, yawning, on the second morning. "The Ogress woke me up at three a.m. to make her peppermint tea."

"Why couldn't she make it herself?" I stop sweeping the stage to talk to her.

"'My teeth hurt,'" Dorchy says in Aunt Fan's whining voice, 'and tea is the only thing that helps.'" She snaps her fingers. "Rye whiskey. That was my dad's cure for a toothache. Too bad she's teetotal."

"You should get some from Gar and put it in her tea."

We giggle as Dorchy staggers across the stage imitating a drunken Aunt Fan.

"Dorchy," Aunt Fan calls, "come here at once. I told you not to talk to *them*."

Dorchy winks at me and jumps off the stage.

After our last show, she comes looking for me. I'm fanning myself in the open entrance to the tent, watching crowds walk past.

"You'll never guess what happened in the cottage just now." Dorchy pulls me over to sit on an empty bench. She's out of breath, and her face is damp with sweat.

"What?" I wave the fan in her direction. "I wish we had ice cream cones, don't you?"

"A couple brought their baby into the cottage just now. Wanted to fill out a questionnaire." Dorchy's eyes sparkle.

I find a way to use the fan to cool us both. "So?"

"So they're Negroes. The Council ladies went into a dither, whispering, running in circles, hiding behind doors."

"They did not."

"Did so. Aunt Fan looked ready to faint. One lady got up the courage to say, 'You don't mean *our* questionnaire, do you?' The man said, 'Yes,' and looked around at all the white families who were there."

"What's the matter with that?"

"Wake up, Rowan. Do Negroes ever come to the Unfit Family show?"

"I never noticed."

"They don't because the Council believes white people are the only fit race. Everybody else, everybody *interesting*, is *un*fit—carnies, Negroes, American Indians, Chinese, and Italians. Didn't your father tell you that?"

"Father says bettering our race is a patriotic duty. 'It's a law of nature that the fittest should rule. You might as well question gravity.'" The words sound hollow to me as I say them. A dull ache starts in the pit of my stomach.

"*Gravity?*" Dorchy laughs. "Sorry, but that should make you wonder if *any* of his ideas are worth spit." She leans closer. "I hate to give Mr. O. credit, but he saved the day. He pulled out a map of the Expo and showed the couple where to find the National Association for the Advancement of Colored People tent. 'They even have a Better Baby contest!' he said, as if it that was the greatest thing at the Expo."

"Did the Negroes leave?"

"Immediately. I felt sorry for them, but it was worth it to see the herd upset."

"The herd?"

"The *cows* on the *Cow*ncil. Bye!" She rushes off.

I watch her go. Her story reminds me of something I haven't thought of in years. I was five when Bernard, the man who took care of the furnace at our house, found a kitten in the coal bin. After he gave her a bath, he brought her upstairs to me. She was a tiger kitten, but I named her Coal. At breakfast I asked Father, "Is Bernard from a best family like we are?"

"Bernard is a fine man," Father said, placing his coffee cup on the saucer. "Why do you ask?"

"Because he is *very* kind to animals. You told me that is a sign of people from the best families."

"It is." Father dabbed his mouth with his napkin. "But keeping the races separate is a basic belief of the Betterment movement."

I thought this over. "So Bernard can't be the best because he is a different race?"

Father gave me a look.

"Separate how?" I pressed.

"Well, for one thing, people of different races should not marry." He picked up the newspaper.

"Why not?"

In a tone of finality he said, "You don't need to worry about *that.*"

I didn't give a thought to questions like these for years. Then I met Dorchy.

CHAPTER 13

Bellevue Hospital,
New York City, 1917–18

Stella and I didn't become friends right away, even though our beds were next to each other on the polio ward for girls ages eight and up. Stella was tall and pretty, with long, dark hair and a weak right leg. At eleven, we were the oldest girls on the ward. Dr. Friedlander was our doctor. But I saw her as a rival, and I was determined to walk on crutches before she did. I had to. I was a Collier.

One day Dr. Friedlander challenged us to a race in the therapy room. We would hang on to wooden railings on either side of a narrow walkway. Using our arms and good legs we were to hop-walk to the middle, about twenty feet. I started at one end and Stella at the other. Whoever got to the middle first could choose a record from Dr. Friedlander's collection to play for the next exercise.

"'Trip the light fantastic,' girls," he said, and put on his favorite, "The Sidewalks of New York."

Stella and I were well matched for this, but I believed I could win.

"*East side, west side, all around the town,*" the lively tune and familiar words gave me confidence. *I am a Collier of Manhattan,* I told myself. *She lives in Brooklyn.* But after only a few feet, I was struggling. Stella surged toward me.

I tried to go faster. But the more I tried, the slower I went.

Then Stella's weak leg folded and she dropped to her knees on the walkway.

I win, I told myself and stopped where I was.

"Keep going, Rowan," shouted Dr. Friedlander.

I stood still, resenting him. *Why go on? I won.*

"*Boys and girls together, me and Mamie O'Rourke,*" sang the quartet on the record.

Stella, her face red, struggled to stand.

"*Tripped the light fantastic on the sidewalks...*"

"You fall, you get up," was one of Dr. Friedlander's mottoes. "Keep moving," was another.

I win, I said to myself and stood still.

Stella managed to get up and start moving again, her smile as wide as Central Park, her breath coming in gasps. She stopped in the middle.

"And the winner is Stella," said Dr. Friedlander, clapping loudly. "For fortitude in the face of adversity. Bravo!"

"*You are the best of the best, Rowan.*" Father's voice rang inside my head. But, I realized, he wouldn't say that now.

Later, as the nurse massaged my legs, Dr. Friedlander rolled a stool over next to me. "Tell me what happened today, Rowan."

I stared at the ceiling. *I'll ask Julia to take me home. Find me a better doctor. A doctor worthy of a Collier. I'm too good for this hospital. I am the best.*

"I knew you would fail today as soon as you stood up between the railings."

Curiosity got the better of me. "How could you know that?"

He took a deep breath. "I've learned to observe people who are getting well. As soon as one starts to do better, he or she wants to do *better than* someone else. Every move you made today announced, 'I am superior to Stella and I will crush her.'"

"I never said that."

"Your body said it. When Stella fell, you stopped because you thought you'd won. That's not winning. Winning is keeping going. As Stella did. You were privileged to see an act of real courage today. Recognize it; use it."

My face burned.

As he walked away, he said, "The key to recovery is *you*, Rowan, not your family."

* * *

Later lying in my bed next to Stella's, I whispered, "What made you keep going?" The words sounded forced.

"Oh, Rowan," she said. "When I fall it is hard to get up because you won. 'Why not rest?' I think."

"Why didn't you?" I was honestly curious.

Stella sighed. "I could not. Maybe I die trying, but I will stand and walk."

Maybe I die trying, but I will stand and walk.

Tears filled my eyes.

"And you, Rowan," she said, "you will too."

Stella and I became friends. We encouraged each other on the rings suspended from ropes that helped us strengthen our arms. We staggered and fell on crutches until we got the hang of them. We strapped steel and leather braces on our weak legs for an hour every day. Using crutches with the brace on was hard work, but we cheered for each other and Dr. Friedlander used us to teach the younger kids how to do it.

"You'll make a good nurse one day," he said to me after one of our demonstrations. "You have a knack few people have around polio patients."

"I have a good teacher," I said.

"I'm serious. In five years you'll be walking without these"—he tapped my crutches—"and old enough to start nursing school. Think about it."

When I left Bellevue and went to the Home, all thoughts of Dr. Friedlander and nursing school were driven out of my head by the effort of surviving. But here at the Expo, the memories are starting to come back. Dorchy is bringing me back to life.

CHAPTER 14

Just before supper, Minnie and Gar join me in the doorway. As a woman walks by pushing a baby in a stroller, Minnie waggles her fingers and the baby smiles.

Minnie says sadly, "I love babies, but I'll never have one of my own."

"Why not?" I ask. Gar gives me a warning shake of his head.

Minnie sighs. "A woman came to the house and offered to take me to see a doctor. She came to all the houses in the Falls."

"Where is that?" I ask.

"Down by the river where the poor folks live." Her eyes flash. "Good folks. All of them."

"What did the woman say?"

"She sat with Mama and me and said she was offering me and other kids in the Falls a chance to get checked out by a doctor. I didn't want to go, but Mama said I had to because she couldn't afford a doctor and this one was free. So the woman took me and some other kids from the Falls in a big car. Drove it herself."

"How old were you?"

Minnie shrugs. "Fourteen. She took us to a hospital, and a doctor said I needed an operation that would give me a better chance in life. He gave me gas so it didn't hurt, and I had ice cream afterward. Chocolate. The next day another woman took us home. But later." She frowns. "Later a man told me and Mama that the operation keeps me from ever having a baby. I felt so bad to be tricked by those people with their lies and big car and ice cream." Tears roll down her cheeks. "I was always good with babies. Not like they make out here in the show."

"The Unfit Family show and all that Fitter Families blarney is a damn lie." Anger pulses in Gar's voice. "I signed on for the money, but I'll be glad when it ends."

"I'm so sorry, Minnie," I say, patting her hand. How dare those people trick her? And then I wonder, with a shiver of dread, if Father and Julia believe in tricking people into sterilization.

* * *

Later Mr. Ogilvie locks us in. As soon as he's gone, I reach under my pillow. Another rose. This one is yellow. I throw it into the still-empty pail. *Does Aunt Fan know he's taking her precious roses?* Then I unlock our door and open it. A muffled thumping comes from the other end of the hall. Minnie, smoking on her cot, shrinks back against the wall. "Don't worry." I pat her shoulder. "Jimmy's having a seizure. Gar and I will help him."

She nods her head, and the tip of her cigarette glows red.

I grab my crutch and go down the hall to Gar and Jimmy's room.

In the light from the small window, Jimmy lies on the floor by his cot. His eyes are rolled back; his mouth is open; blood wells from a cut over his ear. Gar gently turns him on his side and pulls out a handkerchief. "He had a seizure and hit his head. Hold this on the cut."

He turns on the flashlight he brought back one night and studies Jimmy's face. "He's pale," Gar says.

"He's unconscious." I mop blood off Jimmy's cheek and return the handkerchief to the oozing cut.

"Something's wrong. He should be coming out of it by now." Gar strikes another match and holds it in front of Jimmy's eyes. "See, he's not blinking. I saw this in France when I was a medic."

It's true that Jimmy's seizures usually don't last more than a couple of minutes. "Maybe it's because he hit his head."

Gar sucks in a breath. "I'm going for help. If anybody complains, I'll tell them I quit the show. It's a crime to lock up someone sick."

He touches my shoulder. "Don't fret if it takes me awhile. At this hour, I'll have to go all the way to the midway to get help."

After Gar leaves, Minnie comes down the hall to sit with me while I look after Jimmy. He's shivering and his skin feels cold even in the stored-up heat of the cottage. I cover him with a blanket. His head has stopped bleeding and he's starting to come out of the seizure, but he isn't fully awake. I shine the flashlight on his face, and this time he blinks and tries to cover his eyes. I turn it off and say, "He's fine," hoping it's true.

In the sudden darkness Minnie shrieks. The anguished sound rakes my spine with icy fingers. I force myself to stay calm and flick the light on Jimmy. "See, he's better already."

I smell smoke, just as she screams, "Fire!"

I point the flashlight beam at the hall. A haze of gray smoke hangs at the far end outside our room. Behind it is the crackling orange glow of fire.

Minnie is usually careful to put out her cigarettes, but tonight she must have dropped one on the rug. With a sick feeling, I watch the glow get brighter. I bite back a scream of my own and say in an authoritative voice, "Stay with Jimmy, Minnie. Don't let him see it."

I start down the hall into thickening smoke. The straw carpet is burning, sending sparks into the air, blocking the back door Gar unlocked when he left. Coughing, I force myself to keep going. Sparks land on the hall carpet in front of me and flare up. I try to stamp them out, but the fire is moving toward me. Its terrible heat and choking smoke push me back to the front of the cottage.

A wave of fear breaks inside me. We're trapped. I have to do something. Now.

Think. At the Home, we have water buckets, pails of sand, fire extinguishers. Here, nothing. Even our pails are empty at this time of night.

In Gar and Jimmy's room the smoke is getting heavier, but Jimmy is sitting up, a good sign. He's holding his head and coughing, not so good. "What happened?" he asks.

"You had a seizure and hit your head," I say matter-of-factly. In the far corner of the room, Minnie hunches over, crying.

I close the door behind me. It feels like I'm sealing our tomb. Every muscle in my body screams, *Get moving. Find a way out!*

Jimmy tries to stand up. "We have to get out," he says, choking.

"The fire is blocking the back door," I say, "but I have an idea." I climb on Gar's cot and use the flashlight to break the little locked window, too small to use for escape. Pieces of glass sprinkle my arms. "Fire!" I scream through the opening. "Help! Fire!" *Why doesn't anyone hear me? Come running? Save us?* By now smoke and maybe even flames should be visible outside the cottage. *Why isn't Gar back yet?*

For a second, fear paralyzes me. Then anger, hotter than the flames, sweeps that away. *How dare the Ogilvies lock us up, trap us like rats, sentence us to death?*

The cot shakes as Minnie scrambles up behind me, drawn by the thin draft of fresh air in this smoky room.

As I climb down, she howls out the broken window, "Help us!" over and over.

"Minnie's louder than you," Jimmy says between coughs. He's still lying on the floor.

"Keep that up, Minnie," I say when she pauses for breath. "I'm going out in the hall now. Keep the bedroom door closed."

"Get us out," Jimmy says as I crawl past him. His panic ignites mine.

When I open the bedroom door a crack, flames flare up higher and brighter. Smoke presses against my face like a hand. Coughing and gagging, I drop to my knees and crawl.

I pound on the front door and rattle the handle, willing it to open, but it's locked on my side. I take my crutch and break some of the small glass panes that frame the door. Smoke clogs my nose, throat, lungs. I put my face against a small opening and suck in air. *Breathe.* I send a thin stream of words—"Fire! Help! Fire!"—out into the night.

"Where are you?" Jimmy yells from the bedroom.

I take another precious gulp of air.

Then some instinct guides my hand through the lowest broken pane. I stretch my hand down. Broken glass along the edge of the frame tears my skin. I reach farther and then farther still. My fingers brush the key sticking out of the lock. I turn it and feel the lock release.

Run. For a second I imagine opening the door, running outside, escaping. Instead I crawl to the bedroom door and open it. Minnie and Jimmy are huddled on the floor coughing.

"Follow me! Crawl!"

The fire's roar is so loud and the smoke is so thick that I can't tell if they're coming or not. I crawl back to the front door, reach up to turn the handle, burning my fingers, and open it. Then, with Minnie and Jimmy pushing me, I fall out onto the porch.

Behind us the fire leaps up, its breath hot on my legs.

CHAPTER 15

I try to speak, but I can't open my mouth.

"Here's one of them," says a man and scoops me up as easily as if I were a kitten.

"That's her," Dorchy shouts.

Air moves across my face as the man carries me, but I can't inhale it.

"She's not breathing." Dorchy sounds scared. I want to see her, but I can't open my eyes.

"We're too late," another man says in a matter-of-fact voice.

No, I just need air.

"Aw, look at that poor leg," the first man says. "She's been through too much to give up."

Air. Now.

"Here." A wet cloth covers my face. Brandy fumes bite at my nose and throat. "Wake up, Ruthie," Dorchy yells and yanks the cloth away. "Breathe." She slaps the cloth over my nose again.

She knows I hate the name Ruthie. I try to twist my head away from the cloth. She lifts it. Coughing and retching, I struggle for a breath, find one, then another, and another. My eyes open.

"What were you doing in the cottage?" asks the man holding me. He wears a gray uniform with a New England States Exposition nameplate. His face is streaked black.

"I told you," Dorchy says. "She's with the Unfit Family show. There are four of them that sleep in there. *Locked* in."

I paw at Dorchy's arm. I have to tell her Jimmy and Minnie got out, but my throat hurts too much to speak.

"It's a good thing your friend saw the smoke, dearie," the man says as he sets me down under a tree. "Rest here for a while. We got here just in time, thanks to her."

I take another breath. Dorchy crouches beside me. She hands me a dented tin cup. Light from the fire flickers on her face.

I swallow. But my throat is so scorched and dry I can't make a sound.

A steady thumping starts up from the West Springfield Fire Department truck in front of the cottage. Firemen in black coats pull a hose across the screen porch and aim a stream of water through the front door. Spray lands on my face and legs. A hiss of steam and smells of wet wood and smoke coil over us. The cottage—screens torn off the porch, front door hanging open, smoke pouring out—looks destitute. *Unfit.*

Cheers go up as the flames die down. The fire has attracted a crowd almost as big as a midway sideshow.

I bury my face in my hands. My chest burns and my throat aches.

Dorchy pats my hand. "They put Jimmy and Minnie in the tent. Bet you're wondering how *I* got here. The Ogress brought me along to a lecture the Ogre's giving at the Rotary pavilion. I was there to hand her brandy when the pain got too bad, doctor's orders. When I saw the smoke I ran."

I choke the words, "Gar isn't here" and start coughing again. Dorchy goes for more water.

"I thought you were dead," she says, holding a tin cup to my mouth. Her voice catches. "Jimmy said they dragged you as far as they could. He says you could have got out, but you went back for him and Minnie."

I close my eyes. A pile of bricks is crushing my chest.

"Why didn't you leave when you could?" she asks, angry now. "Why did you go back?"

My first thought—*I couldn't let Father down*—I keep to myself. "I had to," I say, and the words sound watered down, untrue.

Dorchy shrugs this off. "No, really, why *did* you go back for them?" she asks.

At that moment our differences feel like a stone wall between us. I shrug. "I had to," I say again, hoping she'll leave it there.

"Well, then you're a hero," Dorchy says. "And I've got good news about your name."

"So do I. It's not Ruthie."

She laughs. "I wanted to make you mad so you'd start breathing. No, this is important."

"What is?"

"Your name comes from the rowan tree."

"No, it's a family name."

"Well, your family got it from a tree. And not any old tree. The rowan tree protects people from witchcraft. Didn't you ever hear the rhyme: 'Rowan tree, red thread, holds the witches all in dread?'"

My laugh turns to a cough. When I can speak, I say, "The Colliers aren't afraid of witches."

"Of course not." Dorchy leans closer, her green eyes burning. "But the rowan tree also protects people from fire." She sits back, waiting for me to thank her.

"There you are, Ruthie." Aunt Fan's voice sounds muffled, as if she's speaking through a wadded-up handkerchief. She bends down, eyes blazing. "How did you get out here? Who unlocked your room and the front door?"

"Aunt Fan," Gar says. "Let me explain." He's breathing hard, and his hands and clothes are soot-streaked. "I unlocked the doors. I used my skills as I saw fit. For Jimmy's safety."

"*Safety?*" she shrieks. "Don't you dare use that word with me. You unlocked doors and the cottage burned down."

"Begging your pardon," Gar says, "but I see it differently."

"What do you mean?" Her hands twitch at her sides.

"If those rooms had been locked, we'd have three dead bodies."

"What we *have* is a disaster." She points at the still smoking, water-soaked cottage. "A destroyed building and the loss of important records. Not to mention a runaway."

"A runaway?" Gar sounds puzzled.

"You," she says triumphantly.

"I went for help," Gar says stubbornly, "and I'd do it again."

"You took your time getting back." Aunt Fan brushes at her dress as spray from the hoses blows over us. "The cottage was practically ashes before the firemen got here."

"I went for an ambulance," Gar says stiffly. "To get help for Jimmy."

"Then the other three must have started the fire," Aunt Fan looks at me. "What was it? A cigarette? Minnie smokes, doesn't she? Despite it being against the rules? Don't lie to me. I swear it's natural selection, that's what it is."

I stand up, leaning on Dorchy. My crutch burned up in the cottage. "It wasn't any of us."

"Then who started it? A cottage doesn't spontaneously combust."

Gar and Dorchy look at me expectantly. Like Aunt Fan they must assume Minnie started the fire with a dropped cigarette.

"I don't know." I can see why they believe it was Minnie, but she is such a creature of habit that I'm suddenly sure that she did not let her cigarette drop on the floor. There has to be another explanation.

Gar takes my hand. "I'm sorry I wasn't there."

I manage a smile. "It came out all right. We're all alive."

* * *

Later, I lie awake on the stage in the tent, wrapped in a blanket roll the Betterment Council ladies brought for us. Minnie sleeps peacefully next to me, but my heart is still racing from the dream that woke me up. In it I was back at Bellevue telling Julia about the fire and how I saved myself and two others.

In real life Julia came every visiting day with flowers or fruit, sometimes a bag of cookies. She didn't seem to enjoy being there. She sat stiffly, eyes down so she wouldn't have to see a nurse carrying a bedpan or a girl with a twisted foot or Stella's father, waving his arms and speaking Italian. Stella's parents brought her an overflowing basket of Italian food every week. They also brought wine, until a horrified nurse discovered it.

I told Julia about the exercises I'd done, equipment I'd mastered, and about reading to the younger patients. Julia always brought two new books with her. One for me and one for the "children," but she never asked to meet them or watched me read to them.

For the first months at some point in every visit she would say, "No word from Father, I'm afraid. But letters do take time to come from France."

But in January when she said it, I burst out with, "Unless every ship from France since September sank, you'd think one letter would have reached you by now. Maybe he's dead. Would they tell you if he was?"

Julia went white and gripped her black briefcase tightly. She opened her mouth to speak, but just then Stella's mother burst out laughing over a picture Stella was showing her in a book.

"Come on," Julia said. "I'll wheel you down to the sunroom where we can hear ourselves think."

Once she had parked me by the window so I could admire the view of the East River, she said, "Father isn't dead." She twisted her gloved hands in her lap. "I have had letters from him, but he hasn't written to you. I didn't want to tell you." She had tears in her eyes.

Shocked, I asked, "Well, what does he say?"

"He's not allowed to say much, nothing about the war or his work," she said in a rush. "So he writes about five-course dinners he's eaten or admirals he's met. Very boring."

I sat frozen. *Father doesn't write to me. He writes to Julia. He doesn't mention me.*

"Well," I said finally, "do you write to him about me? About my progress? Because it *is* progress. One leg isn't paralyzed any more, and the other is getting stronger. Have you told him that?" My voice rose.

"Shh," Julia said. "I write to him and tell him all about you. Of course, I do. I don't understand why he..." She looked stricken. "It's been so hard *not* to tell you. I keep hoping he will write you."

"You should have told me," I said. My voice was as hard and small as a marble. The words *Father's forgotten me* rolled closer. I pushed them away. I'd made progress, and I'd done it without him.

"Father thinks I died when I got polio," I said. "But *you* know I didn't. My legs *seemed* dead when he carried me into the doctor's office, but they're alive. Tell him that."

I started to wheel myself out of the sunroom. I had never even tried that before. The startled look on her face was worth the effort it took to turn the big wheels with my hands.

"See what I can do?" I called over my shoulder. "Not because I'm a Collier. Because I'm me."

* * *

Lying awake in the dark tent, still smelling smoke, I understand that the fire is a turning point, a hinge. It opened a door inside me that I had given up looking for. In the cottage when my fingers found the key that saved our lives, that other door opened. After tonight I'm no longer someone who lets people do things *to* her.

CHAPTER 16

I wake up with the taste of smoke in my mouth and Minnie tapping my shoulder. Mr. Ogilvie arrives with Dorchy and four Council ladies. Over breakfast of bread and butter and cold tea, he says, "The Unfit Family show is canceled today. We'll conduct Fitter Family evaluations here in the tent and find a place for you to perform tomorrow." He speaks slowly and loudly, as if we're all deaf and feebleminded.

I catch Dorchy's eye and we both smile. Deep down I was sure the Council would cancel our shows and send me back to the Boston Home. Now I'll have a few more days here.

"I hope you'll find us a comfortable place to sleep." Gar rubs his back. "This tent floor is rock hard."

Mr. Ogilvie eyes him coldly. "Since you didn't suffer the effects of the fire, you'll help us here in the tent today."

The cold tea soothes my raw throat. Jimmy is pale as a fish and complains of a splitting headache. Minnie bursts into tears when anyone speaks to her. I wonder if Gar will be punished for leaving through the back door.

The fire department claims they have no evidence of what started the fire, but the Ogilvies and the Council are unanimous: Minnie did it. "An accident" is what the Springfield newspaper calls it.

This morning we were given new clothes to replace our soot-covered ones. But we have to stay in our dirty clothes until we have baths. My new dress is blue dotted swiss with a drop waist. It's short and little-girlish, but the underclothes look like they'll fit and there's a new hairbrush and lavender hair pomade. No replacement book for *Little Women*, but I do have a new crutch.

After breakfast Dorchy leaves and Minnie, Jimmy, and I sit outside on camp stools breathing in the smoky, wet wood smell of the blackened cottage while the Council members, with Gar's help, move furniture and boxes of Fitter Families materials into the tent.

A Council lady comes out of the tent holding up the silver Fittest Family trophy for us to admire. "Glory be," she shouts. "It's unharmed!"

"So are we," I whisper. "No thanks to you."

After an hour, Mr. Ogilvie herds us through the Exposition to our new home, one of the medical pavilions. The walkways are deserted, the Expo's gates not open yet.

We go into a small white building, about twice the size of the cottage. Eight cubicles walled off with sheets line a central hall where a table, four chairs, and a tall step-on scale await us. Aunt Fan and Dorchy are already there. We stare at Aunt Fan. Her face has a greenish tinge, and a paisley scarf is tied around her swollen jaw.

"You'll have a bath and rest here today and sleep here tonight," Mr. Ogilvie says. "The medical staff has been relocated. You must stay inside and call no attention to yourselves. No smoking, Minnie!

Dorchy will bring you your meals. A bathroom with a tub is at the other end of the hall."

He puts his hand on Aunt Fan's shoulder. "We'll be going back to the dentist."

She closes her eyes and cradles her jaw.

Gar and Dorchy leave to help with the Fitter Families exhibit, and Mrs. Aubrey, a morose Council lady with a "bum ankle," comes to sit with Minnie, Jimmy, and me. We each take two baths. The first one gets the worst of the soot off and the second gets us clean. Minnie and Jimmy take naps in their cubicles.

I comb out my clean hair. No braids today. Without performances, why bother? I put on the dotted swiss dress. It's even shorter than it looked, but it is clean.

At noon Dorchy appears with our lunch in a basket. Her eyes and face glow; she practically gives off sparks.

She announces she has a message for me from Aunt Fan. She delivers it loud enough for everyone to hear. "Ruthie is requested to return to the Fitter Families tent forthwith. That means right now," Dorchy says. "No lunch."

Once outside, she grabs my hand. "I have a plan. We can talk while we eat fried chicken on the midway."

"What about Aunt Fan?"

"Oh, I made that up. The Ogress is still at the dentist."

We walk for a minute in the direction of the food stalls. Then Dorchy ducks behind a John Deere tractor display. She rubs her foot in the dirt and then blurts out, "They're shutting down the Unfit Family show."

"No, it's only canceled for today. Mr. Ogilvie told us."

"I don't care what he told you. It's canceled."

I look at her doubtfully, and she digs her fingers into my arm.

"Two men with Expo badges came into the tent. The first one said, 'Who's in charge?' Mrs. Clarke said, 'I am the Council president. And I want you to know the Unfit Family show is discontinued.'" Dorchy laughs. "Like she knew why the men had come and wanted to get there first. You should have seen the Ogre's face. He went dead white and opened his mouth like a fish. I thought Aunt Fan was going to cry.

"'Good,' says the other man. 'Because we're here to inform you that no further shows or residence by the Unfit Family actors on the Expo grounds will be tolerated. It's a miracle they aren't all dead.'

"Then they walked away. Mrs. Clarke rushed after them. When she came back, she said to the Ogilvies, 'Your negligence destroyed Exposition property and exposed the Council to a lawsuit. You and the unfit must leave before five o'clock today.' I think the Council cows despise the Ogilvies."

"What did the Ogre say?"

Dorchy imitates his high-pitched voice. "'Of course, Mrs. Clarke. Right away, Mrs. Clarke. Anything you say.' And then he took Aunt Fan to the dentist."

My throat closes, and I rub my sore eyes. "I don't want to leave today."

"Don't worry. I have a plan to get both of us away from here." Her voice tightens around me. "First, I'll take the Ogre's wallet."

"No, Dorchy."

"Oh, I'll give it back. *After* I take out our pay. He hasn't paid you, has he?" She doesn't wait for an answer. "The next part is where you come in. You're the key." Her words tumble out. "He's in love with you."

I shiver. "*What?*"

"All those roses he leaves for you. The photographs. The way he looks at you." She grips my hand so tightly I wince.

"And"—she pauses—"he told me when we were in his car. He's teaching me to drive."

"*Drive?*" Jealousy washes over me. With my weak leg, I'll never be able to drive.

"Mr. Ogilvie convinced the Ogress she needs another driver besides him. She claims she's too old to learn. So he's been giving me lessons. They want me to go on working for them when the Expo ends. But I won't. And I won't go back to the orphanage either."

She goes on, "And all he wants to talk about, when the Ogress isn't around, is you."

I stare at her. "Why didn't you tell me?"

"Because I knew it would make you mad. And he can't know how angry we are until it's too late. The perfect con."

"Dorchy, take the money he owes you, if you want, but I'm not going to help you steal."

"I don't need your help *stealing*," she says. "You're going to rip out his heart and stomp on it." She spits in her palm and holds out her hand. "Are you with me?"

CHAPTER 17

I am. Dr. Friedlander got me on my feet and gave me back my legs; Dorchy gave me back myself. She showed me I don't need to be protected because I walk with a limp. She gave me my book. She told me what my name means.

I spit on my hand and shake hers.

The plan she lays out over fried chicken and biscuits on the midway sounds foolproof. I will accept Mr. Ogilvie's invitation to go to his favorite place today at three o'clock. Dorchy says, "Remember how he cried at the Narda exhibit and how he sometimes says, 'Your poor leg'? Well, play up how weak and crippled you are and how you almost died in the fire."

When he and I go to his car (always parked in the same place, Dorchy says), Dorchy will meet us. She'll insist on going with us— if necessary, threatening to tell Aunt Fan about his feelings for me.

Once we get to the place, he'll park and get out of the car to help me get out. But before he opens my door, Dorchy will climb over the seat and drive off with me. She'll throw his wallet out the window, having removed our "pay," and drive to the Springfield train station. "There's enough salary owed me to get us both tickets to New York on the five o'clock train," she says.

When I don't say anything, she grabs my hand. "I can find my uncle with the carnies at Coney Island and you can go *home*. Isn't that what you want?"

"What if Mr. Ogilvie won't let you come with us?"

"He will."

She has no doubts about the plan; I have plenty. But a steady drumbeat of anger is drowning them out.

"I'll do it," I say. "But what if he goes to the police and they find out where we've gone?"

"He'll be too embarrassed to tell anyone, especially the police. Believe me, he won't want the Ogress to know."

We walk back to the Unfit Family tent where a row of scorched wooden file cabinets gape open. Council women in aprons and head scarves paw through folders and papers spread out on a picnic table.

"We'll open the Fitter Families exhibit here tomorrow," one woman is saying as we come in, and a few of the women applaud. Mr. Ogilvie has been emptying a file cabinet drawer, but he hurries over to us.

"Ruthie, I'm glad you're here," he says, touching my arm. "I have news just for you. Now take a seat here and wait while I talk to Dorchy. Will you do that?"

I sit on a wooden chair, wondering what news he has that is "just for me." Mr. Ogilvie tells Dorchy, "Since you were at the scene, you're just the person I need to go to the Administration Building with Miss Latigue to fill out the fire report."

"I was *in* the fire," I say loud enough for him to hear. My heart is beating so fast I'm sure everyone can see it. *In fact, I almost died in the fire. Thanks to you locking us in.*

He smiles at me and puts his finger to his lips. Then he leads Dorchy over to a tall, young woman in a blue dress. They talk with Mr. Ogilvie for a few minutes. As Dorchy leaves the tent, she grins and gives me a thumbs-up. I shake my head. Now I'll have to speak to *him* without Dorchy nearby. And what if she's gone a long time?

He takes me by the arm. "Come, Ruthie," he says, and we follow Dorchy and Miss Latigue out the front entrance. He shows me the *Fitter Families for a Better America* banner that two men on ladders are hanging on the side of the tent.

"My dear," he says, "we have decided regretfully to end the Unfit Family show. I must return you to Boston this afternoon."

I stare at him. "*End* it? But you said..."

"Things changed." He opens his hands in a what-can-you-do gesture. "The Unfit Family show is over, but the Fitter Families exhibit will go on."

As if I cared about *that*. "What about Jimmy?" I ask, my mind racing. *What do I do now?*

"We'll pick up Jimmy after our picnic," he says cheerfully. "Now we must be off."

"But I have to say good-bye." My chest tightens and I can hardly swallow. "To Minnie and Gar. And Aunt Fan. And Dorchy."

He looks at his watch. "No time for that." His voice is still cheerful. "You can write them letters in care of the New England Betterment Council, Post Office Box 102, Springfield, Massachusetts." He licks his lips. "Thanks to the fire, you have nothing to pack, so we can leave right now. I want to take you to my special place."

But it's too soon! "I was hoping to see your special place," I say, forcing my voice to stay calm. "At three o'clock today, in fact."

"No, no. That's too late. To have time for our picnic we must go *now*, dear heart." He reaches for my hand, then stops himself. "The Buick is parked right over there. You have made me so very happy."

I grip the crutch so hard my knuckles turn white. Our plan is in shreds. I'm going to be alone with him. I walk very slowly, exaggerating my limp, looking around for Dorchy. She has to see us and coming running back.

He grips my free arm and hurries me over to the car parked on the lawn next to the tent.

He lets go of me to open the passenger door. I slide in. He puts my crutch on the backseat and gets behind the wheel. My fingers grip the door handle.

"Ruthie," he says, putting his hand on my shoulder, "thank you for keeping our secret. Poor Fan has just about all she can deal with right now."

"No more shows, no more Ruthie," I say. "I'm Rowan again." My mouth is dry. *Should I get out now? Stay in the car and see what happens?*

The engine rumbles to life. "We'll come back for Jimmy after our outing. How does that sound?"

"Fine," I say in a calm voice. *We'll come back, and Dorchy and I can still run away.* I press back against the seat. I just have to figure out how to cut this outing short.

He drives slowly away from the tent, past a row of booths, to the Expo gate. Then he turns onto a smooth, blacktop road. Cool air rushes in the open side windows as he speeds up.

CHAPTER 18

"You'll like going fast," Mr. Ogilvie shouts, the wind whipping the words away. "Edith did."

I take deep breaths and dig my fingers into the soft leather seat. I lock away Dorchy and our failed plan in a deep part of my mind. It's time for a new plan.

We drive north, away from the fairgrounds. Lining the wide avenue are big houses with rolling lawns. Tall trees arch overhead, their leaves swaying in the light breeze. In spite of being with Mr. Ogilvie, I'm thrilled to see the world outside the Exposition.

"Where are we going?" I shout over the noise of the engine.

He smiles and puts a finger to his lips.

After a few minutes, I lean forward, clutching my stomach. "Mr. Ogilvie, I feel sick," I say. "I want to go back."

"Dear girl"—he pats my shoulder—"you're not used to automobiles. And call me Edward, please. See, I'm slowing down. We're almost there."

We turn onto a narrow paved road and slowly roll through a wide, iron gate. Filigreed letters across the top spell out "St. Thomas Cemetery." A grassy field dotted with white headstones stretches in front of us under the overcast sky. We pass a few automobiles, heading in the opposite direction. No one on foot. Still, we won't be all alone. Other people do come here.

"The cemetery closes at sunset," he says, "but that's hours from now. We don't need to worry about outstaying our welcome."

I want to laugh. What kind of "welcome" does a cemetery offer?

Now the paved drive narrows and gravel crunches under the tires as we pass through a grove of maple trees. Beyond it looms a marble forest of tall monuments and mausoleums, small marble buildings surrounded by knee-high black chains.

On our right a pond reflects the early afternoon sky. Water cascades from a pile of rocks in the center. They look as fake as the ones on Gilda's stage. I wonder if snakes live in the pond.

Mr. Ogilvie pulls off the gravel road onto the grass and stops. Turns off the engine. My curiosity gets the better of my fear.

"Why is this your favorite place?" Over the ticking of the engine and splashing water, a mourning dove croons.

"You remind me so much of my cousin Edith." His voice trembles like a raindrop on a leaf. "I wanted to bring you to her special place." He reaches toward my hair, but doesn't touch it. "She's buried right there under that angel. Do you see?"

I breathe in the scent of his sweat and hair oil, wet earth and stagnant water. The idea that I am similar in any way to dead Edith makes me sick.

"Can we get out and look?" I reach around to grab my crutch, wanting its solid weight in my hand, needing to be on my feet.

"Not yet." He puts his hand on my arm and leaves it there. "That ride with the wind blowing in your face. And you feeling sick." He speaks to me as if I'm six, not sixteen. "I brought ginger beer." He's waiting for me to clap my hands and bounce up and down saying, "Oh goody, yes, please." But I concentrate on one thought, getting back to the Expo and Dorchy.

"We'll stay right here by Edith's pond," he says. "That's what I call it." He gets out of the car, then pulls my crutch, the blanket, and a basket from the backseat, and walks away.

I yell to him, "I need my crutch."

He calls over his shoulder. "Don't worry, I'll carry you."

He lays my crutch on the ground next to the picnic basket and spreads the blanket close to the edge of the pond. Then he takes off his suit jacket. His blue shirt is soaked under the arms. As he walks back to the car, I take a good look at him—weak chin, no beard, hair combed straight back and slick with pomade. Ears that stick out. *He's ludicrous*, I tell myself. *And he has no idea how strong I am.*

He lifts me out of the car and gasps, "You're much heavier than Edith."

Panting, he sets me down on the blanket and pulls a ginger beer bottle from the picnic basket and opens it.

"Can you drink from the bottle?" he says, holding it out. "I forgot to bring a tumbler." He kneels next to me, rummaging in the picnic basket.

"What happened to your cousin?" I ask.

His mouth trembles, and in that instant, I know I can use Edith to get away from here.

"She died." He takes embroidered linen napkins and a box of chocolate cookies out of the picnic basket. With a sigh he sinks down next to me, his left leg pressed against my right. I shift my leg away from his. "She made these," he says. He offers me a thick chocolate cookie on an embroidered yellow napkin.

"The cookies?" My throat closes. *Isn't she dead?*

"No, silly. Fan made the cookies. Edith made the napkins." He takes a bite, and crumbs cascade down his shirt.

"Did Edith have polio?" Maybe if I poke and prod him about her, he'll give up and drive me back.

"Edith was born whole and healthy," he says in a soft voice. "But at age twelve she had the infantile paralysis, long before you did. Her poor right leg was like your left." He takes a bite and speaks while he chews. "I've watched you onstage, trying so hard to manage. And failing. I know your leg must hurt terribly." He helps himself to another cookie. "I hope you'll let me massage it after we eat."

His words catch and tear at me like claws. "We don't have time, Mr. Ogilvie." I force a regretful smile. "We have to get Jimmy and drive to Boston, remember?"

"Oh, my dear." He rests his hand on my left leg, squeezing it through the fabric of my dress. "Call me Edward. I insist."

Then he twitches the hem of my dress up a few inches.

I push his hand away and take a last swallow of warm ginger beer. The bottle feels like a weapon.

I pull my knees up and wrap my arms around them. Still holding the bottle.

"Allow me." Before I can stop him, he takes the bottle and puts it in the basket. "I hate the thought of you so far away in Boston." He pulls a brown envelope out of the basket. "But until I can visit you, I'll have these." Snapshots flutter down onto the blanket.

I stare at them, cold with revulsion. Pictures of me. Lying on the stage, skirt pulled up, left leg exposed. Laughing with Minnie backstage. Talking to Gar in the tent after the show.

My stomach contracts. "What's this?" I shove a picture at him. He took it when I was asleep on my cot, a sliver of morning light on my face.

"You looked so beautiful," he says. "I came in to get some papers from the file cabinet. I didn't want to wake you."

"How could you?" My words are a white-hot poker jabbing at him. "You had no right to come in our room. I was *sleeping*." On the last word my voice screeches.

I tear up the picture and scatter the pieces on the grass. Then I reach for the other photographs.

"Stop." His voice trembles. He collects the torn scraps with shaking fingers and slides them back in the envelope. "I have the negatives," he says in a petulant voice.

The sun breaks through the clouds, and a shaft of light turns the pond to gold. My breath feels trapped in my throat. Whatever I expected, it wasn't this.

"I can tell you're upset," he says. "But you mustn't be. Edith never minded when I photographed her"—his voice breaks—"even her poor legs."

"How old was she when you did that?" I force myself to speak naturally. *Get his attention on her.*

"She was your age, thirteen."

I stare at him. He believes his own lie. "You know I'm really sixteen. Thirteen is what you say in the show."

"I know." He smiles. "Ruthie is thirteen. And you're Ruthie."

"No, there is no more Ruthie, remember?" I speak slowly and firmly. "I'm Rowan and I'm sixteen."

He locks his right arm around my shoulders, squeezing. "Oh, my darling. Let me have my dream of you, all right? Just for this afternoon? Another cookie?"

I shake my head, and he strokes my left leg again, pushing my skirt higher, pressing harder. For a few heartbeats I stare at his long, white fingers as if they were stroking someone else's leg.

"*We* is such a powerful word," he murmurs, putting his lips against my ear. "'*We have all afternoon.*' Is there a sweeter sentence for two lovers?"

"*Lovers?*" My voice is strong, mocking. "We're not lovers. Did Edith love you?"

He sucks in a breath and flinches away, releasing my leg.

"And speaking of Edith," I go on, "she probably wasn't thirteen any more than I am."

He says calmly, "Ruthie, stop. I understand you're jealous of Edith, but you mustn't be cruel. This is Edith's pond. She is buried over there under the angel." He turns and reaches for his suit jacket.

I slide back a few inches and reach for my crutch.

He picks up his jacket. "I always carry the photograph of her in her coffin, the last one I took of her."

My hand closes around the crutch, and the solid feel of it gives me a jolt of courage. I drag it toward me.

"*No!*" he roars. He jumps up and shakes the jacket. "No!" The sound startles two ducks into flight.

I freeze.

He twists the jacket. His body jerks as if he has a wasp in his pants. "My wallet!"

Dorchy! She must have taken it from him in the tent, before she left with Miss Latigue.

I keep my face blank and use the crutch to push myself up. Power floods through me as soon as I'm standing.

His eyes narrow. "My wallet with Edith's picture in it is gone."

He takes a step toward me. "You know who took it, don't you?" His anger inflates him like a balloon with every word.

I back away from him, moving closer to the pond.

He stabs a finger at me. "Who did this? You?"

I shake my head. "I don't know where Edith's picture is."

He barks out a laugh. "*Dorchy*. Of course. I told Fan to lock up the silver when she hired her, but Fan said, 'Dorchy's a hard worker, a real find.' Just wait till I find her."

I move back another step.

"I see it all now. You two have a nice little scheme going, don't you?" He lunges at me. "Thieving carny brats!"

CHAPTER 19

I put my hand up to cover my face.

"*You* bait the hook and reel me in. *She* robs me blind." His mouth twists. "And now you think you're going to split my money."

"Mr. Ogilvie, wait. It wasn't Dorchy." I stretch out my hand in appeal. "She wouldn't do anything to hurt you. She likes working for you."

"No, it was Dorchy all right." He grabs the blanket and basket and starts walking fast for the car. "Hurry up and get in. I'm going to hunt that girl down and get my wallet back."

So Dorchy saved me after all. I try not to laugh with relief.

Now we just have to find her.

* * *

Dorchy turns out to be easy to find; she's waiting for us by the Expo gate. She runs up as Mr. Ogilvie brakes hard. He leans out the window and starts to shout at her, but she holds up her hand.

"Mr. Ogilvie, wait." She jabs her finger toward the back of the car. "There's black smoke coming from under the car."

"I don't smell any smoke," he says. "Give me my wallet right now or I'll call the police."

"Are you OK, Rowan?" Dorchy peers around Mr. Ogilvie.

I sniff loudly and wink at her. "I'm fine, but I smell smoke."

"It's pouring out from under the car," Dorchy says. "Mr. Ogilvie, look!"

He sets the hand brake, pushes open the door, and climbs out. "Where is it? Show me."

"Bend down and look."

As soon as he crouches to look underneath the car, Dorchy jumps in, slams the door shut, drops her knapsack in my lap, and shoves the car in gear. By the time she releases the brake and wrenches the steering wheel around, Mr. Ogilvie is hammering on the side of the car.

"You took his wallet?"

She nods and accelerates so fast I'm thrown back against the seat.

"I thought he taught you to drive."

"Very funny. Now which pedal is the brake?"

"Come back here," screeches Mr. Ogilvie.

I look back. "He's jumping up and down. Is there really smoke coming out of the car?"

Dorchy laughs. "I *was* pretty convincing. I impress myself sometimes." She shifts, and the car coughs and bucks.

"Don't stall," she yells, and the car resumes speed. "Is he chasing us?"

"I'm afraid to look. Go faster." I'm breathless with laughter and fear.

We speed down the blacktop road away from Mr. Ogilvie and the Expo.

"Do you know where the railroad station is?" I look over to see her face is flushed and she's choking with laughter.

"Yes, doubting Thomas, and the train leaves soon. I have a plan."

"I hope it's better than the last one."

"We got the car, didn't we?" She looks over at me, and the car veers crazily.

"Watch the road. And tell me your new plan."

"We're going to leave the wallet in the car at the station. I took out the money he owes us. Together we'll buy two tickets to New York. They'll expect that and follow us there, I hope. Then separately we'll each buy a ticket to Boston."

"Boston?" I go rigid. "I am *not* going back to the Home."

"Of course, you're not, but from Boston we can get anywhere, including New York." She makes a quick turn and then another, and ahead of us is the Springfield train station. The most beautiful sight I've ever seen. "Quick," I say. "Leave the car here."

She laughs. "We'll get as close as we can."

She stops behind a line of taxis and gets out. I grab my crutch and hand her the knapsack.

"Come on," she says, grabbing my free hand. "Let's go!"

PART 2
UNBOUND

Cape Cod,
August 1922

CHAPTER 20

I feel numb as we climb the steps to the train car. The only seat for two is all the way at the opposite end. I take the window seat and look out at the platform. No Ogilvies. No police. I imagine them running through the station. *Oh, why doesn't this train move? Or maybe they are on board already, moving through the cars looking for us.* I finger the ticket in my pocket. Boston, one way.

We sit in silence until the conductor comes by. He holds out his hand, and we put our tickets in it, then he punches and pockets them. Not once looking at us. He opens the door to the next car, and I let out my breath.

"Are you all right?" Dorchy squeezes my hand.

I nod. "But the police could be looking for us," I whisper. "I should sit somewhere else. They'll be looking for two girls together."

"Not on this train," she says. "They'll be looking for us on the next one to New York."

I consider this. "You're right." Tears sting my eyes. I close them, and the afternoon unfolds like a moving picture in my head. Mr. Ogilvie's face close to mine, his hand on my leg, the photographs drifting like leaves across the blanket. I open my eyes.

"We'll wait in Boston and go to New York tomorrow," Dorchy says. "After that..."

"Will they really follow us?" Tiredness floods through me.

"I don't know." She bites her thumb. "He'll be embarrassed I stole his car, but he'll have it back, safe and sound soon. Aunt Fan holds a grudge though. And she'll want to punish me for taking the money."

I close my eyes. *I'm walking up the stone steps of our house on Gramercy Park West...*

My eyes snap open. "Dorchy, we can't go to New York."

"Why not?"

"My father is in Europe with my sister, Julia." My heart turns to stone. "The house is locked up."

Dorchy shrugs. "Then we'll go somewhere else. I'm not going to New York without you."

Directly in front of our seat hangs a colorful poster: "Cape Cod: Come in Summer, Fall in Love!" I stare at grassy dunes, yellow sand, and blue, white-capped waves.

An ocean beach! "How much money do we have?"

"Thirty-five dollars," Dorchy says. "Why?"

"It's enough for tickets and food"—my voice rises with excitement—"and we can sleep on the beach." In my mind we're already there, cooking over a driftwood fire, sleeping under the stars.

Dorchy snorts. "Not me. I hate the ocean."

"What?" Her words don't register at first.

"I almost drowned." She hunches forward, hands between her knees. "I sneaked off while my parents were working the boardwalk at Coney Island. I ran into the waves and got pulled under. A lifeguard yelled and called me a carny numskull, but he saved me." She leans back in her seat. "I swore then I'd never go near the water again."

To hide my disappointment, I lean forward to study the poster. A small map shows Cape Cod looking like a bent, upraised arm. *I have to convince her.* "Cape Cod is close to Boston." I tap the map. "This line is the train route. It wouldn't cost much to get us there." I sit back. "We don't have to swim. I can't anyway with my leg."

I look out the window. Every turn of the wheels takes us closer to Boston. Closer to the Cape. *Come on, Dorchy.*

"All right," she says finally. "You win. Cape Cod." She grins at me.

"Thank you." My heart soars.

"You've camped on the beach before?"

"Of course." I can build a fire and cook on the beach because that's what Julia and I did with our friends, before polio kept us away from everyone. And I slept on the beach once too. Father, Julia, and I took blankets into the dunes to watch the Perseid meteor shower. I counted ten shooting stars before I fell asleep.

But on Cape Cod, Father won't be there to carry me home to a warm cottage.

No Father. No Julia. The words echo the sound of the train's wheels.

Dorchy taps me on the shoulder. "What's our plan?"

"Well, first we go to a general store for supplies. Then we find a good place to camp in the dunes." *And then I'll cure you of your fear of the ocean. If I can't enjoy the waves, at least you can.* But I keep that to myself.

* * *

No trains to the Cape leave Boston's South Station that evening. So we buy tickets on the first morning train. Our destination is Eastham, a town on the Cape's bent elbow, chosen at random.

Dorchy and I buy two candy bars, an apple, and a box of Cracker Jack. We drink from a marble water fountain and sleep sitting up on a bench in the big, echoing waiting room. Trains arrive and depart all night, bringing travelers who bustle past us.

But all night, under the blared announcements for trains and the excited cries of travelers uniting with loved ones or snapping at tired children, another sound rings in my ears. The distant roar of the ocean.

CHAPTER 21

At seven o'clock the next morning, clutching our tickets and Dorchy's knapsack, we wash in the ladies' lounge and then run down the platform to the first car of the Cape Cod Flyer.

As the engine jolts and bumps out of the station, Dorchy opens the window and leans out.

"Watch out," I warn her. "Something could hit you on the head." I sound like Julia or worse.

"Don't tell me what to do," Dorchy says. "I'm free." She lets out a joyful whoop that makes other people in the car turn to look.

I'm free too. It feels like that heady moment on the midway. Only this is better. We have weeks, not an hour or two, of no one telling us what to do.

Dorchy drops back in her seat and echoes my thought. "No Ogres. No orphanage matron."

"No Dr. Pynchon. No Julia."

Dorchy grins. "No Council cows."

"You still have your apron."

She grimaces. "We'll buy new clothes in Eastham."

"We might find a general store, not a dress store."

"Then we'll buy overalls and straw hats and look like boys. I won't wear this hideous dress another minute."

"Mine is the hideous one." Overnight my too-short dress seems to have shrunk. I tug it down to cover my knees.

"It really is," Dorchy says with a shudder. "I wouldn't wear your dress to a hog-calling contest."

"Well, I wouldn't wear it to see Narda wake up in her coffin."

Dorchy giggles. "I wouldn't wear it to see Gilda's fake snake."

"I wouldn't wear it to the Unfit Family show."

We're laughing so hard that we hold our stomachs and rock back and forth. We can't stop, even when the conductor collects our tickets. "What's so funny, young ladies?" he asks.

"Nothing," we gasp.

Dorchy stops laughing. "It's your turn now," she says.

"What do you mean?"

She tears the paper off our second Hershey's bar. "I got us *away*." She hands me a square of chocolate. "Say it."

I smile at her. "Dorchy, you got us away."

"So now it's up to you."

"So now it's up to you."

"No, *you*." She splits the last of the chocolate with me. "We're on this train because you love the ocean and know how to camp on the beach, right?"

"Well, yes."

"So you're the leader. I follow you."

* * *

We stand on the platform at Eastham under a blazing sun and clear blue sky. The only other passengers who got off are two noisy twin boys about six years old, a tired-looking mother with a bulging knapsack, and a distracted father carrying suitcases. With a burst of steam and a long whistle, the train chugs away.

A man pulls up in a rusty automobile and calls out the window, "Need a lift?" Dorchy walks straight past him down the steps and across the street. I hurry after her. We're walking east, toward the ocean, and the breeze strokes my face. I suck in a deep breath of warm, salty air.

"Randolph, Rudolph!" the mother shouts. The names make me laugh. Ahead of me, Dorchy's shoulders shake.

I catch up to her.

She says, "We need to buy new clothes and blankets. And a cooking pot and…"

"No." I hold up my hand. "I'm the leader, like you said. And I say *you* need to take a deep breath. Right now."

Dorchy closes her eyes and breathes in.

"You're breathing in the Atlantic Ocean," I tell her. "That salt air came across three thousand miles of ocean to reach us."

She opens her eyes. "It smells good, like seaweed and clams, but…look at that." She points at a building across the street. *Chandler Dry Goods and Sundries* says the sign out front. "What are sundries?" she asks.

"Anything under the *sun*, I guess." As we walk to the store, I concentrate on the smell and taste of salt air. It will cure me. I know it will. Already my leg feels stronger. The practical, organized part of my mind is being blown away. All I want to do is see, feel, taste, and be the ocean. But I watch my step on the rutted, unpaved street.

* * *

Inside the store a tall woman in a gray smock, face creased in wrinkles, comes from behind a pile of lobster pots, fishing poles, and galvanized buckets. "We need one of those buckets for clams," I tell Dorchy.

The woman smiles. "You girls visitin' our fair town?" The smile doesn't reach her pale-blue eyes.

Dorchy puts down the knapsack and sighs. "We are," she says.

"You wouldn't be with the artist ladies down the beach, would you?"

"Why, yes," Dorchy says. I poke her ankle with my crutch. *What is she doing?* "Or at least we hope to be. You wouldn't know exactly where we could find them, do you?"

The woman runs her finger over some jelly glasses on the counter. "They're stayin' in a cottage down toward Nauset Light. But on a day like today they'll be on the shore painting, easels and all." She shakes her head. "I don't understand the appeal myself, but to each her own, I guess."

Women artists. And we're free to meet them.

"We'll be camping," Dorchy says. "Near the cottage."

The woman looks at my crutch. I shift my weight. "I broke my leg, but it's almost healed." The lie rolls off my tongue.

The woman makes a *tsk* sound, reaches up to a shelf, and hands me a small tin of Gurdey's Farmer-Tested Udder Cream. "Rub that on your leg three times a day, and it will feel a hundred percent better. It's good for lots more than sore udders."

"We also need clothes," Dorchy says. "We lost our suitcase back in Boston."

The woman points to a corner of the store. "Clothes on a rack back there next to the brooms. You're out of luck if you're lookin' for fashion."

The dresses on the rack look like uniforms. Tan, white, and light blue, buttons from collar to hem, round collars with dark-blue trim. I finger the material. Heavy cotton. Dorchy looks doubtful. "Try them on," the woman urges.

"We should have shopped in Boston when we had the chance," Dorchy mutters. I shoot her a silencing look. We don't want this woman to know any more than she already does.

"You girls employed?" the woman asks Dorchy while I'm behind a curtain, trying on the light blue dress. She's either nosy or bored. Either way we don't want to give her information.

"My friend is a student, and I work for a wealthy family in New York City," Dorchy says. "We're on vacation."

I pull open the curtain, feeling a hundred times better in this surprisingly comfortable dress. "It fits," I say. "But it will be too long for Dorchy."

"I can hem it for you for twenty-five cents," the woman says quickly.

Dorchy says, "I'll take a tan one. Better to look like a soldier than a nurse. And my friend here is a quick hand with a needle and thread. We'll take the rest of our supplies, but she'll wear the dress."

When we leave, we have spent ten dollars and now have a bucket, needle and thread, two heavy sweaters, two blankets, a waterproof ground cloth, cans of soup and beans, a loaf of bread, a cooking pot, a tin box of matches, two canteens of fresh water, a can opener, and a gift—a small tin of Gurdey's Udder Cream.

"Now as you're going down the beach, my son Jeb can give you a lift," Mrs. Chandler says. We have exchanged names. I'm Clara and Dorchy is Rose.

Jeb, a pimply boy who looks annoyed and says nothing, piles everything we bought into the back of his pickup truck and then helps me climb in. Dorchy winks at me as she gets in the front seat next to him. The wink says, "He'll be eating out of my hand before we get there."

Sure enough, he's all smiles when he stops at the edge of the sand. "Can I give you a hand carrying things?" he asks. "The artists are a ways down there." He points toward the shimmering shape of a lighthouse far down the beach.

I nod, but Dorchy says, "Thanks, we'll manage. And thanks for the ride. Are you sure I can't pay you?"

He shakes his head. "Service of the store." He points to a small pond next to the road. A metal pipe gushes water into it. "There's the spring for your water. Otherwise it's a mile back to town center."

"He was nice," I say as the truck coughs back down the sandy road. "What changed his mood?"

"Me. I was smooth as udder cream," Dorchy says. "According to him, the artists are 'a bunch of dumb Doras who think they're the bee's knees and ain't.' We'll steer clear of them, I think."

This is pure Dorchy. What she doesn't understand or think is important she discards.

"Well, I want to meet them." I fill our bucket with some of our supplies and tie one sweater around my waist. "They sound interesting and independent. Like us."

The sun beats down and hurts my eyes when I look at the beach stretching into the distance. Due east is the heaving chest of the Atlantic, and that sight hurts my soul. How can it be five years since I stood on a beach up to my ankles in sand? Regret for lost time piles up like a wave and threatens to sweep me away.

CHAPTER 22

I take a deep breath and pick up the bucket. As my lungs expand, the regret vanishes. I feel dizzy with relief. At last. I haven't drawn a breath like this for five years. "Let's go." The sound of the ocean is as familiar as a beloved nursery rhyme.

We walk a short way in the sand; it's slow going with the crutch. Dorchy stays with me, carrying most of our things. "We'll pick out a spot together," she insists when I tell her to go ahead.

Without even knowing exactly what I'm looking for, I find it—a perfect spot where the sloping sides of two dunes come together to form a protected hollow. We drop our supplies.

"Home," Dorchy says. "We lived in a carny caravan," she says. "Mother, Father, and me."

Where else would a snake lady live? I realize I know nothing about Dorchy's life with her parents. "Was she a normal mother?" I want to bite back that *normal* as soon as I say it.

"More normal than yours," Dorchy snaps.

I bite my lip. "Sorry." I spread out my blanket and put the sweater on top. I left my old dress in a dustbin outside the store.

Dorchy says, "I'll get some driftwood," and runs down to the beach. I follow slowly, soaking in the white-fringed breaking waves, hot sand, and endless quicksilver ocean.

Better than any home with Father and Julia.

Better than the beach where I lost both my legs and Father in the same day. The legs came back, which is more than I can say for him. In the deep sand, I can't pretend walking with a crutch feels anything like walking on the beach before. Dorchy runs back and forth above the tide line collecting driftwood. She has two strong legs. It's not fair. But Dr. Friedlander's voice comes back to me, "Don't waste time comparing yourself to anyone else. Jealousy and self-pity delay your progress."

Dorchy comes toward me with an armful of wood, and we walk together back to the dunes. It's too early for a cooking fire, so we pile the wood and I begin hemming Dorchy's new dress.

"We should have paid Mrs. Chandler twenty-five cents to do this," I complain after stabbing my finger with the needle for the fourth time. "Blasted thing."

"But you do know how to sew," Dorchy says.

It's hot in our sheltered spot between the dunes. A drop of sweat falls on Dorchy's dress as I hem it. "No, I sat in a room at the Home shoving a needle and thread through unbleached muslin to make a curtain, but I wouldn't say I learned anything from that." I bite off the thread and hold up the dress. "Oh, except for curse words. Hattie, a girl from Boston, would make you blush, Dorchy."

"Oh, I know a few choice ones myself," Dorchy says. She slips on the dress; it looks good on her now.

She spreads the ground cloth, lies down, and is instantly asleep.

I have never seen her so completely relaxed. I stretch out on my blanket and fall asleep too.

* * *

When we wake up, after an hour or so, we drink some water and head back to the beach. The sun is no longer directly overhead, and the breeze has picked up, so we don't feel hot.

This time I stay on the hard-packed, damp sand, close to the incoming waves. I can move faster here; my crutch leaves slight depressions that slowly fill with water. Dorchy stays in the deeper, dry sand, keeping me between her and ocean.

"There they are." Dorchy points down the beach.

"Who?"

"The artists you're so interested in."

Women in hats and colorful, billowing dresses surround three easels. A burst of laughter reaches us. It sounds like sweet bells chiming.

Their easels are very close to the incoming waves that I read as a flood tide, maybe halfway in. "If they stay there, the easels will wash out to sea," I say.

"How long till that happens?"

"Maybe three hours."

"What time do you think it is?"

I look at the sky. "Four o'clock."

She pulls a gold watch out of her dress pocket. "Not bad. It's three forty-five."

I stop. "That's Mr. Ogilvie's watch!" I can't believe she took it. Now they *will* come after us. "He said it was his grandfather's."

"It's not his. I found it." She drops it back in her pocket without meeting my eyes.

"Give it to me. For my 'pain and suffering.'"

She shakes her head.

I'm about to argue with her when one of the artists shrieks. A piece of white paper skims across the sand, pushed by the breeze, and lands in the ocean, just beyond the knee-high surf. The woman runs down the beach toward us, holding her hat on with one hand.

"It's gone now, Daisy," calls one of the others. "Nature's verdict on your painting."

The woman stops to shake her fist at the others, and Dorchy calls out, "I'll get it." She runs past me straight into the water. Dorchy, who's so afraid of the ocean that she won't walk near it, is up to her knees in the foam, now up to her thighs in calm water behind the breakers. She grabs the paper just before the breeze snatches it again.

She waves it over her head. "I got it."

Cheers and applause and a sharp whistle erupt from the other artists, who are coming down the beach toward us.

As Dorchy wades out, her dress soaked to the waist, the artist— slim and blond, with a streak of red paint on her chin—embraces her. "Oh, thank you, kind stranger." Then she takes the painting — violet streaked with black above blue-green hills or waves; it's hard to tell which—and runs to meet her friends.

"Dorchy." I grab her arm. "You did it! Were you afraid?"

She looks surprised. "You know, I wasn't. I knew I could get the picture, so I did." She smiles, remembering. Then she adds in a low voice, "But from the looks of it, I don't understand all the fuss."

"It was a mess before it landed in the water," I say, "but it meant a lot to *her*."

One of the artists—fuchsia turban, black wool bathing suit, and round, dark glasses—strides up to us.

"Good afternoon," she says to Dorchy, holding out her hand.

"Thank you from the bottom of my heart. My sister Daisy wouldn't let me hear the end of this, were it not for you." She speaks in a slow, sarcastic drawl.

She takes off the dark glasses, the first pair I've ever seen, and shakes my hand too. "April Keene. I'm here with Daisy and her friends. Heaven knows why." She laughs. "They smoke cigarettes, drink wine, and constantly talk about Art with a capital A. If it weren't for my sister, I would beg you to rescue *me* as you did the watercolor. What are your names? Where are you staying?"

Alarm bells go off. We can't reveal anything about ourselves, but I would like to. April has a warm smile and sparkling brown eyes.

Dorchy looks at me.

April presses on. "Are you in a cottage too? We're here for another week." She looks closely at us. "Forgive me if this sounds rude, but are you here with your employers? Is this your afternoon off?"

She thinks we're servants. "Yes," I say. "We must get back."

Dorchy turns a laugh into a cough.

"Look at them." April waves at the four women now regrouped around one of the easels. They break apart with little cries of delight and laughter. "They are watercolorists," she goes on. "Sometimes I wish a wave would rear up"—she raises her arms and then lowers them as she speaks—"and splash down on their precious Prussian blue, cadmium red, and China white palettes and give them *saltwater* watercolors."

Dorchy wrings out the skirt of her dress.

"Aren't *you* interested in watercolor?" I ask April.

"No." She holds up a sketchbook. "I draw. The dunes mostly, in pencil and charcoal. Their lines and shadows fascinate me more than the ocean's million shades of blue, impossible to capture with a camel-hair brush."

"My mother loved the dunes too." I speak without thinking. "She used to photograph them and develop the pictures herself."

"A photographer," April says reverently. "I envy her. Alas, all that is beyond my librarian's salary."

A librarian. My heart leaps. I could talk to her about books. I feel tipsy on the wealth and variety of the world beyond the Boston Home and the Unfit Family show. "Where is your library?"

Dorchy shifts impatiently; she's uncomfortable around this woman who holds the key to what I used to have. But I'm too excited to care. "You may read any book in here," Father told me on the day I received my own public library card.

"Boston Public Library, Children's Room," April says, "but I didn't take you girls for readers."

"We're not," Dorchy assures her, grabbing my elbow. "Now we'd better start back. We have a long way to go."

I nod to April and turn away. The difference between me and Dorchy opens like a chasm between us. I can talk to April, to any of these women, even though I haven't been to real school in five years. Father saw to that. "Collier women are interest*ing* and interest*ed*" was one of his sayings. I haven't felt so proudly and firmly and completely a Collier since I got polio.

* * *

"You said we had to be careful," Dorchy scolds me as we walk back down the beach. She quotes me, "Don't give anyone information they could use when asked if they've seen us."

"No one will come after us out here," I say, and I believe it.

She shakes her head. "The Ogilvies might, not the police. I doubt they would even go to the police, but they'll want to catch us. I *know* them."

"I know them too. And this place is way out of their orbit. We don't have to worry here."

"They know your real name."

I shiver. "So what? Father will protect me."

"Really? When has he ever protected you?"

I say nothing. She's right. The weight of my disappointment in Father threatens to crush me, to drive me to my knees in the sand. *Where was Father when I was at the Home?* Even Julia couldn't explain his absence.

"I'm dead to him, aren't I?" I asked her once, and even though she said no and waved her hands and said I was an ungrateful daughter, I knew I was right.

"Look," Dorchy says. "On the other hand, by now the Ogilvies know we bought tickets for New York. They know I wanted to find my uncle there. They know your family lives there. They'll waste a lot of time looking for us there."

"And don't forget"—I grab her arm—"they think we're stupid."

"I know." Dorchy grins. "But stealing the car and getting his wallet and watch, that had to make him think."

"You gave back the car and the wallet," I remind her. "And you said it wasn't his watch."

She runs down the beach ahead of me, her wet dress flapping.

I stop to look back at the artists, but the beach is empty. Poking up above the dunes, its glass top catching the sun, is the lighthouse. Mrs. Chandler at the store called it Nauset Light.

I dig my crutch into the hard sand at the water's edge and hurry after Dorchy. Long ago, Father built a lighthouse out of sand on our beach. Even in the warm sun, I shiver at the memory of the day a storm stole Father's creation and polio stole my legs.

CHAPTER 23

In the dunes, we build a fire, and Dorchy, wrapped in a blanket, dries her wet dress in its heat. Then she opens a can and we heat soup in our pot. It tastes delicious.

"Our first meal in freedom," Dorchy says. As the fire burns down, she puts on her almost-dry dress and we go down to the beach. The tide is all the way in, and the ocean reflects the dark lavender sky and pinpoints of starlight. It's so beautiful that my eyes fill with tears. I wipe them away, hoping Dorchy doesn't notice.

"I have something for you," she says when we get back to our home in the dunes. I inch closer to the dying fire to see what she's holding out.

"Oh, Dorchy." I suck in a breath. "But it can't be my mother's camera."

"No, but it is an old Kodak Brownie." Dorchy sounds excited. "I found it at the Expo yesterday."

I turn the camera in my hands. It fits perfectly, just as Mother's did. "I had to leave mine behind," I whisper, "the day I got sick. And I couldn't have it at the Home. Julia said Father put it away to keep for me. He framed a photograph I took at the beach and hung it with Mother's pictures."

Which is not the same as thinking I'm alive.

Holding the camera, I sit on the drop cloth, fighting back tears again. Dorchy has given me *Little Women*, my life, this camera. What can I give her?

"Tell me about your mother," says Dorchy, sitting next to me. "You must know something else about her besides that she took pictures."

"I'd like to know more. Like why she died. There must be a reason she died without ever seeing me. Her family must have passed some fatal weakness down to her."

"That sounds like your father's idea." Dorchy pokes the fire and sparks spray into the dark.

"No, it's Julia's idea too." I press my hands together. Dorchy is silhouetted against the fire. It's a beautiful silhouette, but the chin might be a little weak. No one would ever say *she* was from one of the best families. "Julia once said, 'Mother was a Collier in name only. She must have had a fatal weakness in her bloodline.'"

Dorchy jumps up. "Listen to yourself," she shouts, angrier than I have ever seen her. "How can you sit there and say that about your own mother? After weeks with the awful Ogilvies and the Council cows you still don't question that 'better blood' garbage?" She punches her fist against her palm. "You *still* think people are fit or unfit because of their family bloodlines? You know as well as I do that Gar and Jimmy and Minnie are as fit as you and your precious father."

"I didn't say I believed Julia," I point out, as cold as Dorchy is hot. We've never fought before or even disagreed for long. "But sometimes I don't know what to think."

A hole opens before me. Dorchy is right. I didn't question the Ogilvies' beliefs about Fitter Families or those of the Council. I just questioned their making me act unfit. And I never questioned Father either, although that was because I never had a chance to after I got sick. I close my eyes, try to catch my breath, and concentrate on what Dorchy is saying.

But Dr. Friedlander's voice rings in my ears. *Have you forgotten what you learned from Stella and the other children on the ward?*

I had to forget, I silently tell him. *To survive Dr. Pynchon, I had to forget Bellevue.*

"Aunt Fan told *me*," Dorchy is saying, "that 'Any child can better herself and rise to another level, if she applies herself in school.' She blamed me for leaving school, when I had no choice. The orphanage made us girls quit school at fourteen and hired us out to work. The whole idea that Aunt Fan is better than Minnie because Aunt Fan's a teacher is crazy."

"How would you like to have Mr. Ogilvie as a teacher?" I ask, and Dorchy shrieks as I knew she would. Then I shriek and scrub at my arm as if his touch is still on me somehow.

"No more Ogres," Dorchy says.

I nod, hoping she's right. "Why are we arguing?"

"Because you were being foolish about your mother." Dorchy yawns. "Bedtime."

We wrap ourselves in blanket cocoons and stretch out near the fire's glowing coals. Suddenly the ocean sounds very loud and overhead the stars seem to have multiplied. The great hand of the wind soothes me. I tumble into the best sleep I've had in five years.

CHAPTER 24

Seagulls' cries wake me at first light. At first I don't recognize the sound, but as I come fully awake, I do. Their cries woke me every morning of every summer until I was eleven. How could I forget them? A curtain of fog hangs over the ocean, and the air is still and salty.

I take the camera and go down to the beach. The sea is flat calm all the way out to where fog hangs over it like a curtain in the theater. I take a picture of a feather at the edge of the surf, a gentle tumbling of foam. I keep looking down the beach in case an artist comes out to paint this morning world. I advance the film to number three. That means five more pictures are left on the roll.

I'm at the beach, but I can't go into the water. Not with this crutch, this leg. The light begins to glow behind the fogbank. Suddenly I remember Dorchy as she looked yesterday wading into the surf, deeper and deeper, until she grabbed the watercolor. Dorchy, who hates the ocean, wasn't afraid.

* * *

Later we stand together at the edge of the waves. The sun shines in a blue sky, the fog dissolved. "Lean on my shoulder," Dorchy says. "You won't drown. I won't let you."

I lay my crutch next to our blanket and our outer clothes. We're wearing our underwear and slips. Step by shaky step, we wade in up to our knees, my left arm hooked in her right.

She's shivering from the cold water and cool breeze. Her body is slender and strong, all muscle.

"You went in deeper than this yesterday," I tell her.

Yesterday I was terrified of going into the waves. I would be knocked down, helpless to get up. But today, as I fight to keep my balance, something happens. Confidence grows with every step. Both of my legs feel strong, ready to support me or at least help Dorchy support me. When we're up to our waists, a steep wave looms over us, but I know what to do.

"Stand sideways and hold my hands," I say. "I'll tell you when to jump and it will pass under us. I promise."

"Are you sure?" Dorchy sounds nervous. She shrieks as we jump. The wave moves past us, and we're safe. "It worked," she yells, thumping me on the shoulder so hard I almost fall.

"Follow me," I say. "We'll dive through this one." I lean into the wave, push off with my right leg, and dive through it, pulling hard with my arms. I surface and look for Dorchy. I see her head in the foam for a few seconds before it disappears. The wave tumbles her all the way to shore.

When she finally stands up, I wonder if she'll give up, but she shakes her fist in the air. "I can do it," she yells. "You're not going to win, Ocean!"

She races back out to me and ducks her head under an incoming

- 120 -

wave. It catches and tumbles her to shore just like the first one. She comes right back out ready to try again.

Her persistence inspires me. I decide to ride a wave one-legged. A perfect wave rolls toward me. Pushing off with my right foot, I fling myself in front of it, hands outstretched, kicking with my right leg. But one-leg kicking is too slow. The wave rolls on, leaving me behind. I feel a surge of power because I know what to do. I can't kick my way ahead of the wave, so I have to time my jump closer to the crest.

I let a few waves pass before I try riding one again. This time I make it. The wave lifts me up and propels me forward, even though I'm kicking with only one leg.

It is the best moment of my life. I can do anything. Polio did not win.

I rest on shore and watch Dorchy practice diving through waves. "Come back in," she yells. "I'm ready to ride."

I let a receding wave sweep me out to Dorchy, waiting for me beyond the breakers.

On the third try we catch the same wave and glide into shore, laughing and shrieking.

"Hello, there."

I look up, startled. April in her turban and dark glasses smiles down at me. She's wearing a Chinese silk robe tied at the waist. "That looks like fun."

She looks from us to our clothes piled on the sand, then back to us, and starts to laugh. "Poor dears, you have no bathing suits."

I stand up and balance on one foot. "Please hand us the crutch and blanket and turn around. My friend is shy."

April laughs and turns her back to us. "She's swimming in her underwear in broad daylight on a public beach," she says. "She can't be *that* shy."

Dorchy wraps the blanket around her. I tuck my crutch under my arm.

"I saw you in the water," April says, still with her back turned. "So I came to invite you to join us in town this afternoon. We're having an art show on the village green as part of Old Eastham Days. You can see my dune drawings, which are much nicer than that muddy watercolor you rescued."

Dorchy says, "You can turn around now."

April studies us. "Where *are* you staying?" she asks. "There's no cottage around here." When we exchange a look, she says, "I promise I won't tell anyone."

I shrug. "We're camping in the dunes."

"Oh, that sounds wonderful." April looks wistfully at the dunes, then back at me. "I couldn't talk you into showing me your campsite, could I? I'm fascinated by the dunes and the thought of camping in one makes me quake with jealousy."

"We want to keep it private," I say quickly. "What are Old Eastham Days?"

"It's like a miniature county fair," April says. "Besides our art show there are pony rides, food booths, even a turnip tent. Something for everybody."

I can feel Dorchy's excitement. "Games of chance?" she asks.

April looks surprised. "Probably. But for a real midway, you have to go to the big fair in Barnstable next week. The whole Cape comes to that, I hear."

"Thanks for the invitation," Dorchy says. "We'd like to come."

My heart contracts. *It's not safe*, I want to tell her. *The Council could have a Fitter Families booth there*. I'm thrilled April invited us, but it's not worth the risk.

And I'm nervous about Dorchy. What if there *are* carnies there?

What if she decides to stay with them?

April walks with us back to the dunes. I stop to lean on my crutch. Walking in the deep sand is much harder than wave riding. I make a sudden decision. "How will we get to town, April?"

"Do you know Jeb?"

I nod.

"He's going to meet us with the truck at noon by the spring. Some of my group went in this morning to set up."

I smile at her. "We'll see you at noon."

"I'm really glad you're coming. Ta-ta!" She walks away, the wind tugging at her and swirling her long robe.

I pull the blanket around me and hurry to the campsite to dress. Dorchy beats me there, of course. She combs her hair and pulls her midway clothes—the red dress and hair ribbon—out of her knapsack.

"That's awfully wrinkled," I say in a neutral voice.

"It's fine," she snaps.

"What if the Council has a tent or a booth?"

"They won't. All they care about is Barnstable next week."

"There's still a chance they'll be there," I insist. "How could you possibly know for sure?"

"I don't." She fastens the skirt and ties the ribbon in her hair. It looks beautiful. She touches my shoulder. "But if there are carnies there, I want to see them."

"You want to run away with them." My voice shakes. I turn my back and watch the waves calling, *Come ride us, Rowan.*

"I'm not going to 'run away,'" Dorchy says calmly. "I'm going to New York with you. That's our plan."

I draw a shaky breath. "I'm still afraid someone will recognize us."

"We have to go to town for food anyway," Dorchy says. "It will be safer with lots of people around. And when are you going to break down and call me by my new name?"

"Which is?"

"Wave Rider." She pirouettes, laughing.

"Oh no, it takes years to earn that name."

Dorchy mumbles something that sounds like "twenty minutes." Then she thrusts a wad of bills at me. "Ten dollars for your pain and suffering."

I stuff the money in the pocket of my dress and say, "No wallets will be taken today." I try to say it lightly, but her face tightens.

"Carny code says if a rube offers, take."

"Come on, Dorchy. We can't risk getting in trouble."

"I'm kidding." She strikes a pose and raises her hand. "Come-a one, come-a all," she says in the ringing voice of a carny talker. "Little lady"—she points at me—"you're a cute little doll, ain't you? Too bad about that crutch, but your spirit ain't lame, is it now? Step right up here and try your luck! Come on, don't be afraid. Should she be afraid, folks?"

I can't help laughing. But I *am* afraid.

"It's probably just kids' games and pie-eating contests," I say, trying to keep my voice steady. I point to her clothes. "All that for nothing."

She twirls around so the skirt flies out. "This could never be for nothing. Come on."

CHAPTER 25

We start out looking at watercolors in a large tent surrounded by the artists from the beach. The four watercolorists are dressed alike in loose silk dresses and multicolored scarves. Their paintings look alike too.

April—in a rose linen dress and a large white hat—leads us over to her mounted charcoal drawings of the dunes. "The artists are very upset with me for showing these," she says. "My dear sister said, 'But, April, you're not a *real* artist.' The others agree, but they're too polite to say so." She points to a printed "Sold" tag clipped to one of the dune drawings. "The public disagrees. This one found a buyer right away. The only one so far, but still. I wish I'd been here when it happened, just to see their faces."

"That's rich," says Dorchy. "Good for you, April." She looks toward the tent opening. "We'd better get going," she says. "We want to see everything."

I smile an apology at April and whisper, "I love your drawings."

"I would come with you if I could," she says, "but I have to take my turn as saleswoman."

We walk around the village green under a cloudless sky. Boys and girls fish for metal toys in a canvas pool using magnets on long lines. Next to the pool is a mound of sand where other children dig for "treasure." A row of booths offers handwork for sale, and cranberry, turnip, and asparagus displays. No "Fitter Families" tent. No carnival rides. I start to enjoy myself.

"There they are!" Dorchy takes off at a run, weaving through the crowd of locals in Sunday-best dresses and overalls, and tourists in stylish sailor dresses and seersucker suits.

I follow Dorchy to a row of booths close to the old windmill. It stands unmoving, its wings still and some of its weathered shingles missing. "The oldest windmill on Cape Cod" claims a lopsided sign.

"Pop a balloon, miss. Win a prize!" A man waves a fistful of darts at me. I smile and keep moving.

Dorchy stops in front of "Ralphie's Ring Toss—Ring the Bottle, Win a Prize, 3 Tries, 1 Penny!" As she stands there, a short red-haired man comes from behind the booth and does a double take. "Dorchy? That you?" He rubs his eyes. "As I live and breathe, girl, where have you been all this time? Maggie," he yells. "Come see Dorchy."

"Ralph." Dorchy's face lights up as if she's won a jackpot.

A little boy in short pants reaches up to put two pennies on the counter of the booth. Ralph pushes the coins back. "We're closed, sonny." He pulls a balloon from under the counter and hands it to the boy. "Come back later."

A plump, gray-haired woman in a red dress envelops Dorchy in a hug and then holds her at arm's length. "Let me see you," she says in a warm, gentle voice. "You always look so precious in those earrings."

I get a glimpse of Dorchy's face. Alive and joyful. The way she looked this morning when she rode her first wave.

They lead her away, around the booth. *Oh, Dorchy, please don't stay with them. Please.*

I walk up to the counter and study the game. Under a shelf crammed with stuffed toys—teddy bears, dogs, and cats—a slanted board bristles with painted wooden pegs. Rope rings in colors matching the pegs lie on the counter. I lift one, note the rope feels scratchy, and eye the distance to the pegs.

I'm preparing for Dorchy to say, "Ralph and Maggie are my carny family. I'm going to stay with them."

But right then the three of them come back, all smiles, and Dorchy says, "This is Rowan, my friend from New York I told you about."

Ralph grabs my hand. "We're so happy Dorchy has a good friend to go camping with."

Maggie pats my back. "What happened to your leg?"

I tell them the truth. They're so warm and kind that they deserve it.

When I finish, Dorchy says, "You better get back to work, Ralph." She points to a line of restless kids. "I wish I could catch up with you at Barnstable, but we're heading for New York."

"Give our regards to your uncle," Ralph says, "and if it doesn't work out with him, come find us on Long Island. We'll be at the Mineola Fair on September 27. We skipped Expo this year. We do better at the smaller fairs."

Dorchy nods and squeezes their hands. She looks sad. I'm thrilled she isn't staying with them. And angry at myself for doubting her.

"They are really nice people," I say as we walk back across the green.

"Carnies are." She ducks her head. "I didn't know how much I missed those two."

"They knew your parents?"

"Best friends. I'm glad you met them."

I think how good lemonade would taste right now. Dorchy has the same idea so we line up outside the refreshment tent— "Lemonade 5 Cents." As we wait our turn to order, a woman behind us, her voice pitched low, says, "It's them all right."

My blood turns to ice.

Dorchy steps up to the counter, and the woman calls out, "Dorchy! Rowan!"

CHAPTER 26

"Run back to Ralph," I whisper.

Instead Dorchy turns around and a second later I do too.

Two Council ladies.

"I told Gladys it was you," says the tall, younger one in a navy-blue suit.

"You remember us," says the plump, middle-aged one in a lilac dress with a wide, white collar. "I'm Mrs. Clarke and this is Miss Latigue, from the Boston Chapter of the Council. We met you at the Exposition."

"We have to go." I grab Dorchy's arm and start to pull her away. But after two steps, I trip over my crutch and sprawl facedown in the trampled grass.

"Oh, be careful," says Miss Latigue. She and Dorchy help me up and brush off my dress. She holds on to my arm, but her voice is kind. "We've had a hard time finding you. Let's sit and have a lemonade, shall we?"

"We want to hear your side of the story," says Mrs. Clarke.

They guide us to a table inside the tent. Miss Latigue brings a pitcher of lemonade and four glasses. Sitting there on a wooden folding chair, I feel completely drained. *We tried so hard, but they found us anyway. What they don't know is that Dorchy can get away. Why, oh, why doesn't she run to the carnies?*

Mrs. Clarke speaks first. "The Ogilvies want to press criminal charges for thefts committed by you, Dorchy. And they blame you for the fire, Rowan."

"The fire?" I feel faint and gulp my lemonade.

Dorchy looks around. "They're here? On the Cape?"

"No." The two women exchange a glance. Mrs. Clarke continues. "As far as we know. We refused to let them join in our search for you."

Miss Latigue jumps in. "The Council has severed its connection with them."

Dorchy catches my eye. "But they're hunting us on their own." It isn't a question.

"Everything Dorchy did was to protect me," I say. "Mr. Ogilvie said he was taking me to Boston, but he drove into a cemetery..." My voice trails off.

"We know what he did." Mrs. Clarke refills my glass. "We cut our ties with them in part because of Mr. Ogilvie's..."

"...habit of photographing you and other young girls," finishes Miss Latigue. "A most unsavory man. And then there's his wife Fanny's drinking."

"His sister," Dorchy and I say in unison.

"No," Mrs. Clarke says. "That's what they wanted everyone to believe, but in fact they are man and wife, married fifteen years, with no children."

Dorchy says, "But I lived with them during the Expo. They have separate bedrooms."

"That may be," Miss Latigue says, "but they are married. Another mark against them for lying about it."

"Why would they lie?" Dorchy says.

I know the answer to that. "Because being married so long and not having children makes them look unfit," I say.

"What will happen now?" Dorchy helps herself to more lemonade.

You're going to run to Ralph and Maggie. I stare at her, willing her to get the message.

Mrs. Clarke says, "It is in our interest to avoid any publicity about the fire, which means protecting you from the Ogilvies." She blots her damp forehead with a small lilac handkerchief.

Miss Latigue leans forward. "You are Council employees until Labor Day. For all of our sakes, it's best that you come to Boston with us. In September when the school year begins, we believe the Ogilvies will give up trying to find and charge you."

Dorchy tips her chair back. "We're not afraid of the Ogilvies." She smiles at me. "We have insurance."

What?

"Insurance?" Miss Latigue's tone is sharp.

"We have something Mr. Ogilvie wants very badly," Dorchy says calmly. "We'll simply tell him that we'll hand it over if he agrees to leave us alone." She is practically smirking but doesn't meet my eye.

"Dorchy, what…?" I begin.

"Explain yourself," Mrs. Clarke says.

"Here, I'll show you. It's in my shoe." Dorchy bends down and comes up waving a small photograph.

A girl dressed in white, eyes closed, lying in a coffin. *Edith.*

"You took it," I gasp. I don't know whether to slap her or applaud. She's right about it being valuable to him. The memory of Mr. Ogilvie's fury when he realized his wallet and this photograph were gone still terrifies me.

"Who is that?" Mrs. Clarke fans herself vigorously, sending scraps of cool air across the table.

I explain about Edith and describe Mr. Ogilvie's visit to Narda in the tent on the midway.

"Well, well. Still waters run deep." Miss Latigue studies me. "So off you went to the midway on your crutch without so much as a by-your-leave." She sounds impressed.

Mrs. Clarke leaves the table and comes back with a plate of pastries. As she offers the plate to us, Dorchy says, "How did you find us?" She pats her mouth with a paper napkin.

"The day after you disappeared, we showed ticket sellers at the Springfield and Boston railway stations a photograph of Rowan," Miss Latigue says.

"One of Mr. Ogilvie's many photographs of her." Mrs. Clarke smiles grimly.

I squirm and bite into a ladyfinger, remembering those awful, prying pictures.

Miss Latigue nods. "For once his picture-taking came in handy. He turned his photographs and negatives over to us, and in return we agreed not to press charges for endangering lives and our reputation by locking you, Minnie, Jimmy, and Gar in the cottage at night."

"Why do they think I had something to do with fire?" I ask.

"Why?" Mrs. Clarke sniffs. "To distract us from accusing them, I suppose. The fact that you and the others could have died doesn't seem to register in their small minds."

I shift in my chair and look around the tent. It's filling up with people escaping the hot sun. At the counter, two of the artists are accepting glasses of lemonade. I duck my head, and a chill runs through me. What if the Ogilvies are here asking questions? If the Council ladies could find us, so could they.

"We can't stay here." I avoid looking at Dorchy. She believes her insurance will protect us. I don't.

"Then you'll come with us back to Boston," Miss Latigue says, wiping her hands on a paper napkin.

"To work for the Council," Mrs. Clarke adds. "But first we need assurance that you will not steal."

Dorchy sits up straight. "I only took what we were owed. Not one penny more."

"Not paying you was wrong of the Ogilvies," says Mrs. Clarke. "But you should have complained to the Council, not taken his wallet and his car."

"I had to protect Rowan." Dorchy sounds about to cry.

Miss Latigue pats her hand. "You are a loyal friend, Dorchy. We appreciate that. And you will be paid for the work you do for us."

"What work is that?" Dorchy sounds suspicious.

"Assisting the staff at our Camp for Unfortunates in Maine," says Miss Latigue. "We'll pay you two dollars a week. When the camp ends in September, we'll arrange for you…"

"I'll be going home to New York," I say firmly, "as soon as my father, Franklin Collier, returns from Europe. I expect you will arrange for that."

Dorchy clears her throat.

"Dorchy's uncle is there too," I continue. "We'll both need train tickets to New York."

Mrs. Clarke nods. "We agree, pending good reports about you

from the camp."

"Why do you need us so late in the season?" Dorchy asks.

She's right. It sounds fishy. Why should we trust these women?

Miss Latigue says, "They're shorthanded and have asked for help. There have been cases of flu among the campers and some of the staff left." She puts her hand to her mouth. "Oh dear, we should have asked you this first. Have you had the flu?"

We both nod. I had it during my first year at the Home. I don't know when Dorchy had it.

"Is that the only qualification to work there?" I ask.

Miss Latigue smiles. "The Ogilvies won't vouch for either of you, which is a recommendation in itself. We heard good things about you, Dorchy, from the Council ladies in Springfield. 'Resourceful,' 'helpful,' 'cheerful,' and 'a saint to put up with the Ogilvies' are just some of them. And Rowan"—she pats my hand—"you are a hero who saved two lives during the fire."

I like the sound of *hero*. "Dorchy's a hero too. She saved *me*," I say.

"I'm going to the camp tomorrow," Miss Latigue says, "so I will accompany you."

Dorchy nods, but I can tell she's not convinced.

"May we talk this over?" I ask.

The ladies stand up and move away, keeping an eye on us.

"You can still run to Ralph and Maggie," I tell Dorchy. "I'll go to work at this camp of theirs, but you have a choice."

"No, I don't." She glares at me. "We're in this together. If you go, I go."

"Well, I want to go. I don't want to be looking over my shoulder for two more weeks. When we were standing in line and she said our names, my heart stopped."

"Mine did too." Dorchy grins. "So we're back working for the Council."

"No Ogres this time, Wave Rider."

Dorchy grins. "You mean no *Mr. and Mrs.* Ogre."

* * *

Mrs. Clarke arranges for Jed to drive Miss Latigue, Dorchy, and me back to the beach to collect our things. The sky is a deep, late-afternoon blue. I walk down to the edge of the surf while the others gather our belongings from the campsite. Breaking waves greet me with floods of white foam. I rode the waves today. The feeling is the same as that first time, five years ago. But now, with my weak leg, the achievement seems even greater. I make a promise to the ocean that when I leave today, it won't be for long.

From Eastham the four of us catch the evening train back to Boston. The Council ladies were so sure they'd find us, and that we'd agree to go with them, that they already have tickets for us. On the train Miss Latigue gives us shiny color brochures about the camp, a place for unfortunates to savor the outdoors and learn life's lessons. I'm surprised to see it's on an island. They didn't mention that.

"How do we get there?" I ask Miss Latigue.

"By train from Boston to Rockland, Maine, and then the camp ferry from there to a private island. The family provided it to us for the camp this summer. It's called Loup Island. *Loup* is the French word for *wolf*."

"Are there wolves?" I ask.

Miss Latigue laughs. "Not any more."

Dorchy looks dubious. "An island," she mutters.

In Boston we go by taxi to Miss Latigue's home on Beacon Street. Dorchy and I sit up late, talking in the guest room.

"I don't like it," Dorchy says. "I don't trust them. On this island we'll be trapped."

"We're trapped anyway," I say. "At least the Council wants the same thing as we do—no Ogilvies."

"So they *say*." Dorchy pulls aside the heavy curtains covering our bedroom window. "We could go now. This window opens easily enough."

"Loup Island is where I'm going," I say. "And so are you. It could be fun. The brochure says unfortunates deserve fresh air and fun as much as anyone. My father believes that too. We'll be doing good."

Dorchy turns away from the window. She picks up the brochure and waves it at me. "They use this to raise money. People feel sorry for 'unfortunate' orphans and make donations. Then the Council uses the money to sterilize more folks who don't deserve it."

"*We'll* be helping the unfortunates in person," I say. "Think about that."

"I'll bet you anything the camp is a con," she says stubbornly. "Miss *Fatigue* is the carny; you and me and the *unfortunates* are the rubes. You'll see."

"Well, nobody can con you, Dorchy," I say. "And you've taught me a lot. Look, it's a chance to turn the tables on the Ogilvies again. You know you want to do that."

She brightens. "You win. First this island and then New York!"

PART 3
UNDAUNTED

Loup Island, Maine,
August 1922

CHAPTER 27

The wind grabs me by the throat as I stumble out of the hatch and suck in wet, salty air. Every few seconds, it seems, a horn bellows above my head. It must be almost noon, but the fog is so thick it's impossible to tell. Behind me the cabin stews in the stink of vomit. Dorchy is one of the sickest. When I tried to get her to come out on deck, she shook her head and moaned, "I hate the ocean." I wanted to remind her that she loved riding the waves but thought better of it.

Using my crutch, I cross the tilting deck, brace my right leg, and lean over the railing. Fog rubs a clammy hand over my face and burrows through the wool blanket wrapped around me and into my clothes. My stomach calms down. Father always said fresh air prevents seasickness. For once he's a help to me, even if only in memory.

The taste of salt on my lips reminds me of Eastham. *Maybe we should have risked everything and stayed there. Too late now.*

When my right leg gets tired, I move back across the deck and sit on a bench, gripping the wet wooden slats as the ferry rolls from side to side. I breathe deeply, determined not to give in. Sickness is weakness. Another lesson from Father.

A wave sluices across the deck. I lift my feet just in time.

Dorchy and I haven't talked much since we left Boston with Miss Latigue. On the train we were never alone. Ten campers, five girls and five boys, joined us in Boston. Dorchy and I tried to sleep, but Miss Latigue needed our help as the train crawled from Boston to Portland to Rockland with long stops at each station. The two older girls who sat together speaking Italian were no problem, but the twin girls, who seem much younger than fourteen, either cried, fought, or ran up and down the aisle. Posy, a plump girl of fourteen, was very frightened, so Dorchy spent time distracting her with stories about the midway.

When we finally got to Rockland, very early this morning, we had to wait three hours for the ferry in the damp chill of the ferry house. The twins had run out of steam by then, and the other girls fell asleep. The boys played cards for most of the trip and went on playing while we waited. Dorchy decided right away that all the boys were boring. I disagreed because a scrawny one called Ratty, who walks with two crutches because of a clubfoot, can whistle any tune perfectly.

Boys first, we shuffled onto the ferry, everyone except Miss Latigue holding a blanket and a canvas duffel bag. Once the ferry left the harbor, it began to roll and everyone except me got seasick.

* * *

The sun tears open a window in the fog. And there's the heaving gray-green ocean flecked with foam. It looks angrier than it did on our last day at Eastham.

The ferry crests a wave, and I spot an island on the horizon. It disappears as we slide into a trough. As we inch closer, a heap of dark rocks, rimmed in white foam where the waves hit them, comes into clearer view.

The ferry slows and details emerge—a rocky point with a battered wooden lighthouse perched on the end like a seabird on its nest. Cliffs topped with spiky fir trees, a weathered one-story building with a wall of windows blindly reflecting the sky. A cove with a sailboat tied to a dock. On a cliff high above, a three-story red house with a wide porch overlooks the ocean. A shift in the wind brings the scent of warm pine needles and woodsmoke. Steam rises from my damp clothes.

My heart stirs. Maybe we'll stay in that house. Sleep in real beds. Eat real food off china plates with silverware at a cloth-covered table.

The ferry rounds a rocky point into the calm green water of a small bay. The boat is steadier now. Dorchy, Miss Latigue, and the campers straggle out on deck. Boys and girls cough, shiver, and open their mouths to gulp clean air. They're all orphans, Miss Latigue told us, but not all are from orphanages. Some are from institutions for the incorrigible, crippled, or feebleminded. The girls wear shapeless gray or tan shifts; the boys, gray or blue trousers and shirts.

Dorchy and I stand out in our new blue-gingham Council dresses and our sweaters from Eastham. The dresses are an awful reminder of the Ogilvies, but they were all that Miss Latigue could provide at short notice. We don't have to wear the aprons today, but we will wear them on the island to remind everyone that we work for the Council.

The twin girls cling to each other, worn out from the ferry ride.

When one howls, an Italian girl slaps her. The other twin starts to whimper.

Posy comes out on deck with one hand covering her harelip. The other clutches her woolen blanket around her like a shawl. She told us on the train, "It's my harelip got me sent to this camp. My folks were going to get it fixed by a doctor before they died. Matron at the orphanage says it's a punishment for their sins."

"How could a harelip get you sent to camp?" Dorchy asked.

Posy looked down at her hands. "Matron said she picked me because they only want ones older than fourteen and deformed in some way."

Now on deck, Posy's face is creased with worry. Her long, blond braid immediately starts to unravel in the wind. I squeeze her shoulder and tell her everything will be fine once we're on dry land. She doesn't look convinced, but talking to her, I begin to feel like a counselor, not one of the campers.

CHAPTER 28

The ferry rounds a wooded point into a bay. No boats, but a long dock. At the land end of the dock stands a nurse in a white dress and cap, fighting to control her dark-blue cape. Next to her a tall boy in a blue shirt and trousers keeps pushing his dark hair out of his eyes.

I nudge Dorchy. "The welcoming committee."

She closes her eyes and groans.

"You'll feel better on dry land," I say and then, "Look up there."

As the ferry nudges against the dock, a tall, thin man in a long, white coat comes to the edge of a cliff above the bay. He stands completely still, staring down at us. I feel a chill between my shoulder blades.

"Miss Latigue, who is that?" I point to the cliff top.

"I've never met him, but I imagine that's Dr. Jellicoe, the camp physician," she says quietly. "He's the one who's been reporting flu among the campers."

We make our way down a steep gangplank to the dock, first the boys, then Posy, who has taken the twins' hands, and then me. We're almost there when Posy trips and falls flat onto the dock, pulling the twins down with her. I fall on top of them, my crutch flying, our bags and blankets scattering around us. Posy scrambles up to comfort the twins. I reach for my crutch.

"Here, let me help," a deep voice says. A calloused hand grabs mine and pulls me to my feet. I feel a surge of strength and stand up straight. "Thank you."

"I'm Tom." He's the tall, dark-haired boy I saw at the end of the dock. He looks about our age, with kind eyes and a scar on his cheek. His clothes look too big for him, but he's definitely not a camper.

"I'm Rowan."

I hold on to his arm until Dorchy hands me my crutch. She and Posy gather up the blankets and bags. Miss Latigue takes charge of the twins.

"Posy, Dorchy, this is Tom," I say.

Posy giggles. Dorchy gives him a quick look and a nod.

Tom winks at me and walks away.

"Oh, isn't he handsome?" Posy giggles. "He likes you, Rowan."

"No, he doesn't." I'm embarrassed to have fallen at his feet.

The dock seems as unsteady as the ferry deck. I concentrate on moving forward while the wind tries to tug me off balance. Miss Latigue and the twins reach the nurse at the end of the dock. Beyond them a gravel road winds uphill away from the bay.

With a piercing two-note whistle, the ferry casts off and heads out of the bay for open water.

Dorchy stops. "We're stuck here until that boat comes back," she says. "I don't like boats, but it's worse being in a place with no way out."

"There's always a way out." I shiver, remembering the locked door in the burning cottage. "It's an island. I saw a sailboat, and there must be other boats."

Dorchy says, "That Tom fellow has a nasty scar. What are we getting ourselves into?"

She's not really looking for an answer, so I start walking again. Unlike Dorchy, I'm enjoying the island—the salt air, the scent of warm pine needles, the cries of seagulls. I still feel the touch of Tom's hand.

Posy rushes up behind us. "Do you think we'll have far to walk?" Her face is mottled, her breathing rapid. Fear is a flag she waves over her head. I wonder how long she has been in the orphanage. At the Home I learned never to show any feelings, especially fear.

A flatbed truck bounces down the road to the dock and brakes hard, scattering gravel. Climbing out of the cab is Dr. Jellicoe. Up close, his unexpressive face looks waxy. His name is embroidered in red on his white coat.

* * *

Miss Latigue and the nurse start toward him, but Dr. Jellicoe has beckoned Ratty out of the crowd of boys. As Ratty limps over to the truck, Dr. Jellicoe snatches his crutches and holds them up like a trophy. Ratty falls against him, but Tom is there, putting his hands under Ratty's arms to hold him up.

A stab of dread chokes me. *The doctor is a bully.* Dorchy steps in front of me, blocking the doctor's view of my crutch.

"Give me my crutches," Ratty yells, reaching for them, his face streaked with tears.

Dr. Jellicoe puts the crutches behind his back. "You won't need them on the truck."

"I want them." Ratty struggles against Tom's grip, but Tom lifts him easily and lays him in the flatbed of the truck. Then he leans over and talks to Ratty before he goes back to the other boys.

I shrink behind Dorchy, willing the doctor to drive away without noticing me. *But he was watching from the top of the cliff. He must have seen me fall.*

"Follow me," the nurse barks. Miss Latigue smiles at us, and we move forward. "The nurse says it's a half-hour walk," she murmurs. "Rowan, would you be more comfortable on the truck? We can arrange it."

"She'd rather crawl than ride," Dorchy says.

Miss Latigue snaps, "I'm asking Rowan."

"I'll walk," I tell her. "I'd prefer it."

The truck chokes to life, turns around, and rattles up the hill.

I draw a deep breath. Safe. But from what? And for how long?

"If you were a camper, they wouldn't have asked," Dorchy mutters. "You'd be on that truck too."

We follow Miss Latigue up the road away from the dock. In front of us, the nurse herds the girl campers. Ahead of them, Tom and the four remaining boy campers race each other to the top of the hill. A gust of wind shakes the pines that line the road, but above us is a brilliant blue sky.

After a few steps, I have no breath for talking. By the time we get to the top, my right leg feels like rubber.

With Dorchy next to me, I rest on my crutch and look around. From up here, the white-flecked ocean stretches away to the south. The road curves inland where the air is still and warm, and the wind rustling the tops of the tall pines doesn't touch us. Both of my legs ache now, and after a few minutes, I spot a granite boulder the right height for a seat.

Dorchy notices it too. "We have to rest," she yells.

"No stopping," Nurse Blunt calls back. "If the cripple can't walk, she should have taken the truck."

Dorchy says, "Don't be fooled by the limp. Rowan has the stamina of a bloodhound."

"Bloodhound?" I elbow Dorchy. "How about a thoroughbred racehorse?"

"Hmm. No. A donkey," she says. "Racehorses are for speed. You're for distance."

"I'll wait with them, Nurse Blunt," says Miss Latigue.

"Blunt. What a perfect name for her," Dorchy says.

Miss Latigue sighs.

We catch up to the others when they stop to rest. Boys and girls sit on the ground, wide-eyed and panting. I wonder if they were selected for being "deformed," as Posy said she was. One boy is deaf, but the others seem fine. One Italian girl speaks no English, and the other translates for her. Other than language skills, they are fine. The twins are strange but not "deformed." Posy must be wrong.

Dorchy picks a bouquet of feathery white Queen Anne's lace and hands it to Nurse Blunt. *Will the con work?* The nurse swats it out of Dorchy's hand. *Nope. Nurse Blunt is no rube.*

We walk another hundred yards and the road divides. We follow the right fork that curves back to the cliff top and a view of the ocean. Straight ahead is the big red house we saw from the ferry. Maybe we're going to stay there after all. But we walk past it to a one-story weathered building with the word "Gymnasium" burned into the wood above double doors.

As Nurse Blunt and Tom herd the campers inside, the truck rattles to a stop next to us.

Miss Latigue exclaims, "Where's Ratty?"

Dorchy clutches my arm.

"Dr. Jellicoe." Miss Latigue strides over to the truck as he climbs out. "Did that poor boy fall off?"

He shakes his head and pushes past her into the building.

"If he didn't fall, what happened to him?" Dorchy demands. She's thinking, as I am, that it could have been me.

Miss Latigue says briskly, "Come along. I expect he'll tell us when we get inside."

I stare at the empty truck bed. Nothing here makes sense. First the doctor teased Ratty by taking his crutches and holding them over his head. Then Tom loaded Ratty on the truck, and now Ratty's gone. Miss Latigue hired us to work at this camp, but she doesn't know the doctor and is as confused about Ratty as we are. *What's going on here?*

CHAPTER 29

Nurse Blunt waves us inside a big room smelling of sweat and pine oil. Opposite the doors, sunlight streams in through long windows overlooking the ocean. My crutch thumps on the polished wooden floor as I walk over the painted yellow lines of a tennis court. No net. A balcony runs around three sides of the room. The stairs are roped off: "Staff Only."

"Line up in front of the table," Nurse Blunt sings out. "Mrs. Van Giesen will check you in."

The name runs through me like an electric shock. Father knew her, but I'm not going to tell Dorchy yet. I keep my eyes straight ahead and hope Dorchy didn't notice. Posy gets in the end of the line behind a stocky black-haired boy. Dorchy and I line up behind her. One by one, each camper approaches a middle-aged woman sitting at a card table. Mrs. Van Giesen's gray hair is pulled back in a chignon. In a blue tweed suit, pearls, and a large sapphire ring, she looks out of place among the campers.

"Who's Mrs. Van Giesen when she's at home?" Dorchy asks in a low voice.

"She *is* at home. This island belongs to her."

Dorchy's eyes open wide. "How do you know *that*?"

"I just do."

"I need water," the taller of the two Italian girls calls out from her spot in line. "Where is water, please?"

"Silence in the line." Nurse Blunt raps the girl's head with her knuckles, and she yelps like a puppy.

"Is there a problem, Nurse?" Mrs. Van Giesen calls out in a clear, pleasant voice.

"Not at all, ma'am," barks the nurse.

Tom comes over to us. "Are you the new girls' counselors?"

Dorchy looks at the floor. She's not in a friendly mood.

"Yes," I say. "We came with Miss Latigue. She's a member of the New England Council and—"

"Be quiet," Dorchy interrupts. "We don't know him."

"We met on the dock," I remind her.

Tom holds out his hand to Dorchy. "Tom Hollenbeck, boys' counselor. Pleased to meet you."

Dorchy gives him a long look. "What happened to Ratty? The truck came without him." She doesn't shake his hand.

Tom shrugs. "I'll ask the doctor once we get checked in."

I turn and watch the dark-haired boy in front of Posy step up to Mrs. Van Giesen. She smiles at him. In front of her are an open ledger and an assortment of colorful cloth squares.

"Name?" she says.

The boy speaks so quietly that she asks him to repeat it. "Jack Gillen," he says as if the words taste unfamiliar.

"And you are from?"

"The Worcester Home," Jack mumbles.

"...for Incorrigible Boys," Tom adds, as he joins the boy at the table.

Mrs. Van Giesen purses her lips and hands Jack a red patch with a capital *I* sewn on it.

"Get your uniform and a needle and thread in the locker room downstairs, and sew on the patch. Then put on your uniform. It's hard to sew a patch on clothing you're wearing." She laughs a tinkling laugh that makes me wince. I remember that laugh—and her. So probably she will remember me.

"And what do I do with this uniform?" Jack has an Irish brogue. *Being Irish is reason enough for sterilization,* Julia said once.

"Tom will take it once you've sewn the badge on the new one. If you can't sew, ask someone to do it for you. 'One for all, and all for one.'"

Tom turns to me. "Remember that," he says. Then he leads Jack away to join three boys waiting at the other end of the gym.

Posy steps up to the table, covering her mouth. "Lower your hand," Mrs. Van Giesen says.

Posy looks back at us, then lowers her hand. "Harelip. Physical deformity," Mrs. Van Giesen says and hands her a gold patch with *PD* on it.

Dorchy and I step forward. We stand close enough to Mrs. Van Giesen for me to read the words engraved on a gold pin on her suit jacket: Detection + Selection + Correction = Perfection. I know I've seen that before—but where?

Miss Latigue joins us. "Cecily," she says, smiling, "these girls are here at my request. They'll work in any capacity you wish. I'm sure you'll find them useful. They have been employed by the Council all summer, and I vouch for them wholeheartedly. They'll wear the uniforms we have provided."

Mrs. Van Giesen touches her hair. "I'm sure Nurse Blunt could use some help with the girl campers," she says. Something much more interesting than me or Dorchy seems to have caught her attention at the other end of the room.

"Excellent." Miss Latigue beams. "The Council is very appreciative. Just let me know where these two will be sleeping and I'll show them around. I know you're busy."

Mrs. Van Giesen stands up and walks away, calling over her shoulder, "If you can just wait until the campers are settled..."

Now I remember where I saw the words on her pin. It was five years ago, at the beginning of the summer that ended with polio. Father, Julia, and I were eating breakfast on the screen porch of the beach house. As usual, Julia was opening Father's mail. As I began spreading strawberry jam on my toast, she handed him a typewritten letter.

Father glanced at it. Then he crumpled it in one hand and threw it across the porch. Julia and I exchanged a shocked look. Father never lost his temper.

"Those fools," he roared. He splashed a sugar lump in his coffee. Then another, and another. Father never took sugar. "Send a telegram, Julia." His voice grated. "One word." He stirred the coffee so fast that most of it sloshed out.

"What word, Father?" I asked.

Julia kicked me under the table.

"*No!*" Father shouted. "En-oh. A word that pigheaded woman and her addled daughter and friends need to hear more often."

Later on, when I was sweeping the porch, I picked up the letter and smoothed it out. I told myself that it was jetsam, something thrown away and free for the taking. The words *Detection* + *Selection* + *Correction* = *Perfection* were printed in raised letters at the top of the cream linen page. They were all I had time to read before Julia came out.

Mrs. Van Giesen walks back, smiling graciously. "I'm so sorry I had to leave you," she says. "Now, please, tell me your names."

Before Dorchy can speak, the double front doors bang open and an animal sound, bright as a knife blade, slashes the air.

* * *

A chestnut horse backlit by the bright afternoon sun whinnies again as it comes through the doors and clops across the floor into the middle of the tennis court. A girl screams like a teakettle going off. Everyone else is silent. I grab Dorchy's arm.

A woman rider sits astride the horse in a western saddle. Her black jacket, fawn jodhpurs, and black boots set her apart from every other woman in the room. She has a jutting chin, bruised-looking eyes, and thick auburn hair. A shaft of sunlight from the tall windows creates a spotlight effect where she comes to a stop. "I am Vera Van," she says in a loud, hard voice, "and this is my gelding, Viking. Stay well away. He's nervous." She rubs the horse's neck with her riding crop, and he tosses his head, eyes rolling.

A honking laugh erupts from one of the boys.

I lean on my crutch and observe how Mrs. Van Giesen's mouth tightens whenever Viking's hooves move on the polished floor. *She hates having a horse in here, and she also hates the rider.*

Miss Latigue starts to smile and quickly covers her mouth with a handkerchief. *She feels superior to this performance.*

Vera Van ignores the adults and speaks to the campers herded up against the windows by Viking. "I will now explain the procedures here at camp," Vera says in a high, clear voice. "Can you all hear me? Any deaf ones in this batch?"

The campers shuffle their feet. *Who is in charge here? I wonder.*

Mrs. Van Giesen or Vera Van?

The campers shuffle their feet.

Tom calls out, "One, Miss Van."

"Only one? Dear me, what a fit group we have here. Well, I'm sure no one has told you anything." She points her whip handle at Mrs. Van Giesen. "You didn't spoil the surprise, did you, Mother?"

Mrs. Van Giesen frowns as if she just spotted a weed in a flower arrangement.

Dorchy nudges me in the ribs with her elbow and raises her eyebrows.

"The girls will stay here in the gym." Vera turns in the saddle and waggles the fingers of one hand at the clump of girls. "All set, Nurse?"

"Yes, Miss Van," says the nurse.

"Tom will take the boys camping," Vera Van says. "Ready, Tom?"

"Ready." Tom stares at the floor.

"He hates her," I say in a low voice.

Crrrack. Vera snaps the whip in the air. Viking whinnies. "Silence over there," Vera shouts at us. "Who are those two, Mother?"

"Vera," Mrs. Van Giesen says gently. "Miss Latigue has brought them with her to help us out. They work for the Council." She gives Vera a warning look.

"I don't care if they work for J. P. Morgan," Vera says. "One is a cripple and the other one looks like a gypsy." She kicks Viking's side and the horse advances on us. He places his feet as carefully as a ballet dancer. I shrink back. Dorchy stands still. Before Viking takes another step, Tom runs over and grabs the bridle. He speaks quietly and Viking flicks his ears. Then Tom looks up at Vera.

I hold my breath, waiting for her to lash him with the whip. Instead she laughs. "You have a way with the boys and my horse and an eye for the girls. Well, well."

Tom strokes Viking's nose.

"Hire whomever you like to work in the house, Mother," Vera says. "But keep them well clear of the campers."

Dorchy steps forward. "Miss Van, where is that boy Ratty who was taken away from the dock and put in a truck?"

Vera keeps her erect posture, but her face freezes. Then she says in a calm, friendly tone, "The doctor tells me he was exposed to influenza, so he's been quarantined for the good of all. We'll be monitoring everyone who was on the train with him, because if he does have it, all of you are at risk." She slides off Viking and hands the reins to Tom.

"While Tom takes Viking to the stable, we'll have lunch here," Vera says, "served by our new helpers." She snaps her fingers. "Their names, Miss Latigue."

Miss Latigue says loudly, "Dorchy Miller and Rowan Collier."

Mrs. Van Giesen lets out a cry and covers her mouth with her hand.

CHAPTER 30

Mrs. Van Giesen collects herself and says, "Which one of you is Rowan?"

Dorchy pokes me.

"I am."

"*Rowan.*" Mrs. Van Giesen reaches out her hand. I take it. She squeezes it between both of hers, and the sapphire digs into my skin. "I'm so very pleased to see you." She looks at my crutch. "We heard you had died."

Died? I don't know whether to laugh or cry.

"Do call me Cecily." Her hand trembles and she lets go of mine. "I know your father—or used to know him, I should say." She takes a deep breath. "He traveled so much during the war, and afterward too, I'm told. I'm sure *you* hear from him, but…"

"No," I say firmly. "I don't. Not once in five years."

She nods. "Well, I'm sorry, but before we go further, I must vet you."

"*Vet* me?"

"Establish that you are who you claim to be." She laughs and clicks open her handbag. "Though you do bear an uncanny resemblance to Franklin." She pulls out a leather notebook and gold pen. "Your father's date of birth?"

It's my turn to laugh. "Father doesn't share information about himself, but I can tell you this." I take a breath and recite so fast the words run together, "HiramFaithJeremiahSarahGalenKatherine PeterSukeyHiramBetsyObadiahAnn—"

"Stop." Cecily holds up her hand; her nose wrinkles. "What on earth does that mean?"

"It's the Collier family tree. I started with the first Colliers in America, Hiram and Faith, 1634, and continued up the trunk to Father. Or I would have, if you hadn't stopped me. He made me memorize their names in order when I was five." Reciting the old names has an odd effect on me. I feel a surge of confidence. Father once said no to this woman, and she has no idea that I know.

Cecily beams at me. "That sounds just like Franklin. His lineage was so important to him." Her chin juts out. "As ours is to us, of course."

Of course.

"So now that I know you are who you say you are, I have to ask." Her voice hardens. "Did he send you here to spy on us?"

What? I would laugh except that her eyes look as cold as her voice sounds. "I told you the truth. I haven't heard from him for five years," I say slowly. "He has no idea where I am." Saying that aloud makes me feel strong. "I wouldn't spy for him if he asked."

"Then you will be my new assistant." Cecily's voice sparkles like her eyes. She is all sweetness again. "We'll work together at the house. The other girl who came with you...what is her name again? She'll stay here and help Nurse Blunt with the girls. I'm sure Vera didn't mean it when she said to keep you two away from the campers. Miss Latigue will be staying at the house too." She looks at me expectantly.

"Thank you, Mrs. Van Giesen."

"Oh, please call me Cecily."

My mind is racing. Miss Latigue never mentioned the possibility that Dorchy and I would be separated. I look for Dorchy to see if she heard, but she has her back to me, talking to Posy and the twins.

Cecily waves at Vera and says, "I want you to meet my daughter, Vera Van. She shortened her last name during the war because Van Giesen sounded too German."

Vera strides over to us, tapping her whip against her leg. I take a step back.

Cecily says, "Vera, darling, look. This is Franklin Collier's daughter Rowan. She has satisfied me that she is, beyond a doubt, Rowan Collier."

Vera says impatiently, "What's wrong with your leg? And what on earth can you do for the Council using a crutch?"

I answer the first question. "Polio paralyzed my legs five years ago. I was in Bellevue for a year, treated by Dr. Friedlander. I then spent four years with Dr. Pynchon at the Boston Home." No one has asked me anything about myself for a long time. I consider the next words, testing them before I add, "Father went to France during the war, and I haven't seen him since. My sister, Julia, is my guardian. They are both in Europe."

"Julia Collier," murmurs Cecily. "A delightful young woman. Devoted to the cause of sterilization as I recall. You know her too, Vera."

Vera sniffs and walks away.

* * *

As Dorchy and I hand out sandwiches and cups of water to the campers, I keep thinking, *If we show that we work well together, they'll keep us together*. But as soon as the campers start eating, Cecily says, "Come, Rowan. I'll take you over to the house for a bath and some decent clothes."

Dorchy gapes at me. "What does she mean?"

"It's a mistake. I'll be back here as soon as I talk to Miss Latigue."

"Class sticks together," Dorchy says, her face blotchy red with anger. "The carny gets pushed back."

"It's not like that," I plead. "I don't want to go, but she knew my father and…"

Dorchy turns her back on me.

Sick at heart, I say, loud enough for Dorchy to hear, "Miss Latigue promised us that Dorchy and I would work together while we're here. And she specifically said we would wear these uniforms and our aprons."

"No, no," Cecily says. "You'll work wherever I think best. And I need you in the house with me. As far as clothes, girls your age like pretty things, and while you work for me, you shall have them."

I look back, hoping for a sign from Dorchy, but she is standing stiff-backed, staring out the wall of windows at the ocean.

I'm so sorry I got us into this, I tell her silently and promise, *I'll be back as soon as I can.* It sounds like Father's promise to me at Bellevue.

Outside, as Cecily and I walk along the gravel drive, the red house calls to me, *You belong here.* Maybe I did once, but now I belong where Dorchy is. On our right are the woods, as thick and green and dark as a fairy-tale forest. I feel like Gretel following the witch to the candy house. Compelled to go forward, but more suspicious with every step.

Cecily opens the heavy front door. After the noise of the gym, the big house seems very quiet. And airy. And beautiful. I suck in a deep breath of salt air pouring through the screen door at the far end of the hall on a shaft of sunlight.

"Come with me," Cecily says. I follow her halfway down the hall—polished hardwood with islands of oriental rugs—into a small office. Behind the big wooden desk, a window looks out on an overgrown garden, and beyond that, I catch a glimpse of the cliff and the bay where the ferry landed. The warm room smells of lemon oil. The desk chair is wooden, not leather like Father's. On the wall hangs a yellow and brown poster. Under the words "Sow your family's seed in healthy soil," a farmer scatters seeds from a basket onto a plowed field. An Underwood typewriter is centered on a typing table next to tall, wooden file cabinets.

"This is the camp office," Cecily says, "and here you can be of great help to me." She points to the file cabinets. "This summer's records are kept in the top drawer. You will confine yourself to that." She opens the drawer and shows me the files. "The other drawers are locked, and if you ever discover one that isn't, you must tell me immediately. I need your word on that."

"Of course, you have my word," I say, and then, "Why are they locked?"

Cecily's cheeks turn a deep red. "They contain notes on research projects conducted by Vera and Dr. Jellicoe." She rests her hand on the file cabinet. "The files shouldn't be in here. They have nothing to do with the camp."

My heart beats faster. She's lying about that. Why?

She turns her back on the file cabinet. "When Vera is in the house, you will work in my private office next door. Is that clear? She is very, um, picky about who may use this room."

"Miss Latigue told us she was here to examine files," I say. "Will she be working in this office?"

"Yes." Cecily draws herself up taller. "I personally will select the files for her. As I told you, she will be staying here in the house."

Cecily waits for me to leave and then closes the office door. "Now, my dear, a bath and some fresh clothes. Cook can wash the ones you traveled in. I will pick some more suitable outfits and leave them on your bed while you bathe." She puts her hand on my arm. "I am so very pleased to meet you," she says. "I will take good care of you while you're here. Your father will have no complaints."

She's right, but for the wrong reason. Father will have no complaints because he has no interest in me.

* * *

I slip into warm water in a pink marble bathtub. A kerosene heater pulses warmth, an electric light casts a pink glow, and lavender bath salts scent the air. I used to take baths like this for granted. In two weeks I could be back home having baths like this again. Hope bubbles up like the lavender bath salts.

I rub soap on my arms and neck and head, happy to have shed my salty gingham dress. After my bath, I'll put on different clothes.

I lie back and stretch out my left leg, the stranger. The scar from the operation I had two years ago slashes red across my thigh. The one wonderful thing Julia did for me in those years at the Boston Home was to make sure I received that operation. Her usual visits were so unsatisfactory that they could have been scripted by someone who didn't know how sisters are supposed to speak and act.

But at the start of my second year, she tracked down Dr. Friedlander at Boston Children's Hospital. He had left Bellevue but agreed to accept me as a patient again and perform the operation. Julia came to Boston and stayed in a hotel, visiting me daily while I was in the hospital. She promised me and Dr. Friedlander that I would see him regularly for the next three months and made all the arrangements. Thanks to her, my left leg has a real chance of being as strong as the right.

But she didn't keep her promise to bring me home to New York after my sixteenth birthday in June.

Dr. Friedlander talked to me alone after the operation. He was very quiet when I told him about Dr. Pynchon and the Home. He told me my leg could get stronger, but only with use and the proper exercise. "In time you'll be able to walk with a barely noticeable limp, I promise you. So now you need to start thinking about what you want to do with your life."

"I want to go home to New York."

He ignored that. "I told you back at Bellevue that you would make a fine nurse," he said. He was facing the window, playing with the curtain cord. From the hall came a rattle of wheels, the lunch trays being delivered. I sat very still on the edge of my bed.

He turned and said quietly, "There is an excellent nursing school at this hospital. I can speak to your sister if you'd like. You understand the disease and have a gift for connecting with children, the essential qualification for a polio nurse. I saw how the other patients on your ward at Bellevue responded to you. You say you are as helpful as you can be to the little ones at the Home. Think about a career working with children who are terrified and alone in the hospital dealing with a crippling disease."

"That's your gift," I said, tears welling in my eyes. "At Bellevue, we felt better even if you only poked your head into the ward and said, 'Good morning.'" I started to cry.

"You will make a fine nurse," he said again. "But first"—his tone was now light and playful—"strengthen and put weight on that leg as often as you can. It *will* get stronger. Sadly your exercise has been neglected at the Boston Home by that woman…"

Julia arrived then and Dr. Friedlander said, "We were discussing the possibility—with your father's permission, of course—of Rowan training to be a nurse, specifically to work with me here in the polio ward after she leaves the Home."

Julia frowned. "But surely a cripple cannot be a nurse."

Dr. Friedlander's voice was icy as he said, "Her mind and hands and heart are unaffected by polio, Miss Collier, and they are what count in nursing."

* * *

Well, this summer I've used my leg and strengthened it in ways Dr. Friedlander never imagined. I leave the bathtub and pull the chain to empty it. Wrapped in a huge purple towel, as soft and thick as a quilt, I wipe a sponge around the tub and rinse it carefully. At the Home I learned to keep common spaces clean for the next user.

I dry off and go through a connecting door into my bedroom, a big, comfortable room at the back of the house, away from the ocean. I put on the clothes Cecily laid out on the bed—silk underwear, a white sailor blouse with a navy-blue tie, and a navy flannel skirt. The skirt is too big so I roll the waistband over and push up the sleeves. Long black stockings and beautiful black leather boots. Real clothes like these seem like a dream.

Cecily is waiting for me at the foot of the wide staircase. She clasps her hands and says, "You look much better, my dear. In those clothes even your father would recognize you."

I consider telling her that after all this time, Father probably couldn't recognize me even if he wanted to.

She leads the way to a sitting room at the front of the house, overlooking the ocean. We eat sugar cookies and drink tea. I'm so hungry I eat two cookies before remembering my manners. "Thank you for these, and the bath and clothes," I say.

Cecily nods and smooths her skirt. "Do you have any questions about Loup Island, dear? Anything you need?"

I need to be with Dorchy. "Will I be eating dinner at the gymnasium tonight, Mrs...um, Cecily?"

"No, you'll dine here with me, Vera, and Miss Latigue. Better company for you. Some of the campers' manners can be quite rough around the edges."

Rough around the edges?

"We are more your type than that Dorchy," she adds.

"Dorchy is exactly my type." My voice rises. "She is an orphan like me. And we are friends."

"I see you feel strongly about this." Cecily puts down her teacup. "I won't speak of it again, except to say I know your father would expect me to open my home and my arms to you, and protect you while you are on my island."

I bite back another comment about Father's long absence. It's clear that Cecily intends to keep me away from the gym and Dorchy until we leave. I am her prize possession, and she is going to "protect" me here in her castle. *But protect me from what?*

I'll look for answers as soon as I have some time alone in the office. Thanks to Gar's training, the locks on those file drawers don't have a chance.

CHAPTER 31

The dining room table, covered with a cream damask cloth, is set with silverware, china plates, and crystal goblets. A candelabra bathes us in a warm glow. Miss Latigue and I drink water; Vera and Cecily have wine. Everything looks familiar. How many dinners did I eat in New York at a table just like this? But I feel disconnected, as if I've floated up and am looking down at the room.

"The Council has had troubling reports of children here dying of the flu," Miss Latigue says, spreading her napkin on her lap. "I look forward to learning more."

"They aren't children!" Vera slams down her wineglass.

"Vera, please." Cecily sounds weary.

"I'm sorry, Miss Latigue," Vera says in an un-sorry tone, "but as you know, our campers this summer are fourteen or older, hardly 'children.'"

"Except for the twins, Lolly and Dolly," says Miss Latigue, patting her lips with her napkin. "They act much younger than fourteen."

Vera helps herself to a roll from a silver basket. "Well, the twins are a special case. Technically they are research subjects, not campers. But all the other campers this summer have been at least fourteen."

"And how many of them have died?" Miss Latigue speaks softly, but she's like a terrier on the trail of a savory rat.

"Influenza is so unpredictable, isn't it?" Cecily says. "I lost six healthy members of my family in the epidemic of 1918. Six. In two weeks. Some were only sick for hours before they died." She goes on, quoting statistics about flu cases in institutions and at summer camps in New England, including a Connecticut camp where three teenagers died of flu in July.

"Those were measles cases," says Miss Latigue. "And only two campers died. I don't know how this false information spreads."

"Well, here at Loup Island"—Cecily sounds nervous—"we have done what's best for the majority of campers, and that is inoculation."

"I had no idea there was a vaccine for influenza." Miss Latigue looks shocked. "Why isn't this more widely known?"

"Because it's experimental." Vera leans forward. In the candle-light her bushy auburn hair gleams. "Hiram, Dr. Jellicoe, has done brilliant research. He'll explain it all to you tomorrow. There are risks, of course, as with any experimental vaccine. But we feel the risks are worth it, because the benefit is so great."

Miss Latigue frowns and taps her finger on the table. "The Council will take a dim view of any experiments carried out on these unfortunates. Heaven help all of us if the press catches wind of it."

I almost miss the look of panic that flashes between Vera and her mother.

"There are always accidents," says Vera. "And yes, some campers did die. But"—she jabs her finger at Miss Latigue—"only those who had never been exposed to flu before they came here. As a test, Dr. Jellicoe injected himself and then Mother and me, and look, we are all still standing. As are the majority of campers."

Injected himself? Miss Latigue raises her eyebrows. I don't believe it either.

"Please give me a head count of campers who died of the flu this summer," Miss Latigue says. "I know you've had a lot to contend with and have done your best to protect all of the campers. Still the Council must have the facts."

"Sadly, fourteen campers reacted badly to the inoculation or came here so ill it did no good," Cecily says bleakly. "Every one of those deaths tears at my heart. Their bodies have been buried here and their institutions advised. But when they come here infected, what can we do? It would be criminal not to use the means at hand."

She and Vera watch Miss Latigue. I would swear they're holding their breaths. Cecily twists her string of pearls so tightly that I'm afraid it will break. It makes me wonder about Father's reaction to Cecily's letter all those years ago. Did he suspect her and Vera of something?

Finally Miss Latigue nods. "The perception might be that we are *experimenting* on the campers with this vaccine, so for now the information about the inoculations and the deaths will remain private. I will inform the Council, and it will stop there."

Did Father find out they wanted to experiment on the campers?

She turns to me. "I'm sorry to burden you with this, Rowan, but you must promise to tell no one about this conversation. No one. Not even Dorchy."

"Of course." I look down at the table, afraid they'll see I'm lying. But what I said wasn't really a lie. I meant, *Of course, I will tell Dorchy.*

"What will the Council say?" The words burst from Cecily.

"That depends on what I find out tomorrow at the medical tent." Miss Latigue turns to me. "I'd like Rowan to come to the gym tomorrow with her camera. I'll be interviewing the girls and would like a photograph of each one. You do have a darkroom, Cecily, do you not? That Rowan can use?"

My heart leaps. *I'll be back in the gym with Dorchy.*

Cecily frowns. "I need Rowan's help filing tomorrow."

"Well, after she assists me, she's all yours," Miss Latigue says. "What about the darkroom?"

"Mother," says Vera. It's a warning.

"Vera is very proprietary about the darkroom," Cecily says.

"I don't care who does the job, but the Council needs to have the film developed and prints made here," says Miss Latigue. "I hope that won't be a problem."

Vera shrugs. "If Rowan knows what she's doing, I guess...."

"I do know." I haven't been in a darkroom in years, but Father taught me well.

"One last question," Miss Latigue says brightly. "I'd like to contact the Boston office at some point tomorrow. What is the best way to communicate with the mainland?"

Another glance between Vera and Cecily; this time it's surprise.

"We don't have a way to contact them," Cecily says. "I'm afraid you'll have to wait until you're back on the mainland."

"No contact?" Miss Latigue sounds horrified. "What about emergencies? How would you call for help?"

"Dr. Jellicoe is here to handle any medical emergencies, with Dr. Ritter as backup," says Vera.

"And we have the lighthouse," Cecily says. "Although it was damaged by fire some time ago."

"We saw it from the ferry," says Miss Latigue doubtfully. "It's in ruins."

Cecily smiles. "Oh, it's workable. Reuben, the caretaker, assured us of that."

"But how would a lighthouse summon help?" Miss Latigue says.

I wonder the same thing.

"We'll light the lamp. It's unusual these days, so when people on the mainland see it, they will send a boat to offer assistance. The townspeople were quite fond of our lighthouse in its day and have told us many times, 'If we see the light, we'll know you need help.'"

Miss Latigue shakes her head. "Surely you could establish radio contact with the mainland?"

"We *could*," says Vera with finality, "but we see no reason to. The lighthouse will work for a nonmedical emergency. Otherwise we handle things ourselves. How on earth do you think people got by before radio and telephone?"

Miss Latigue flushes and grips the table. "I will recommend the Council immediately look for another location for the camp. I always said an island was asking for trouble."

She stands up. "And now, please excuse me. I want to make a final inspection at the gym."

I stand up too, putting my napkin by my plate. "I'd like to speak to you before you go, please," I say.

She nods and I follow her out of the dining room.

"May I go with you?" I ask. "I need to explain things to Dorchy. And really I would like to be assigned to work with her."

Miss Latigue sighs. "They need both of you to work with the campers, and that's a fact. Nurse Blunt is a nurse, not a counselor for healthy campers. But Cecily has decided she needs you, so my hands are tied for the moment."

She puts her hand on my arm. "Stay here tonight and say nothing to Cecily for now. Dorchy is fine with the girls, and you'll see her tomorrow. I'll tell her you wanted to come but had no choice."

I want to follow Miss Latigue when she opens the front door, but Cecily calls me back to the dining room. I go reluctantly.

CHAPTER 32

After breakfast with Cecily the next morning, Miss Latigue and I head out to the gym. I'm anxious to see Dorchy and tell her about the flu deaths. She's sitting on the gym floor watching over the girls doing needlework. I only have time to give her a brief wave. She lifts the hem of her apron with the Council's initials on it and glares at me in my new clothes. I shrug and hope I'll have a chance to explain later.

Miss Latigue sits at the table where Cecily sat yesterday, with the interview forms in front of her and the window behind her. Sitting opposite her, the girl she interviews is forced to squint into the bright sunlight. I sit behind Miss Latigue with her camera, a newer Brownie, loaded with film. "Several photographs of each girl, please," says Miss Latigue. "I like to have choices."

This afternoon I'll type the interviews on clean forms and develop and print the photographs.

"We'll start with Lolly," Miss Latigue calls to Dorchy.

"Not the twins," Vera's voice booms as she strides across the floor in her boots and riding clothes.

Posy jumps, and the short Italian girl lets out high-pitched squeal. Lolly and Dolly start jabbering in their private language.

"Why not?" Miss Latigue says sharply.

"My mother should have explained." Vera comes to a stop, facing Miss Latigue and me. I'm tempted to take a picture of Vera's angry scowl, but she would probably rip the film out of the camera. "Dr. Jellicoe and I have a special research interest in the twins," she says in her loud voice. "We're keeping all information about them private for the moment."

"How very unusual." Miss Latigue frowns. I look over to catch Dorchy's eye, but she's helping Posy thread a needle.

"Why don't you start with Elsa." Vera laughs. "She's a rich source of material by the look of her. Get your camera ready, Rowan."

Miss Latigue reads questions printed on a form and records Elsa's answers in pencil. The first questions are: *What defects, deformities, or birthmarks do you have? Did your parents have? Did your grandparents have? Were any of them vagrants? Feebleminded? Drunkards?*

What childhood diseases did you have?

How are your teeth: Any decay? Extractions? Pain?

Are your vision and hearing good? Failing? Defective?

Elsa speaks no English. Her answers are: "Um." "*Scusi?*" "*Niente.*"

"Miss Latigue," I interrupt. "Maybe the other Italian girl could translate for…"

"No, no, *no*." Vera, who has been listening to the interview, shakes her finger at me. I back away from her and catch sight of Dorchy staring at us.

"It's a logical suggestion, Vera," says Miss Latigue. "What is your objection? This girl, Elsa, cannot understand my questions."

Vera turns on her. "We never allow the unfit to interview the unfit. Simply note any responses you get. She understands you better than you think. Proceed."

Miss Latigue purses her lips. I can tell she's not used to taking orders or being corrected. Vera has gone too far.

But Miss Latigue only says mildly, "All right, I will continue in my own way. Now, Elsa, please try to understand. Only a few more."

From my vantage point, I can read the questions over her shoulder:

Condition of speech: enunciation—clear, lisping, stammering, stuttering, mumbling, hand gestures?

Miss Latigue circles *mumbling.*

Unfit. Vera's use of the word sets off an alarm in me. Is the point of these interviews to *confirm* the unfitness of the campers? That seems to be exactly what Miss Latigue is doing. And I'm part of the process. Just as I was part of the Unfit Family show, reminding audiences how "fit" they were compared to us. A wave of disgust sweeps through me. I lower the camera.

"Posy, please come over here," calls Miss Latigue. "I will evaluate your walk. Please photograph her, Rowan."

Posy walks over to the table, unsmiling. I raise the camera and press the shutter release.

Over Miss Latigue's shoulder I read: *Walking gait—Brisk? Leisurely? Shuffling?*

Miss Latigue circles *Shuffling.* Then she says, "Now we'll test your sense of direction, Posy. Close your eyes and walk to the front doors."

Posy closes her eyes and walks in an ever-widening circle, closer and closer to the windows.

"Stop," Miss Latigue shouts just before Posy bumps against the wall. For *Sense of direction*, Miss Latigue circles *Easily lost*.

For defect or deformity, she writes in, *Harelip*.

Miss Latigue chooses words that make Posy sound unfit, because Miss Latigue sees her as unfit. The questions aren't fair. The questioner isn't fair. None of it is fair.

Then it's the other Italian girl, Magdalena's, turn. After a short conversation with her, Miss Latigue circles the following words for *Temperament—Excitable, Low self-control, Talks to self.*

She later circles *Below-average intelligence* and *Poor grammar.*

On one of the forms she writes Lolly's and Dolly's names and "No access to subjects, by order of Vera Van."

When she's through with the interviews, she turns to me and makes a face. "Well, Rowan, what do you think?"

I'm so surprised that I barely manage to say, "It's hard to make sense of it all." But that's not true. I know exactly what I think. The interviews are meaningless. They confirm the interviewer's opinions about the interviewee. They are as fake as Gilda, Half Woman, Half Snake; as prejudiced and demeaning as the Unfit Family show.

How many hours, how many *years* has Julia wasted interviewing people to determine if they should be sterilized when she already knew the answers? Does Father know he's basing his lectures and articles on data collected by prejudiced interviewers?

A hot, furious fire kindles inside me. I wall it off.

Miss Latigue sighs. "The interview questions about parents' and grandparents' health and traits are ridiculous to use with orphans, wouldn't you say? So much of their family information is unknown."

"Yes. So why interview them at all?"

She looks startled. "How else can we determine who is fit to have children? From what Cecily tells me, your own father and sister are dedicated to our mission." She looks at me thoughtfully. "I assume you are too."

Cecily arrives to escort me back to her house for lunch, the darkroom, and note typing.

"The interviews won't take long to type up," says Miss Latigue. "Remember to make a carbon copy for me to take back to the Council. I'm off to inspect the medical tent."

As I leave the gym, I look around for Dorchy. I haven't had a chance to speak to her. She sits with her arm around Posy, who is weeping. When Dorchy sees me, she scowls and looks away.

That's unfair. I *didn't make Posy cry.* So why do I feel like the enemy?

CHAPTER 33

For "luncheon," as Cecily calls it, the cook, a plain, sturdy woman in a long white apron, serves us consommé, cornmeal biscuits, and lobster salad.

As she hands me my bowl of consommé, I ask her what her name is. Cecily calls her Cook.

"Louise," she says, looking surprised and pleased.

When she comes to clear our plates, I say, "Louise, the lobster was delicious."

A look of triumph crosses her face at the compliment. "Much obliged," she says.

After that, I have an hour to work without supervision while Cecily takes a nap. I go to the office as soon as she disappears upstairs. I'm determined to make the most of my time alone.

My first job is typing the interviews. I'm tempted to change what Miss Latigue wrote, but Father and Julia instilled a reverence for research in me, so I type what I was given, hating every word. I finish typing and file the originals in the top drawer of the file cabinet.

Now is my chance. I take a deep breath, unfold a paper clip, and pick the lock on the first forbidden file drawer.

I open the drawer and pull out a folder labeled *Summer 1922 Special*. The first page is headed *Betty Riordan, Camper*. The notes about Betty's deceased parents call them "non churchgoing," "shiftless," and "degenerate." Her own traits are as bad as the ones Miss Latigue came up with for Posy and Elsa and Magdalena: "bad teeth," "below-average intelligence," "gets lost easily," and "mumbles."

Betty's photograph is a shock. In it she's lying down, eyes closed, wrapped to the neck in a white sheet. *Riordan, B. Died 7/5/22 Influenza* is written on the back of the picture. I drop it as if it burned me.

Betty died here. This summer.

Cecily said that fourteen campers died this summer, but I never expected to see a photograph of one of the corpses.

I flip through all the pages in the folder and count twenty-five photographs of a dead boy or girl.

Twenty-five campers died here this summer of influenza. Cecily lied at dinner last night. I put a new roll of film in the camera and turn on the desk lamp. Then I snap pictures of a few of the photographs to show Miss Latigue. After that I relock the forbidden drawer.

"What are you doin' in here?" I jump and turn around. Louise stands in the doorway, arms folded.

"You scared me." My heart thunders. I force myself not to look at the camera on the desk. *Did she see me taking photographs?*

"Mrs. Van Giesen and Miss Van are in charge of the files," she says. "Do they know you're lookin' in there?"

I frown at her. "What business is it of yours?"

"Oh, it's my business all right." She leans on the doorjamb. "Reuben, my brother, is the caretaker, and we know all there is to know about this island," she says. "Ask anybody on the mainland about the Dubuques of Van Giesen Island. We have different views from the Van Giesens sometimes, always have, but we're family all the same."

"Well," I say carefully, "I'm not hurting the island. But I thought its name was Loup Island."

"That name's just for the camp," Louise says in a disgusted tone. "Miss Vera's idea. She's made a lot of changes. Not one of them any good, if you ask me. And if I read you right, you don't trust her either. But be careful. She's a step ahead of most folks when she wants something."

"What *does* she want?"

"I couldn't say for sure." She abruptly leaves the doorway, and by the time I get to the hall to look for her, she's disappeared.

Dust motes float through a shaft of sunlight from the west-facing window. So Vera's "a step ahead of most folks" is she? *But not you, Louise Dubuque.*

Cecily didn't tell me where to find the darkroom. I go back and look around the office. Then I go next door to Cecily's. From there I follow my nose, because here the closet has been turned into a chemical-smelling darkroom. When I open it and go in, I'm back in our darkroom at the beach.

Father stood over his pans of chemicals, the amber safelight adding to the magic. His hands in black rubber gloves rose from the sink. He hung wet prints to dry and flattened the dried ones under a towel with a dictionary on top. "Your mother took the photographs, and I developed the film and printed them," he told me that summer while he was teaching me. "Until she got so she could do a better job herself."

I click on the amber light in this darkroom and close the door. This is a much smaller space, but the same brown glass jugs of developer, stop, and fixer rest on a shelf above the workbench where the paper safe, enlarger, and paper cutter sit. Above my head is a wire with clothespins for drying negatives and prints.

I get to work. First I develop the negatives and then print the photographs I took of the girls for Miss Latigue. Then I develop the negatives and make prints of the pictures I took of the "Special" campers and other items in the files. Miss Latigue will get these too.

A while later Cecily finds me back in "my" office arranging today's prints. "All done?" she says. "I've asked Cook to make us some tea. I'm sorry I forgot to tell you where to find the darkroom. But it looks like you found it."

"Yes," I say. "I found everything."

* * *

Cecily loans me a blue dress with a dropped waist and a wide, white collar to put on after my second bath in one week. She also insists on washing my hair. I wear a bathrobe and lean over the sink, but still it feels much too close. I only let her do it because I'm nervous that Louise will tell her I went in the file drawer. I plan to say, "It was unlocked and I was going to tell you." Which sounds unbelievable even to me.

So I let her do what no one has done in five years—touch my hair. At Bellevue, as soon as I could stand in braces, Dr. Friedlander told me I had to take care of myself.

Cecily has strong hands and works up a lather with her sweet-smelling Palmolive shampoo. She towels my hair dry and wants to comb it, but I insist on doing that myself.

"I think you'd look sweet in a bob," she says wistfully as I comb out my long hair. At the Home, Dr. Pynchon cuts every girl's hair shoulder length once a year. Usually I wear braids. A bob is a new idea and I think I like it. But Cecily's attention bothers me. She's failed miserably with her own daughter, I think, so she's adopting me. But she's also trapped me here. I have no chance to speak privately to Miss Latigue before dinner. But after the interviews this morning, I feel like keeping my distance from her as well.

At dinner Cecily seats me on her right opposite Miss Latigue. Vera and Dr. Jellicoe, who has joined us, sit across from each other, and Dr. Ritter, a red-faced, blond-haired young man, faces Cecily. Cecily calls him "our German visitor." I was often included at dinners like this at home with Father and Julia. Even after four years in the Home, I remember when to use each fork, how to keep my napkin in my lap, and to keep my elbows off the table. The food is delicious. Louise serves efficiently, but her face is locked in a cold frown most of the time, even when Dr. Jellicoe stiffly compliments her.

Other than pale Dr. Jellicoe, who has very hairy fingers and cuts his fish with a surgeon-like precision that makes me feel queasy, the others all look civilized in the glow of candlelight. A nicely tailored suit on Dr. Ritter; fashionable dresses on Cecily, Vera, and Miss Latigue. She smiles at me when we sit down and I smile politely back. But my heart is hardened against her. She is an enemy who believes, like Father and Julia and everyone here, that they can decide who should be sterilized.

As the meal goes on, I let the conversation wash over me and try to make sense of what I found in those files.

Then Dr. Jellicoe hammers on the table and shouts, "Anyone who disagrees has his head in the sand," and I start to pay attention.

"We want only one thing, to better the prime stock of this nation," he says. "It is our patriotic duty. I felt it strongly as an army surgeon in France. We didn't have enough resources to save every wounded soldier. Once I had to choose between a Negro soldier and a white one."

"Goodness," said Cecily with a laugh, "that must have been an easy choice."

"Oh, it was," he says, eyes flashing, "but not in the way you think."

I squirm in my seat. How I wish I were at the gymnasium with Dorchy and not here.

"Many people, like yourself, Cecily," says Dr. Jellicoe, "believe race alone determines worth. 'White is right.' I presume you've all heard that poisonous saying?" He takes a sip of water and looks around the table. Vera and Dr. Ritter nod. Cecily looks as though her fish doesn't agree with her. Miss Latigue puts down her water glass.

"Well, *I* believe that in every race there are both fit and unfit individuals. A radical view to all of you, no doubt."

I speak up. "My father, Dr. Franklin Collier..."

"Mother, send her to bed," Vera says in a bored voice. "This is an adult conversation, or at least it's trying to be."

"Dr. Franklin Collier"—I repeat the name loudly and force-fully—"agrees with Dr. Jellicoe."

"Do tell," mutters Vera.

The doctor goes on without reacting. "In the war, I saved the more intelligent man, the Negro. He survived and now runs a clinic for poor children in Pittsburgh. He is a man many would do well to emulate."

"I assume you share your father's views," Vera says to me.

Being around Dorchy I've learned a few tricks. "Of course." I stare down at my plate, as if embarrassed by her attention.

"Of course she does," echoes Cecily, my protector. "I'm so glad, Miss Latigue, that you brought Rowan to us."

"Her father won't be glad," Vera says. "Oh, no indeed. Are you sure he didn't send you here to spy on us, Rowan?" Her eyes twin-kle, but she can't hide an edge of concern in her voice.

I take a sip of water. "No one sent me here to spy or for any other reason. I'm here to learn." *Which, if you think about it, is the same thing.*

"Miss Latigue," Cecily says, her voice calm but her hands grip-ping the table like a drowning sailor clinging to a raft, "have you decided what you will tell the Council?"

Dr. Ritter puts down his wineglass. Vera coughs. Dr. Jellicoe leans forward.

Miss Latigue smiles. "I will tell them that having Dr. Jellicoe here has been a blessing for the majority of campers."

Cecily puts her hands in her lap. Vera nods. Both doctors pick up their glasses and drink. What else, besides the number of camp-ers who died from influenza, were they afraid Miss Latigue would find out?

* * *

Loud voices in the hall outside my bedroom wake me. I sit up in bed, clutching the blanket.

"I *own* this island," Cecily says.

Vera tries to shush her. She must know that if I wake up, I'll hear them. Then she says so quietly that I have to strain to hear, "You agreed, Mother. Surely you're not so senile you've forgotten signing our agreement?"

"You forged my name," Cecily says. And louder, "I own this island and I can throw you off."

"I'd like to see you try."

The two of them move past my door, still arguing, and then a door slams. I want to tell Dorchy about the dead campers, and the dinner and what I just overheard. The wanting is so strong I go to the door and open it a crack. A murmur of voices reaches me from downstairs. I can't hear the words, but the deep voice tells me Dr. Jellicoe is still here, probably talking to Vera. I can't get out of the house without them hearing me.

I close the door and get back in bed. But I lie awake a long time imagining that Dorchy and I are back at our camping spot on the beach, under the stars, lulled by the ocean, talking until we fall asleep.

CHAPTER 34

From my bedroom window I watch Miss Latigue and Dorchy come up the road from the gym. My heart leaps. *Dorchy. At last.* They're in the hall when I arrive downstairs out of breath. Cecily calls, "Who's there?" and appears with her coffee cup in hand. "Oh, Miss Latigue, what a pleasant surprise." She ignores Dorchy. "I assumed you had left for the ferry dock."

"I'll be off before you know it," Miss Latigue says. "But I brought Dorchy here because I want a word in private with her and Rowan before I go."

Cecily nods and disappears. Dorchy looks around. It's impossible to tell from her expression if she's impressed. I try to see the hall through her eyes. Light glints off gold-framed paintings and polished floorboards and intensifies the colors in the oriental rugs.

"Come into the sitting room," Miss Latigue says. She perches on the arm of a blue-linen-covered couch. "I have a proposal for you two."

Dorchy and I stand facing her. I'm in my sailor suit shirt, blue flannel skirt, and house slippers provided by Cecily. In her gingham dress, dingy apron, and scuffed boots, Dorchy looks like a fish out of water. Sheer white curtains flutter in the breeze from tall, open windows that look down on the gym.

The realization that I'm looking down on Dorchy hits me like a fist in the stomach. After two days among the comforts of this house, part of me has effortlessly reverted to the spoiled girl I used to be. Now as I look at Dorchy, I come to my senses and kick off the slippers.

"I am ordering Cecily to release you, Rowan." Miss Latigue smiles at me. "And I'm assigning you and Dorchy to be co-counselors to the girls for the rest of the week. Luckily Nurse Blunt is needed at the medical tent."

"Why is she needed?" Dorchy asks. She still doesn't look at me.

"Because I told Dr. Jellicoe she was." Miss Latigue laughs. "But keep that to yourselves. Dr. Jellicoe understands a direct order when he hears one, and he actually looked relieved. Vera decided to make Nurse Blunt a counselor when the last girls' counselor got the flu and left three weeks ago.

"But you girls have had flu and are terrific with the girls. I will inform Cecily of the new arrangement, effective immediately. How does that sound to you?"

"Oh, thank you, Miss Latigue." I want to be with Dorchy. She studies her scuffed boots.

"Dorchy?" says Miss Latigue. "You have excellent rapport with the girls right now, but surely another counselor will make things easier."

"Yes, Miss Latigue," says Dorchy flatly.

"I have another recommendation," Miss Latigue says. "The girl campers would benefit from a visit to the quarry lake where the boys' camp is. It will be a nice change from the gym for all of you."

She leans toward Dorchy. "You know the girls better than I at this point. Do you think they would enjoy a ride in the truck and some socializing with the boys today?"

Dorchy nods. "The older girls, definitely. It's hard to predict what the twins enjoy."

"That's why it will be useful to have Rowan along." Miss Latigue smiles at me. "Tom has a good head on his shoulders. I talked with him yesterday on my way back from the medical tent. *He's* in favor of the girls and boys spending time together."

"I bet he is," Dorchy mutters.

Miss Latigue stands up. "Come with me. We'll find Cecily and give her the news. By then Reuben will be here with the truck to give me a ride to the ferry. After that he can take you and the girls to the lake."

I want to tell Miss Latigue that Cecily and Vera lied about how many campers have died and give her the proof, but I'm so thrilled to be leaving Cecily's that I don't say a word.

Cecily isn't at all happy about losing me. But she has no choice. She works for Miss Latigue too.

Miss Latigue surprises us again. She gives us each ten dollars in an envelope for travel to New York via Boston when camp is over. She says, "You're both doing very well here, so I have a request. I want you to be my eyes and ears. Vera, Cecily, and Dr. Jellicoe have not been as forthcoming as I'd hoped. Will you give me your impressions when camp is over? Come to me at the address on the envelope. Not a word about this to anyone here."

"Yes," we say in unison. A smile twitches Dorchy's lips.

As Miss Latigue is about to get in the truck with Reuben, I ask her to mail a letter for me. I've written to Julia explaining where I am and why and telling her I'll be in New York by September 1.

As the truck pulls away, Dorchy and I wave to Miss Latigue. "She saved us from the Ogres," Dorchy says, "but what did she get us into here?"

"I'll tell you everything I know," I say, "just as soon as I get out of these clothes."

Dorchy goes to be with her campers in the gym, and I go inside the house to change and pack up. I take off my new things and put on my now-washed-and-ironed old clothes—underwear, gingham dress, and apron. I hesitate over the boots. The new ones are more comfortable, and I decide that for spying I need to be comfortable. Every other piece of clothing from Cecily I leave on the bed.

* * *

At the quarry lake, Reuben, the gruff, uniformed caretaker, stops the truck and we climb down from the truck bed. The girls stand silent, except for the whimpering twins. Posy covers her mouth and stays near them. Elsa—with her blotchy skin and red-rimmed eyes—chatters in rapid-fire Italian to tall, beautiful Magdalena. Tom is perched on a rock by the lake, watching the boys fish. The boys ignore us all.

As I walk over to Tom, I take in the narrow, blue-green lake cupped in a bowl of granite slabs and cubes. Smaller blocks are scattered like a giant's toy blocks around the lake. *An abandoned granite quarry.* The words come into my head as if I were back in our beach house reading *The Bobbsey Twins in Maine.*

"Lunch?" I ask Tom hopefully.

"Reuben brings our meals; he'll be back soon. What do you do for meals at the gym?"

"Cecily's cook, Louise, brings our food," Dorchy says, walking up behind us. Farther away, Posy shies a small stone into the lake as Dolly claps and cheers.

"Who's Cecily?" Tom says.

"Mrs. Van Giesen. Vera's mother," I say.

"You mean the Harassed and the Harridan."

Dorchy's lips twitch into a grin.

"I thought the girls might like to go fishing," Tom says, "but the boys never seem to have any luck."

Dorchy claps her hands. "Girls, let's collect wood for a fire."

They all stare at her, unmoving. She waves her hand in a circle. "Go around the edge of the quarry and bring back twigs and branches." She picks up some examples lying near the fire pit. "We'll have a nice fire later."

Tom looks impressed. "I should have thought of that."

Posy comes to life and starts off; the twins follow her like ducklings. Elsa and Magdalena watch them go.

"You two can get some flowers." I point and make gathering motions at the goldenrod and wild roses growing in cracks between the granite blocks around the quarry lake.

Elsa looks confused, but Magdalena smiles and nods. After she speaks quietly to Elsa, they start picking flowers. Tom nods. "You had a good idea there. Keep them busy."

I nod at the boys engrossed in fishing. "I got the idea from you."

* * *

When Posy and the twins come back with twigs and sticks, Tom gives them a sweeping bow. "Thank you, ladies."

The twins giggle. Posy turns purple with embarrassment. Tom piles their contributions in the fire pit.

Then Posy and the twins gather granite chips and toss them into the lake, making interlocking ripples. The sun warms our faces, and I wish we had hats.

A tall, skinny boy with red curly hair puts down his fishing pole and starts walking toward Elsa and Magdalena, who have moved to the meadow by the boys' tents.

"That's Christophe. He's harmless," Tom says. "In fact, it's good for him to show initiative for once."

Dorchy looks dubious. "Nurse Blunt will raise hell if she sees boys and girls talking."

Tom shrugs. "I don't think you'll be seeing much of Nurse Bludgeon. She hated being a counselor. Now with you two to do all the work she'll make herself scarce."

"Really?" Dorchy studies Tom's face to see if he means it. I can read her thoughts now. "Well, if Nurse Blunt does see them, she'll take it out on the girls." She starts walking to head off Christophe.

Tom whistles. "She's tough as nails. Nothing gets past her. What's her story?"

"Ask her," I say and then, because he's still watching Dorchy, I ask him, "What's *your* story?" Spoken out loud, it sounds like one of the interview questions on Miss Latigue's form. "I mean, how did you become a counselor here?"

He turns to me, pain in his warm brown eyes. "You're looking at a trustee from the Home for Incorrigible Boys in Portland, Maine. I brought four of our boys here. We were the only boys here that week, so I became their counselor. Not one is left to go home with me."

"What happened to them?"

"Flu. I had it in 1918. It raced through the orphanage I was in then. I brought the boys to the camp because I want to make something of myself when I leave the Home. The warden said if I took the boys and brought them home with a good report from the people here, it would help me get a good referral. But now"—he kicks at a granite chip—"I can't bring the boys back. They're dead."

"They all *died*?" With a sickening jolt, I realize I saw their pictures. Dorchy comes over. "Who died?"

"The four boys I came with," Tom says. "They were taken away the second day we were here and never came back. Those boys looked as healthy as horses to me, but the doctor said they had to be quarantined. Not me, because I'd had the flu. I was allowed to visit them in the medical tent, until the third day. That's when the nurse told me they were dying.

"A nurse told me, not the doctor, and that made me mad. I said I wanted to see the boys, and she said, 'Come back in an hour.' When I did, the doctor and Vera took me into a room and said there was nothing they could do; the boys were dead. Somewhere they had been exposed to a carrier of the flu—someone who might have seemed healthy but wasn't."

"That's terrible." Dorchy puts her hand on his arm.

I want to step between them. Instead I ask, "Why did you stay here after the boys died?"

Tom crosses his arms. "Vera said I had proved myself as a counselor and could have a job here for the rest of the summer. They promised me a good referral. It beat going back to the Home empty-handed."

"Didn't you have to take the boys' bodies back?" I say.

"Nope. They were orphans like me. Reuben and I buried them in the woods. Vera called it a family cemetery, but I didn't see any other graves. Then Reuben gave me a nice meal and a tour of the island. He doesn't care much for the doctors or Vera either. He made that clear over a bottle we drank back at his cabin."

"Have other boys died?" I ask to find out what he knows.

His face tightens. "I told Miss Latigue everything I know about that. You'll have to ask her."

"She left this morning. I guess she was satisfied nothing's wrong."

He eyes me and Dorchy and says, "So what qualifications do you two have to be counselors?"

"Miss Latigue hired us," Dorchy snaps. It's like a sparring match and she has to throw a fast punch. She doesn't seem to like him as much now. "Why do so many kids here get the flu?" she says. "It's an island."

"Fresh air releases the germs they were exposed to on the way here or at the Home or orphanage they came from." Tom shrugs. "Or so Dr. Jellicoe says."

"That isn't true," I say. As the boys' counselor, Tom needs facts. "My doctor, Dr. Friedlander, says fresh air, healthy food, and rest *protect* you from disease."

"'*Dr. Friedlander says*,'" Dorchy mimics me. "Too bad he's not here and Dr. Jellicoe is."

"Jellicoe's wrong about a lot of other things," I snap. I don't like being mocked.

"Well, I'm healthy," Tom says. "Most of the campers have been. If you had the flu, you can't get it again."

Dorchy and I speak at the same time, "I had it."

"Well, you're all right then." He smiles at us.

* * *

Magdalena comes over to us with two huge bouquets of goldenrod and cornflowers just as Reuben and Nurse Blunt pull up in the truck. They greet Tom and Dorchy, ignoring me. I guess they still think I am Cecily's assistant. Finally Dorchy says, "Rowan is a counselor like me now. She'll be sleeping in the gym with us. It's Miss Latigue's idea."

Nurse Blunt's eyes light up, and an actual smile creases her usually ironclad face. I look to see if Tom notices. He gives me a *what-did-I-tell-you* look.

Then she says sourly to me, "So Mrs. Van Giesen has had enough of you, eh?"

Posy takes the lunch basket from Reuben and carries it over to a block of granite Tom designated as the table. He hands out ham sandwiches and apples, first to the girls and then to the boys. Reuben ladles cold water from a bucket into two tin cups that get passed around.

"Not very sanitary," I say to Dorchy.

She shrugs. "They can stick their heads into the quarry lake and drink straight from there, for all I care," she says. "They look happy. That's what counts."

She's right. The twins are speaking their own language with animation. Elsa eats daintily without dropping a crumb, and Magdalena talks nonstop to Christophe, waving her hands, one holding a sandwich. Posy sits between two of the boys on a boulder by the lake. They eat while watching Tom point out the different layers of exposed granite on the quarry walls.

"Hey, boys," Reuben says, "where are the fish you caught for supper?"

The boys look at Tom and stay silent, except for dark-haired Jack whom we met in the gym the first day. He says, "*You* ever catch anything in that empty hole?"

Reuben laughs. "Only a twelve-pound catfish."

Tom says, "Then you're the one we need. Show us how it's done. Fellows, give Reuben here a rod."

Nurse Blunt frowns and looks away, disapproval radiating from her. Suddenly her face changes and she stands up, straight-backed.

"On your feet, campers. We have visitors."

Viking, with Vera on his back, steps carefully toward us across a field of stones. Dr. Ritter, in a white coat and straw hat, hurries along behind. "You were supposed to pick me up," he yells, jabbing his finger at Reuben.

Vera says, "Don't worry, Doctor. The walk was good for you." She slides off Viking as Dr. Ritter sinks down on a block of granite and fans himself with his hat.

"We're here to evaluate the campers," Vera says to Nurse Blunt and Tom. She turns to Dorchy. "It's standard procedure after they've been here a day or two." She smiles at the air over our heads. "Tom will attest to that."

"Yes, Miss Van," Tom says. He stands like a condemned man, feet together, head hanging. His voice is expressionless.

Dorchy starts to introduce me as a co-counselor, but I grab her hand and squeeze. I want to be a fly on the wall as long as possible.

Vera swats the fly. "So Mother has consented to let you mix with the unfit, Rowan," she says. "How unlike her. This must be Miss Latigue's idea."

I nod.

"Well, watch and learn from Tom," Vera says. "So very talented, yet so modest."

Then she claps her hands and shouts, "Campers, on your marks, run to the tents and back. Dr. Ritter is the judge. I'm starting my stopwatch. Go *now*!"

The boys tear off, slipping on the loose rocks. Tom cheers them on, cupping his hands around his mouth.

Vera and Dr. Ritter talk quietly, never taking their eyes off the boys.

Nurse Blunt says, "Girls, hurry up now. Show us how fast you can run."

Posy and the twins take off, their good mood still intact. But Magdalena and Elsa shrink back toward the lake. Dr. Ritter scribbles something in his notebook. I wish I could steal it and find out what he wrote.

Without looking up from her watch, Vera says, "Rowan, get those girls in the race. If you start off with that crutch, they'll realize they can easily beat you."

Dorchy says something under her breath, but I smile. "Of course, Miss Van." I cup my hands around my mouth and yell, "Magdalena and Elsa, try to catch me!"

They giggle and look at Dorchy. "Go on," she says.

Before polio I could have outrun them, but now I go slowly, making sure my crutch doesn't slip. The two girls stroll past me laughing. The other runners dash back; Jack gets the prize, a slice of cake that Reuben produces from the truck. Jack shares it with Posy and the twins, the three winning girls, who crossed the imaginary finish line together. Dr. Ritter and Vera talk quietly for a minute and then call Reuben over.

"Miss Van shouldn't have done that," Tom says when I finally finish the "race." His eyes burn. "She had no right to say that to you."

I shrug. "Picking on the weak is what she does. Why else would she be here?"

"Come get more treats," Vera calls, and the campers gather around us. Dorchy pours lemonade, and I hand out sugar cookies made by Louise and delivered by Reuben.

Then I look up and freeze. Dr. Ritter and Reuben are walking away from us with Elsa between them. I'm the first one to notice. I touch Dorchy's arm, and she starts off after them, yelling, "Where are you going with Elsa?"

Now Magdalena screams. Immediately Vera grabs her arm and steers her down to the lake.

Before Dorchy can reach her, Elsa climbs into the cab of the truck, followed by Dr. Ritter. Reuben gets in the driver's seat and guns the truck away from the quarry.

I look around for Tom. "They took Elsa," I tell him.

"It's probably just a precaution," he says, but his eyes don't meet mine.

"Like they took Ratty from the ferry dock?" Dorchy is back now, her hands balled into fists.

"Yes. They are very careful about influenza here. Why are you so upset?"

"Why aren't *you*?"

Magdalena screams as she pulls away from Vera and runs after the truck. Viking whinnies from the meadow.

"Get her back, Tom," Vera yells.

He easily catches up with Magdalena who first slaps his face and then collapses in his arms. Dorchy looks at me. "Magdalena trusts me," she says and walks over to talk to them. After a moment Tom steps away, and Dorchy and Magdalena walk back to the lake.

"Where are they taking Elsa?" I ask Vera, my voice rising in panic. "She isn't sick."

"If that's the case, she'll be back tomorrow." Vera sounds bored. "More lemonade, everyone."

Tom picks up the pitcher and starts filling the cups.

Vera walks out to Viking and rides away without looking back.

* * *

I want to ask Tom, "Is this how they took your boys?" But his face is closed, mouth tight.

The truck returns and bounces to a stop. Nurse Blunt yells,

"Girls, get into the truck."

Magdalena starts screaming again, and the twins kneel on the rocks clinging to Posy's skirt. Reuben gets out of the truck. "Stop that caterwauling," he shouts. "We're just going back to the gym."

"Rowan, stay here and help Tom clean up," Nurse Blunt says. "Dorchy, come with me."

"How will Rowan get back to the gym?" Tom asks.

"She can walk." Nurse Blunt heads for the truck.

"What did they do with Elsa?" I yell after her.

Tom says, "Well, you're free of Nurse Blunt for a while. Enjoy it."

"But poor Elsa. She wasn't sick."

"The doctor will decide that."

Vera's words exactly.

The boys drift back to fishing. They don't seem upset at all.

"They've taken two now," I say. "Ratty and Elsa."

"Well, Miss Latigue investigated," Tom says. "So it's all on the up-and-up."

"You visited the boys," I say. "I want to see Elsa."

"You can try, but the rules have changed."

"Draw me a map."

He clears away scattered stones with his hand and scratches a map in the dirt with a sharp one.

I don't mention it, but determination is forming in me. Let Tom trust the doctors and Vera. I'm going to see for myself.

I wash the plates in the quarry lake. The sea is out of sight beyond the quarry's high walls, but the roar of the surf is a familiar sound. I think longingly of Eastham, the closest Dorchy and I have been. At least we're finally working together.

I'd like to tell Tom about the pictures in the file, but it feels wrong to tell him before Dorchy.

He fills a canteen with water for me to take on my walk back to the gym. "You'll be bringing the girls back here tomorrow," he says. "I'm glad. They seemed to like it."

"They did like it, until Elsa disappeared." I catch his eye. "Who will they take tomorrow?"

CHAPTER 35

The evening air is cool, a hint of fall. Despite everything, I enjoy my walk. At the Boston Home our time outdoors was strictly limited. A few times a week we were allowed out in the yard, closely watched. Other than that, we occasionally had doctor and dentist visits, trips to the library, and once as a special treat, a movie. But meeting Dorchy has meant fresh air every day. And fresh air nights too, when we were on Cape Cod.

Bands of sunlight and shadow stripe the woods as I follow the path away from the quarry lake. Birds sing and the wind rustles in the tall pines and shorter birches. About halfway back to the gym, my legs start to ache, so I step off the path and choose a birch stump to sit on.

When I look down, I freeze.

Two eyes stare up at me out of a pile of leaves. Red-rimmed, human eyes.

A boy pushes the leaves away and sits up. His thin face is dead white except for those enflamed eyes, dark red patches on his cheeks, and blue lips. Heat radiates off him, and his body is shaking.

"You got water?" he says in a strangled voice. He cocks his head, listening for something behind me on the path.

I unscrew the top of the canteen and offer it to him. His hand brushes mine as he takes it, and my stomach lurches. I need a mask. This boy is deathly sick. When he's through drinking, I put down the canteen and scrub my hand with leaves.

I have a lot of questions—*What's wrong with you? Why are you out here in the woods?* But I only ask one, "What's your name?"

"Ratty."

Now I recognize him. But he's changed so much since he was taken away from the dock. "What happened to you?"

He sucks in a wet-sounding breath. "They took me to the medical tent. You saw me go."

I nod. "We asked where you were, and no one would tell us anything."

"I had to sign a paper." After a fit of coughing, he wipes blood off his chin with the back of his hand. "So somewhere they have the names of all of us."

"All of who?"

"The ones they killed."

I grip my crutch tighter as if to protect myself.

"Like you and all the others will be, if you don't do something."

I go ice-cold, lean toward him, and force myself to speak, "Killed how?"

"A shot."

"From a gun?" But he looks sick, not wounded.

"A needle. A vaccine 'to prevent flu,' they say. I said I already had the flu. They didn't believe me and gave me the shot."

"And then what? After the shot?"

"They tied me to a cot." His voice fades to a whisper. The heat coming off him could singe my eyebrows. He starts a desperate, body-shaking cough. When he stops, I ask, "How did you get away?"

"They untied me because that lady came to the tent. 'Close your eyes and lie there,' they said. I just took my crutches and walked out when no one was looking."

"Did she talk to you before you left?"

"She wanted to, but they told her I was too sick to talk. But I was fine. Then."

He spits on the ground; blood gleams in a patch of pale sunlight. He lies back down, staring up at me. His cheeks are flushed darker now. "Now I'm dying."

I force a smile. "You survived the flu once. You'll survive it again."

"This is"—he shakes his head—"different."

I hold the canteen so he can drink and leave it next to him.

"You need help, Ratty," I say. "I can get Tom. He'll know what to do. You can't stay out here."

"No." His voice flares like a struck match. "Don't tell *anyone*. They'll take me back. I don't want to die there."

"What did you mean about killing?" I ask. "They're just inoculating the ones exposed to the flu."

"No." He flares up again. "It's true. That doctor"—he coughs again and blood spills from his nose—"said to that witch Vera, 'No one leaves the island alive.' They thought I was asleep."

I know Ratty's feverish, but I can imagine Dr. Jellicoe saying that. The thought makes my stomach clench. "If that's true, then I have to tell the others. Dr. Jellicoe has to be stopped."

"Don't tell anyone where I am." He spits more blood on the leaves and lies down. "Promise you won't and then cover me."

I mutter a promise with my fingers crossed and then scatter leaves over his body to hide him again. It feels like a burial.

As I turn to go, he grabs hold of my skirt. In a voice as thin and sharp as a needle, he says, "Blue kills."

CHAPTER 36

What is "blue?" How can I help Ratty?

As I get closer to the gym I speed up. Dorchy is standing in the road in front. I have to tell her first. Ratty is important in a way none of my other discoveries about Loup Island have been. Those burning eyes, that terrible accusation, and those haunting words, "Blue kills." Whether we believe him or not, we have to help him. *But how?*

Dorchy grins as I come panting up to her. "What took you so long?" she says. "I want to explore the lighthouse before it gets dark, so I waited for you."

I hold up my hand, still trying to catch my breath.

"Nurse Blunt fell asleep," Dorchy says. "I told Magdalena I was coming to meet you."

Finally I manage to get the words out.

"I found Ratty. He says he's dying."

Dorchy's eyes narrow. "Found him where? In the medical tent?" She sounds horrified.

"No. He got away from there. He's in the woods." I point down the road. "Lying in the bushes."

"Let's go find him." Dorchy is all business. I knew she would be. As we walk back the way I just came, Dorchy matches my pace even though I can feel her impatience in every step.

As we go by Cecily's house, I grab her arm. "Act like we're just out for a stroll. We don't want any of them following us."

Dorchy smiles at the house and takes my arm. "A beautiful night for a stroll," she says loudly. Then she whispers, "Tell me what he said."

Once we pass the house, I use my normal voice. "He said they're—" I stop. "It sounds crazy."

"Spit it out."

"He said the doctor is killing the campers by giving them the flu. He overheard the doctor say to Vera, 'No one leaves here alive.'"

Dorchy stops and chews her bottom lip. "Does Ratty have a fever?"

"He's burning up. Why?"

"He's delirious." She walks on ahead of me. "That was the fever talking, and it's why we need to get him help. When his fever's down, we can get some sense out of him."

The woods thicken, shadowing the road. I stop to peer deeper into the woods. "I think it was here. Yes, there's the stump I sat on."

Dorchy plunges into the bushes around the stump, calling, "Ratty. Ratty. We're here to help you."

"Stop," I say. "You'll scare him. He's hiding for a reason."

He moved since I spoke to him last. Broken bushes and scattered leaves show his desperate effort to get away. He didn't believe my promise. For good reason. I can't imagine the effort it took for him to crawl away.

Dorchy says, "He's gone."

"He's here. Buried in leaves like last time. He can't go far. Wait here."

She sighs, impatient.

I move carefully into the dusky shadows of the taller trees. Drifts of fallen leaves. Low bushes hugging the ground. He could have crawled under one, and unless we crawl under all of them, we won't find him.

"He was coughing a lot," I whisper to Dorchy.

We stand perfectly still listening. Nothing.

Finally Dorchy says quietly, "We'll find him tomorrow with Tom. We couldn't move him ourselves anyway."

Walking away, I say, "The last words he said to me were, 'Blue kills.'"

"What does that mean?"

"I don't know. It sounded like a warning. Is blue a disease?"

She shrugs. "No idea. But remember what I said about fever." She taps the side of her head. "Delirious."

"No, it was a warning. Dr. Jellicoe and Vera admitted to Miss Latigue that campers have died of flu here this summer. But they lied about how many. I found photographs of the bodies in Cecily's files."

"They probably did die," Dorchy says slowly, "but that doesn't mean Ratty isn't delirious."

With the woods behind us, golden early-evening light floods across the road. "Come with me while I climb the lighthouse," Dorchy says. "Reuben told me about it. I feel like he *wants* me to explore it."

I stop and rub my right leg, which is aching again from all the walking. "I don't know. It's getting late, and it's not very close to the gym."

"There's a path along the cliff. Come that far. You can sit and watch the sun go down and wave to me when I get to the top. It could be our only chance."

"OK. But go on ahead. I don't want to rush."

Slowly I follow Dorchy along the road and down onto the cliff path. The view of the ocean spread out below makes me catch my breath. The orange sky streaked with purple clouds is reflected in the water. The colors remind me of the painting Dorchy rescued from the ocean the day we met the artists. At the point where the path starts downhill, I stop to rest. Dorchy is already close to the lighthouse. She picks her way through the tangle of weeds and brambles to reach the back door. The lighthouse isn't very high. From here the wooden tower with its glass crown looks solid enough. But below it the building is a ruin. Dark streaks smear the back of the tower where fire charred most of the shingles. One gaping hole looks like a giant kicked his way in. A broken beam blocks the opening.

"Watch out," I yell. She waves her hand but doesn't turn around. *We should go back*—I feel the words on my tongue, but Dorchy's concentration silences me.

She disappears inside. Long minutes later, she yells, "Hey, Rowan, up here!" And there she is, waving from the metal-rimmed walkway at the top. "Some of the stairs are burned and the ladder is tricky," she shouts, triumphant, "but I made it."

I wave. *Come down*, I beg her silently.

The sun disappears behind a drift of clouds and streaks them red. The only sounds are waves breaking on the rocks below the cliff and cries of gulls circling. *We have to get back to the road before dark.*

"The lamp is still up here," Dorchy shouts. "There's kerosene and matches too. It looks like whoever was here last just walked away."

"That's what you should do," I yell back. "Come down now."

She disappears inside, then comes back out on the walkway again. "I wish I could sleep up here."

That does it. I wave and start picking my way back up the path. Before I reach the road, she catches up with me.

"I know you can climb anything," I say. "But that looked dangerous."

"The stairs were fine, just a few burned out at the bottom, but the ladder was like a pendulum. I thought it was going to fall off the wall, but I made it up and down."

"I know why the lamp is ready to be lit," I say.

"Why?"

"Cecily told Miss Latigue that it's the only way to call for help from the island. If people on the mainland see the light, they'll know there's trouble and come by boat."

"What did Miss Latigue say to that?"

"She said they should have a radio. Now hurry up. I don't want to get in trouble my first night as a counselor."

"*Assistant* counselor." She looks back at the lighthouse. "What a waste. If it was in good condition, we could camp out there with the girls. The boys would be jealous."

She stops. "Oh, Rowan, I'm sorry. It would be hard for you to camp there with your crutch."

"I walked uphill from the dock the first day," I say. "I guess I could get into a lighthouse."

The dock reminds me of Ratty, alive and loudly protesting as Tom put him in the truck.

At the top of the cliff path, we turn around for a last look at the lighthouse. The glass reflects the red sky.

Dorchy says, "Living up to its name."

"Which is?"

"Fever Point Light."

The chill runs straight down my spine.

* * *

In the gym, we sit on our cots at one end of the balcony. We are allowed up here because we're "staff."

On the gym floor below us Magdalena, Posy, and the twins lie on cots covered with their Council blankets. They all seem to be asleep.

Nurse Blunt left as soon as we got back. As she went out the door, she called out, "Thanks to you two, I'll get a good night's sleep for once."

"Tomorrow we'll tell Tom about Ratty," Dorchy says. "He'll know what to do."

I nod, but I don't think Ratty will live through the night. My heart aches for him.

Dorchy pulls at a loose thread in the hem of her nightgown. Miss Latigue gave us the nightgowns in Boston along with our uniforms and carpet bags. None of the clothes were new, and I suddenly wonder who wore them before.

"And then with Tom's help," she says, "we'll find Elsa in the medical tent."

I'm relieved that Dorchy now seems to trust him as much as I do.

"I have an idea how we can get into the medical tent," Dorchy goes on. "It's a good con, if we can forge Miss Latigue's signature."

"I had the same idea yesterday." I reach into my bag and pull out a photograph. "This is Miss Latigue's handwritten reference letter about us. I didn't want to take the original, so I took a picture of it and printed it in the darkroom."

Dorchy takes the photograph:

"To: Mrs. Cecily Van Giesen, President

"Loup Island Camp for Unfortunates

"Loup Island, Maine

"Dear Mrs. Van Giesen:

"It is my pleasure to recommend to you Rowan Collier and Dorchy Miller, two young women who have proven to be outstanding employees…"

She stops reading. "Don't employees get paid? Usually, I mean?"

"Usually," I say, "but sometimes they do it for love."

Dorchy grins. "As you did. Your only payment was a kiss from Mr. Ogilvie."

"Stop," I squeal, and from the cots below Posy shushes us.

"How did you—?" Dorchy studies the photograph of the letter as if it were her own likeness. "What were you *doing* up there at the house?" Her tone is interested, not scornful.

"Magic," I say. "Thanks to you I have a camera"—I bow to her—"and Cecily has film and a darkroom, so naturally…"

"Naturally what? What did you do?"

"I took pictures of some of the documents I found. And I developed the negatives for Miss Latigue. I think she's going to like them."

"OK, but how does this picture of a letter help us find out what happened to Elsa?"

I take out a fountain pen and a sheet of cream linen stationery. "I'm going to write a note from Miss Latigue to anyone we meet in the medical tent. I'll practice on half of this sheet of paper and then write it on the other half."

"How are you going to see to do that?"

I produce a candle and a matchbox from my bag.

Dorchy whistles, impressed. She lights the candle and holds it while I practice Miss Latigue's handwriting. It's very plain, almost like printing, but her signature is a scrawling line with a flourish on the tail of the *e*.

"Read it to me," Dorchy says when I finish.

"To Whom It May Concern: I hereby authorize Council employees Rowan Collier and Dorchy Miller to have full access to all medical reports for the summer of 1922. Please provide them with copies of your records for the last week of August. They will deliver these to me in person on August 29.

"As my agents on Loup Island, they also have full access to all patients in your custody. By my order this 22nd day of August, 1922.

"Please extend them every courtesy.

"Sincerely yours,

"Florence Latigue, New England Betterment Council, Boston Chapter."

Dorchy grins. "'Agents' makes us sound like spies."

"Is it too much?"

"No, it's perfect. I wish I could write half as good as you do."

"I was inspired," I say, glowing from her praise, "to get Elsa back."

"We *will* get her back. I'll make a carny out of you yet."

CHAPTER 37

In the morning Reuben arrives in the truck to bring the four girls, Dorchy, and me to the quarry for breakfast. Magdalena is sure Elsa will be there. She keeps saying, "Elsa is healthy as a horse." At the quarry lake Nurse Blunt is nowhere in sight. Reuben carries a metal pot of porridge over to our granite "table," and Tom spoons it out into metal bowls.

The sky is cloudy, and the brisk wind stirs the silver surface of the lake and makes us shiver.

"I hate porridge," says Dolly clear as a bell.

"Me too," says Lolly.

Posy looks as proud as if the twins had just sung an aria.

"So they *can* talk," says Reuben. He goes back to the truck and brings the twins bread and jam.

"The boys want to know if there's coffee," says Tom.

Reuben shrugs at that and turns away. *Something's wrong.* Yesterday he ate with us. Today he goes back and sits in the truck.

"Reuben's acting strange," Dorchy says in a low voice. "But did you hear Dolly and Lolly?"

"Tom," I say, "I need to talk to you."

He nods as a shrill whinny announces Vera's arrival. This time she rides Viking all the way down to the lake. Fear closes my throat and I gag on my last bite of porridge.

"Why is she here?" Dorchy whispers.

Tom has gone still as a statue. *He's afraid too.*

Vera points her whip at Tom. "Tell Reuben to fetch Dr. Ritter from the staff cottage. Where's Blunt?"

Mouth dry, I say, "Not here and not at the gym. Maybe she's ill."

"Ill, my Aunt Fanny," barks Vera. "She's lazier than a mule at midday. Well, we need Ritter more than we need her."

Tom speaks to Reuben and he drives away. The sky is darker now, and the wind has picked up, ruffling the lake into whitecaps.

Ten minutes later when Dr. Ritter hops out of the truck, he says, "Girls in the first tent, boys in the second."

Posy starts leading the twins over to the tents, followed by Magdalena.

Tom stops them and faces Dr. Ritter. "What are you doing?" he demands.

Dr. Ritter shakes his head. *Is it a warning?*

"We have concerns about flu, Tom," he says. "You, of all people, know that."

"Liar," Dorchy shouts. "You let the campers drink out of a common cup." She shoves in front of the twins. "What's really going on?"

Vera walks Viking toward Dorchy as the first drops of rain hit my face.

Vera reins Viking in. "Just because Miss *Latigue* brought you here," she says to Dorchy, "doesn't mean we'll answer any of *your* questions."

Dorchy immediately becomes a polite, shy version of herself. Eyes down, she says, "Of course, Dr. Van."

"*Miss* Van." Vera whirls Viking around. "Skip the tents," she shouts. "All campers in the truck. *Now.*"

Posy turns to me, face pale. "We want to stay at the quarry." She puts her arms around both twins.

"It's raining," I call to Vera. "Why can't we go back to the gym? The boys could come too."

"Not today," Vera snaps. "Dr. Jellicoe wants to do a further examination of the campers in the medical tent."

Reuben spits onto the rocks and points at the sky. "Weather's foulin' already," he says. "'Tis only going to get worse."

"Be quiet, Reuben," snaps Vera. "It's a little rain, not the apocalypse. Now get in the truck, everybody, twins first."

Reuben juts out his chin. "Mark my words, Miss Van. You best respect this storm or it'll knock you and all of us sideways to Sunday." He climbs into the truck cab.

"What's he talking about?" Dorchy says.

"He's been predicting a big storm all week," Tom says. "He's lived here all his life, and he's usually right about the weather." He frowns. "A storm can't come soon enough for me."

I feel a spike of fear. *Ratty.* "I have to tell you something, Tom."

He turns away. "Not now."

"Can't we stop them?" Dorchy says.

"No," he says through clenched teeth. "They waited until Miss Latigue left and now..."

A gust of wind blows rain into our faces as we watch Posy boost first Lolly and then Dolly up into the truck bed. She climbs in after them and waves to us.

"You can't do this," I call out to Vera. "I'll get Cecily."

She laughs. "*Cecily* has no authority here." She claps her hands and Viking sidesteps into Jack, who pushes back.

"All aboard, campers," Vera calls. Magdalena gets in the truck. She doesn't look back. Deaf Snout and red-haired Christophe follow with fat, asthmatic Lester who is crying. Black-haired Jack is last.

"Stay here." Vera points her whip at Tom, Dorchy, and me. "Reuben will find Nurse Blunt and bring her to the medical tent. Do not move."

The truck lurches up the hill, and the big horse follows, Vera straight as a ramrod on his back.

Dorchy shakes her fist at them.

Tom looks ashen. "They have all of them now. Plus Elsa and Ratty."

"Rowan found Ratty last night," Dorchy says.

"Where?" Tom is instantly alert. "Why didn't you tell me?" He grabs my arm. "Where is he? We have to find him before they do."

"In the woods by the road between here and the house," I say. "About fifty feet into the woods near a boulder. He said he was dying and he looked it. He was burning up and spitting blood. I went to get Dorchy, and we tried to find him again, but he wasn't there."

"You should have told me." Tom's voice shakes. "I'll see if he's still there. Make up a story about where I went."

"No." Dorchy holds up her hand. "We need a plan for when they come back."

Tom draws a deep breath. "Ratty could be dead now." He speaks slowly, thinking aloud. "Come on. There's a cave, a long walk from here, but they won't find us there. Reuben knows about it, but he won't tell on us. I think he hates their guts."

"A cave?" Dorchy wrinkles her nose. "What about going to the house, Rowan? Will Cecily do something?"

"Vera's running the show," Tom says. "We need a place where all of us are *safe*. The cave is big enough, I think."

He starts walking toward the road. "We can go there now and decide what to do. I'm not going to let this happen again. Once was enough."

"Rowan and I are Miss Latigue's 'agents.'" Dorchy uses the word as if it were fact. In a way it is, since Miss Latigue asked us to be her "eyes and ears." But proud as I am of the letter, I'm beginning to think it won't work.

"Agents?" Tom snorts. "That's rich. Don't you get it? Miss Latigue and the Council are the only ones who care about rules. And they aren't here. Vera and the doctors don't give a damn about rules, except the ones they make up. Cecily goes along with them."

"We brought our bags and blankets with us," I say, "along with the letter I forged."

Tom seems unimpressed. "We'll take everything from here and go. They'll be too busy for a while to worry about us. Load up. Especially blankets. I wish we could get Ratty."

Dorchy folds her arms. "You can go hide. Rowan and I are going to the medical tent. We have to do it now while we can get some of them away."

Dorchy is *impulsive*. The word swims into my mind. Sometimes it's a good quality—saving the little boy on the Ferris wheel, getting help during the fire, stealing the car from Mr. Ogilvie—but here it seems dangerous.

Tom flushes with anger. He's not used to anyone standing up to him.

I make my decision. "Dorchy's right," I say quickly. "They banned you from the tent, Tom, not us. We can get in and bring them out with us."

Tom holds up his hands in surrender, but I can tell he doesn't like it.

I'll give him this—he's not so attached to his own ideas that he won't listen or change his mind. Not like Dorchy who digs in her heels, just because something is her idea.

"We'll go to the cave as soon as you get them out of the tent," he says. "But be careful. Take your things and hide them in the bushes. If you hear the truck, hide. Reuben is still obeying orders. But after the storm hits, I guarantee he'll help us. When you leave the tent, hide in the woods by the road. I'll meet you there."

Dorchy salutes him.

"He's very good-looking," she says as we walk away from the quarry lake through the woods, instead of on the road. Tom suggested we try sneaking up on the medical tent.

"Who?"

"He looks a lot like Valentino."

"*Tom?* No, he doesn't."

"Have you ever seen Valentino in a movie? If you had, you'd agree with me."

"They took us to see the *The Shriek* in Boston. Private showing at the theater. A bus with curtained windows."

"Why curtains?"

"To protect us from 'staring eyes and unpleasant comments,' Dr. Pynchon said. Then she told us the real reason. 'No one at a movie theater wants to see crippled children in the audience.'"

"She sounds as bad as Vera," Dorchy says. "Did you think Valentino was handsome?"

"No, I was bored. But the other girls shrieked so I guess that's how the movie got its name."

"It's *The Sheik*, not *The Shriek*. I saw it with the Ogress and..."

"Getting back to Tom." I rest on my crutch.

"He likes you," Dorchy says.

"He trusts Reuben," I say, "and I don't."

We come out of the woods and look down a steep hill onto scattered granite boulders and smaller rocks. Rusting machinery. This is an abandoned quarry without a lake. A road winds down next to a steep granite wall. At the end of the road stands a huge, gray-green tent, as big as the sideshow tent at the Expo. A faded red cross on a white background is painted on the side facing us. The ropes holding the tent in place are weighted down with piles of rocks. Six small windows are evenly spaced along the side of the tent. At the midway point, an outhouse-size structure sticks out. The tent canvas ripples in the wind like a horse's flank.

At the ocean end of the quarry, a low rock wall protects the mouth of the quarry. Skeleton pilings are all that's left of a dock where barges were once loaded with granite. Spray from waves breaking against the wall occasionally splashes over it, leaving puddles.

We hide our bags at the edge of the woods, and I hand Dorchy the letter. Then we use our fingers to comb each other's hair before we start downhill to the tent. When we're ready to go, I grab Dorchy's hand. "Can you do it?" I ask her. "Walk in the front entrance and convince whoever is in there that you're Miss Latigue's assistant?"

"Piece of cake," Dorchy says.

Relief floods through me. I touch my camera hanging on its strap around my neck. I have a plan.

"What are you going to do?"

"As soon as you go inside, I'll walk over to that part that sticks out and crawl under like we did at the sideshow. You keep them distracted in the front of the tent."

"If you can't get underneath, go around to the back entrance," she says, all business. "If you meet anyone..."

"I'm Miss Latigue's agent."

She grins at me. *We're a team again.* I grin back. "We'll meet in these bushes. I'll wait for you. You wait for me."

She nods and gives me a thumbs-up. Then she walks across the quarry to the front entrance of the tent and disappears inside.

CHAPTER 38

Crossing to the tent on the slippery, wet granite slabs of the quarry floor, I feel my boots and crutch slipping out from under me. The rain is light, but the wind coming straight off the ocean shoves me along. I refuse to fall. As I get closer to the tent, the fresh salt air is drowned by the odor of musty canvas. I examine the structure attached like a pilot fish to the side of the tent. At the bottom there's a space big enough for me to crawl under. But what will I find inside?

I get down on my hands and knees and crawl in, pushing my camera and crutch ahead of me. Inside is pitch-dark and smells of disinfectant and something sour. I manage to stand and reach out my hand. A curtain. I open it a crack.

A rattling metallic sound stops me. "Wait," a woman says. "I have to put this in Supply." I hold my breath and step back from the curtain. *Not here. Don't let them come in here.*

A clash of metal on metal, like a galvanized bucket clattering down a fire escape, makes me jump. For a split second I consider crawling back out and limping for the woods. But I'm more curious than scared.

"Darn it," the same woman says in a loud voice. "Give me a hand, will you, Hazel?"

"Fine. But hurry up," says a woman I guess is Hazel. "Blunt isn't here yet."

The first woman says, "I tell you, I'm of a mind to quit. Extra pay or not."

"Why is that?"

"It just seems wrong."

"You know they're not people, not really," says Hazel. "Not like my little Veronica, dead of the flu in four hours on November 5, 1918. Hale and hearty at breakfast. Dead by noon."

"They *are* people, and they suffer just like your poor daughter did."

"I've seen their like in asylums and you haven't, Theta. They eat their bodily wastes. I say thank god for Dr. Jellicoe and Miss Van, and the old lady too."

"I don't say anything against you or the doctors," says Theta. "But I have to live with myself. And lying to that lady who came here day before yesterday asking questions goes against the grain."

So they lied to Miss Latigue!

"Well, you can't quit," Hazel says, "and I'll tell you why. There's a storm coming and we're done on Sunday. We go home with our pockets full and forget this summer ever happened." Their voices and footsteps move away.

I ease open the curtain and move forward. *What did happen this summer?* Light from a small window shines on a glass-fronted metal cabinet with a white enamel basin on top. A bucket and mop stand to one side. This must be Supply. Another curtain. I pull it back and listen. Footsteps on wooden boards move away from me. I take a chance and peek out. To my right, two women in white uniforms and caps walk toward the front of the tent. Nurse Hazel and Nurse Theta. I'll remember them. One shouts, "We're coming." I assume they're talking to Dorchy.

I go the opposite way down a hallway lit only at intervals by watery light from the small windows. Wooden slats creak underfoot, offset by sharp smells of disinfectant, a boy shouting, scuffling sounds, and a high wailing cry that must be Lolly or Dolly.

"...crawling with bugs, Doctor," Vera says from behind a canvas curtain. I stop.

"Where is a nurse when you need one?" Dr. Jellicoe whines.

"Get on with this, or so help me..." Vera says.

I peek into the cubicle. An oil lamp hangs over a metal examining table. Vera stands on one side of it, Dr. Jellicoe on the other. One of the boys, I can't tell which, lies on the table on his stomach violently kicking his legs. The table sways and lets out a metallic shriek. Vera jumps back.

The boy kicks again.

"I'll have to sedate him," the doctor shouts. "If you can't hold him still."

"We're out of sedatives, as you well know," Vera says. "Give *me* the needle." She grabs for it, the boy rears up, and the doctor jerks his hand back. Without thinking, I push through the opening, hold the camera to my eye, and click the shutter.

The doctor yells and stumbles backward against the tent wall. The boy starts to climb off the table. It's Christophe. Vera shouts, "Nurse! Dr. Ritter!" and pushes Christophe back down. He knocks the oil lamp, which swings wildly.

The hypodermic needle in Dr. Jellicoe's hand flashes.

He stabs it at me. I step back and click the shutter again.

"*Stop!*" Vera is purple with anger. "Hiram, get hold of yourself." Her razor-sharp voice makes the doctor back away from me.

I retreat to the doorway and lift the camera again. I manage to wind the film and click the shutter before Vera snatches it, breaking the strap.

"Get out." Vera opens the camera and dumps the film out. "You're just like your goody-goody sister and too-pure-for-this-world father. I *hate* you Colliers."

How can she lump me with Father and Julia? I start to argue, but Dr. Jellicoe catches my eye. Vera doesn't see him smirk and jab the needle in my direction again.

"Go," Vera says, "and if you tell my mother the doctor threatened you, we'll say you're a liar not worthy of her protection."

"Your *friend* here won't be so lucky." Dr. Jellicoe grabs Christophe and jerks his arm up behind his back.

I hurry down the hall to the back of the tent. This is an open space divided in two parts by a canvas curtain. Boys are on one side, girls on the other. I go to the girls' side where Posy and the twins sit on a cot. Posy looks desperate, and the twins look sick, dark circles like bruises under their eyes. Magdalena crouches next to another cot where Elsa lies under a blanket. Her face is blue-tinged with dark-brown streaks on her cheekbones. Blood drips from her nose.

Empty cots have a neatly folded white sheet at the foot and a dark stain across the top, where a patient's head would go. A bleeding patient. The back entrance flaps are tied shut, but the wind shaking the tent finds openings.

"Come on, Posy." I gesture toward the entrance. "Bring the twins. Magdalena, you come too."

Posy shakes her head. "You have to come now, Posy." Desperation washes over me.

"They said me and the twins will be fine if we stay here."

"That's not true," I say. "Look at Elsa. She's sick. They probably said the same thing to her."

Magdalena, her hands over her mouth, runs past us, unties the entrance flaps, and keeps going.

"See that, Posy?" I want to get down on my knees and beg her to come. "Please. Magdalena went. We'll *all* go. Tom has a place we can hide."

Elsa groans and the twins grab Posy's arms. She shakes her head.

If I try to take her without the twins, or the twins without her, they'll scream the tent down.

* * *

I go to the boys' side of the curtain. "Jack, Snout, Lester, follow me," I say.

Jack jumps up. "I've been trying to get them to leave since they took Christophe," he says.

"Come on." I'm crying now. "I can't get Posy to come, but Magdalena already left. We have to go *now*."

"*Ich fand das verlorene im Wald*," Dr. Ritter yells from the front of the tent. "I found the lost one in the woods! He's dead."

Ratty.

"Jack, *go*," I beg. He grabs a blanket and runs through the back flap.

"Lester, you too, follow Jack *now*." Lester gives a raspy cough and lies back on his cot.

"Ritter, put the body in a cubicle," yells Vera, "and go get the other Italian."

I grab Snout's arm, but he pulls away from me.

"He's deaf," says Lester. "And he already got the shot."

As I run out of the tent, a huge sadness, like a black rain cloud, swells inside me. If it splits open, I'll be washed away. I clench my fist and stab my crutch against the rocky quarry floor. Smells of blood and bodily waste and the sound of coughing follow me back into the woods.

What have I done?

Posy. The twins. Lester. I didn't save them.

Hale and hearty at breakfast, dead by noon.

Blue kills.

Ratty's dead.

The dam inside me breaks, and tears pour down my face. We're flies caught in a spiderweb spun by Cecily, Vera, Dr. Jellicoe, and Dr. Ritter. Doctors who don't heal but kill. Who believe they're making the world better by killing. I hate them, hate them, hate them.

From the front of the tent comes Dorchy, wearing a black rubber raincoat and carrying a cardboard file box. She almost drops it when a wind gust blows her sideways. She gives me a thumbs-up and starts to run toward me.

And just like that, my despair lifts. I make a promise to myself, to Tom, to Dorchy: *we* will *stop them.*

CHAPTER 39

Now from the back of the tent comes Snout, bent over and running fast. He joins Dorchy and me at the edge of the woods. We work our way up to the road, collecting Magdalena and Jack along the way. And there is Tom, right where he said he would meet Dorchy and me. Behind him in the bushes he's hidden blankets from the boys' tents.

"What happened?" Dorchy asks me as we follow Tom and the others down a trail that leads away from the quarries. "When Ritter came in with Ratty, I thought he was going to catch you."

"It was a close call. Before that, I tried to stop Dr. Jellicoe and Vera from giving Christophe a shot." I shudder, thinking about the needle. "Then I tried to get everybody to leave." My breath catches in my throat. "Posy and the twins and Lester wouldn't come with me, and Vera and Jellicoe have Christophe. Elsa was too sick."

Feeling sick myself, I describe what she looked like. "She was fine yesterday. They killed her, like Ratty said. And he said they'll kill all of us, unless..." Hysteria seizes me and suddenly I can't stop shaking and crying. Dorchy slaps my face, not hard, but it's such a surprise that I stop crying.

"Listen to me, Rowan. You saved *them*." She waves her hand at Magdalena, Jack, and Snout. "You probably saved Christophe too."

"And what did you do?" I say.

"Well, I kept them away from you, and"—she pats the box of files—"I got this. A nice nurse gave me a raincoat and sandwiches. She really likes Miss Latigue."

* * *

Half an hour later, Tom stops in front of a wall of brush. "We're here."

We push blankets and bags ahead of us through the scratchy branches and come out in front of the open mouth of a cave.

"Bats," Dorchy says and covers her head with her arms. Magdalena does the same. They stay outside in the rain until we give them the all clear.

Then we divide the sandwiches the nurse gave Dorchy.

By late afternoon, it's still raining steadily and no one has come to look for us. Tom says we need more food. He explains we can take food from Reuben's cabin back in the woods. "He showed me where he keeps food in the cabin and said I should help myself in an emergency."

"Come on." He gestures to Jack. "This is an emergency."

"I'll go too," says Dorchy. "Three can carry more than two."

After they leave, Magdalena curls up in a blanket on the cave floor. Snout is asleep farther back. I sit in the opening and stare out at the rain dripping through the leaves. A high-pitched whining note in the wind makes Reuben's storm prediction seem more likely. For just a moment I wish I were back in the darkroom at

Cecily's—sloshing photographic paper in the developer until the image appears, rushing to submerge the print in the "stop" solution and then in the "fix." Then rinsing and hanging it to dry. All those motions and decisions I learned working next to Father. A great aching space opens in my chest. We could die here.

* * *

Tom, Jack, and Dorchy come back laughing and joking, the boys soaked to the skin. They empty a canvas bag of canned food, three canteens of water, a can opener, three spoons, and a knife.

We can't heat the food—it's too dangerous to light a fire, Tom says—so we eat it cold from the cans: stew, corn, tomatoes, and hash. It's dark by the time we finish. Jack and Snout roll up in blankets at the back of the cave. Magdalena wraps hers around her shoulders and sits close to Dorchy and me.

I pull the candle and matches out of my bag, and Tom nods. I light a match and melt wax on the bottom of the candle, then Tom sets it on a rock and I light the wick. The glow fills the cave. Dorchy's eyes sparkle. "How homey," she says.

Magdalena smiles too.

"How do you know they'll look for us?" Dorchy asks. She likes challenging Tom.

"Because we're a threat," Tom says. "We know too much. And we stole their patients from the tent. They'll figure out that both of you were there. They'll tear the island apart, but the storm, and Reuben, will get in their way."

"I think we should find a boat and leave," I say.

Tom snorts. "There isn't a boat here that's big enough to weather this storm. If they had a boat that size, they wouldn't need the ferry. Vera's sailboat would be suicide in this weather. But maybe we can radio for help." He looks at me hopefully.

"No telegraph, no radio. Cecily told Miss Latigue the island has no communication with the mainland."

"Except for the lighthouse," says Dorchy. "But in a storm, no one on the mainland could get here. I say we stay here in the cave and wait. They can't kill us if they can't find us."

Tom asks me to repeat everything Ratty told me. He and Dorchy agree with me that it sounds as though the inoculation infects campers with the flu. It's a "blue" flu that kills in hours or days. I also tell them what I overheard the nurses saying about lying to Miss Latigue.

"My first thought was to get off the island," I tell them. "But I've changed my mind. Now, I want to *stop* them, not *hide* but attack the tent and chase the doctors and Vera into the woods. What do you think?"

Tom nods. "I agree. Tomorrow, or even tonight, they'll be out looking for us. Probably Dr. Ritter and Reuben will come in the truck."

"Did you ever hear the saying about influenza?" Dorchy says. She doesn't wait for an answer. "I had a little bird, his name was Enza. I opened up the window and in flew Enza."

"Never heard it," Tom says. But he smiles at her.

I feel a rush of irritation. "Everybody knows that," I say. "But you wouldn't be reciting it now, if *you'd* seen Ratty lying in a pile of leaves coughing up blood. Or Elsa..." Tears sting my eyes.

"Look," Tom says. "Put Ratty out of your mind. That's what I'm trying to do." He holds my gaze. "As I see it, we have to do three things. See if you agree. First"—he holds up one finger—"find a safe place. We did that."

He holds up a second finger. "Second, protect as many as we can. That means the ones here and—"

"Wait a minute! *First*"—Dorchy waves a mocking finger at Tom—"I'm protecting myself and *second*, Rowan. You can run around protecting the others, but that's what I plan to do."

"We have to protect the weaker ones," Tom says stubbornly. "If we don't, we're as bad as *they* are, with their labels about who's 'unfit' and who can and can't have children. I should know." His voice shakes with emotion, and he stops abruptly.

I look at him closely. *Something happened to him that he's ashamed of.*

"I know all about those labels," I say slowly. "Before I could read, I knew the words 'unfit' and 'sterilization.' And this summer I was the unfit, crippled daughter in the Unfit Family show." Rage flares with the memory. I force out the words. "The people from the Council used that show and us, the actors, to send a message—the unfit don't deserve to have children."

Tom clears his throat. His face is stiff with resolve. "Do you want to know why I was sent to the Home for Incorrigible Boys?" He doesn't wait for us to answer. "Two years ago a doctor came to the orphanage. He offered a painless operation for boys fourteen and older. He said it would make us 'happy.' That was the word he used. I should have run for my life. But I was full of myself, so I volunteered to go first." His face is rigid, but his voice trembles.

My mouth is dry. I know what he's going to say.

"They sterilized me. Took my manhood. Without telling me. I about screamed the place down for pain. But it was when I found out they'd tricked me that I got really mad."

Shame boils up in me—for Father and Julia. For myself too, for once believing, as they do, that sterilization "strengthens our nation."

Tom sucks in a ragged breath and lets it out. "I attacked the doctor. That got me this scar on my face and three years in the Home for Incorrigible Boys.

"Then early this summer they called me in and said I was going to bring four boys to 'summer camp.' I went along because, like I told Rowan, they said I'd get a good reference when I leave the Home."

He leans closer, looking from me to Dorchy. "They lied about my operation. They lied about my boys. And I believed them. Now I know they lie every second of every hour of every day. It's like breathing for them. They can't tell the truth, so we have to."

After a long silence, Dorchy asks, "What's the third thing?"

"What?"

"You said three things. A safe place for us, save the others, and...?"

He slams his fist against his palm. "Like Rowan said. Stop them."

* * *

We blow out the candle and wrap up in blankets. Tom goes to the back with Snout and Jack. Magdalena, Dorchy, and I lie near the front. Dorchy tosses and turns for a while and then taps my shoulder. "You awake?"

"I am now."

"You and Tom seem to think that all you have to do is find out what's going on and then, poof, you'll fix it." She's whispering, but I hear the pain in her voice. "'Save the weak,' Tom says. Well, we're all weak. Look what happened today. None of it makes any sense. Why will tomorrow be any different?

"Why don't you go back to Cecily, tell her what we know, and get *her* to stop it. It's her island. Threaten her with Miss Latigue, the Council, your fancy father, and his connections. You could end this whole mess."

"No, I couldn't," I say, furious at her for thinking it's possible. "Cecily is controlled by Vera. She's afraid of the Council, yes, but she is *more* afraid of Vera. Trust me, I know these people better than you do."

"Maybe it only looks that way because you know they won't stick a needle in *you*," Dorchy says.

Silence grows until it fills the space between us. Not even the rising howl of the wind can displace it.

CHAPTER 40

Things look different in the gray light and pouring rain of morning. "We can fight them," I say as I fold my blanket. "The doctors and Vera aren't all powerful. *We* know what's going on, but they don't know we know."

"Tom's nice," Dorchy says, "but he's not a magician. We are *not* going to stop these people."

"Well, I'm not giving up. First things first. We saved ourselves."

"For now," she says.

"Yes, for now. One thing at a time, OK?"

"You'll never be a carny." Dorchy sighs. "We're always six jumps ahead of the rubes. It's in our blood."

The storm strengthened during the night. Even from inside the cave, we hear the new shrill notes of the wind. Snout moans continuously and Magdalena is crying.

Dorchy, grim-faced, riffles through the folder of papers the nurse gave her. "There's nothing here about killing anybody," she says. "How can we be sure it isn't a vaccine to prevent the flu?"

Because Ratty told me the truth.

Tom brings over an open can of beans, and we take turns eating it. "The storm is coming on hard like Reuben said it would," he says. "That's going to ruin their plans today and maybe permanently. But Snout has a fever. He had the shot yesterday."

I wipe my mouth with my hand. If only Julia could see me now. "They've been killing campers all summer," I say. "Twenty-five dead before we got here. I saw the files. The storm won't stop them from killing the ones they still have in the medical tent. Or us."

"Take a look at these files," Dorchy says. "Here's one from 1917–1920 and I specifically asked for this summer." She sounds disgusted as she hands me a folder. I open it, expecting to see Father's 1917 "No" telegram. Instead I read a typed letter dated June 30, 1920 that changes everything.

"Listen," I say, my voice shaking. I can hardly breathe. "Dorchy, is the nurse who gave you this the one who likes Miss Latigue?"

Dorchy nods.

"Well, she just handed you exactly what we need to bring this place down."

I read the letter out loud.

"Cranston Army Hospital, Leesburg, Virginia

"June 30, 1920

"Dear Mrs. Van Giesen and Members of the Loup Island Board:

"I believe you will be interested in the progress I have made in finding a suitable method to free us from our burden. Below you'll find a description of a certain strain of influenza that appears to be deadly in most cases. From other sources, I have obtained laboratory specimens of it, suitable for our use.

"I hope you will agree that inoculation is a much better solution than gas, which carries a stigma since the war. Inoculation will be interpreted as a sign of our caring for the well-being of our subjects.

"As for the speed of this strain of flu, here are a surgeon's words about his observations at the U.S. Army's Camp Devens in Massachusetts during the second stage of the 1918 flu epidemic:

"'The…men start with what appears to be an ordinary attack of…influenza, [but] when brought to the hospital they very rapidly develop the most viscous type of pneumonia that has ever been seen. Two hours after admission they have the [dark] spots over the cheekbones, and a few hours later you can begin to see the cyanosis extending from their ears and spreading all over the face…It is only a matter of a few hours then until death comes…'

"In layman's terms, cyanosis means 'blue in the face.' I propose, therefore, we refer to our solution as 'blue' in all future correspondence. I predict an 85 percent (or better) success rate with this method.

"Yours for a world free of the unfit.

"Hiram Jellicoe, MD."

"Blue kills," Dorchy says. "Ratty wasn't delirious."

Tom goes pale. "I should have known," he says in a strangled voice. "But I wanted to believe my boys were sick when they came here and that's why they died. How dare he call them 'our burden'?"

Dorchy heads for the mouth of the cave. "In that case, why are we hiding in here? We have to get Posy and the twins and the other boys right now."

Tom says calmly, "Not now. We'll hide until the storm gets worse, then go. If we go now, they'll take us all."

"What's the storm got to do with it?" Dorchy glares at him.

"The tide," I say. As if watching a movie, I can see what will happen.

"The tide comes in and out every day," Dorchy says. "What's different about today?"

"At high tide the wind will send a surge of salt water up into the quarry." Excitement sparks in my voice. "It will flood the tent, maybe even wash it away."

Tom nods. "Reuben says he warned them not to put the tent in there. But for someone who grew up on an island, Vera Van is…"

"Pig-ignorant," Dorchy says, disgusted.

"Exactly. And her 'pignorance' helps *us*. We'll go to the tent in a couple of hours, closer to high tide. In the confusion, we'll have a better chance of getting the others out."

"If they're not all dead by then," Dorchy says.

"If we go before the tent floods, they will kill us too." He turns to us, his eyes bright. "Thank you for getting the files, Dorchy," he says, "and finding the letter, Rowan." He squeezes our hands.

"We have a lot more to do," Dorchy says, but I can tell she's as pleased as I am.

* * *

We decide that Tom and Jack will hide in the woods and watch the trail, ready to distract any searchers who come this way. Dorchy volunteers to climb a tree to get a long-distance view. I don't like to think of her in a tree that's shaking in the wind. But she can climb anything, and the farther away she spots them, the better chance the boys have of distracting them.

"Keep the raincoat," she says, thrusting it at me. "I can't climb a tree in a rubber cocoon."

I stay in the cave, keeping Magdalena and Snout quiet and listening for signals. Dorchy will whistle, one short, one long. Tom will hoot like an owl and Jack will caw like a crow. At any signal, Magdalena and I will move Snout deeper into the cave.

I settle in to wait. Magdalena sits next to me on a blanket. She keeps wiping her face, but I can't tell if it's from raindrops or tears. *They won't come*, I tell myself. *Nothing will get Vera out on her precious horse in this storm.*

A loud blare of noise from the woods sends Magdalena scurrying back to Snout. I move into the cave opening to hear better. Suddenly Vera's voice rings out, louder than usual. "Bring the sick boy to the medical tent. He needs our attention. Bring the…" Her voice dies away. Whatever she's doing, she isn't coming to the cave.

Tom bursts through the bushes. "Did you hear that? She's on Viking. Dr. Ritter is with her on foot. They're off the trail, going through the woods. I wish I could get that horse away from her. She doesn't deserve a beautiful animal like that."

Suddenly, much too close to the cave, we hear a shriek and a loud whinny. Then Dorchy yells, "Move your damn horse."

"Get her!" yells Vera. A man's agonized scream rises over the howling of the wind.

Silence.

Tom and I look at each other. Magdalena comes from the back of the cave. "What was that?" She wrings her hands.

I smile at her. "That was Dorchy, surprising them and saving us."

"From the sound of that scream, I'd say Dr. Ritter got the worst of it," Tom says. "Brave girl."

Jack comes into the cave, dripping wet. He squeezes out his cap and says, "That Dorchy is something. You should have seen her. When that horse came through the woods, headed for the cave, she jumped out of the tree right in front of it." He laughs shakily. "Then Dorchy yelled at Vera to move the horse and that fat doctor started after her. She ran into the thickest clump of brambles I ever saw. He followed her and began screaming."

"They didn't get her." Tom thumps Jack on the shoulder. "They didn't get her…and they're far away by now."

"He'll be picking thorns out his face for a week," Jack says.

I'm excited but scared for Dorchy. She knows nothing about the woods, and if she ran into the same brambles, she's injured too.

"Dorchy?" says Magdalena. "Dorchy?" She looks toward the mouth of the cave, and I remember how Dorchy comforted Magdalena at the quarry after Elsa was taken away. It seems like months ago, not two days.

"Dorchy got away." I smile at Magdalena, and after a few seconds, she smiles back.

Tom goes to check on Snout, and in an instant, fear sweeps through me. I try to recapture the relief I felt hearing about Dorchy's brave jump and escape. Instead icy dread spreads through every cell in my body.

"Snout's sleeping, but his fever is…What's wrong?" Tom stares at me.

I manage to say, "I'm afraid for Dorchy." Then the cold certainty that they have her closes over my head.

Agents of Miss Latigue. Those words seem ridiculous now. I can only hope that Dorchy, the con artist, convinces them of our high standing, our untouchability. But deep down I know we erased that possibility when we invaded the tent and stole the campers.

I spring for the cave opening like an arrow shot from a bow. "We have to get her back."

"No." Tom grabs my arm. "She got away. Jack saw her."

I wrestle free of him. "They'll hunt her down. I know it. She sacrificed herself for us. We have to get her back."

"Listen to me." Tom takes my hands and holds them between his calloused, warm ones. "We'll wait here for an hour in case she comes back. Then we'll go to the medical tent."

With Tom's hands on mine, I feel calmer, but the fear still gnaws at me. I haven't felt this hopeless since Father told the doctor, "Take her to Bellevue."

An hour later—Tom has a good sense of time—Dorchy hasn't come back. She could be out there hiding from the storm, but I know in my bones that she's in the medical tent. In danger.

So Tom, Jack, and I leave, just as Snout starts coughing blood. Magdalena sits next to him, calmly wiping his face with a piece torn from a blanket. She offers him water in the tin cup. I leave them Dorchy's raincoat. "We'll come back for you," Tom tells Magdalena.

When? I wonder. But not for long. I can't worry about anyone but Dorchy.

CHAPTER 41

Screaming wind gusts drive the rain sideways as we walk along the trail. The storm is flexing its muscles. The wind is a steady roar in the tall trees. Rain soaks us through. With a tearing crack, a white pine topples next to the trail. At times the wind comes straight at us out of the west—a giant hand holding us back.

"Viking must be in the stable by now," Tom says. "And Ritter is both hurt *and* a lazybones. You won't find him out hunting us in this mess."

"And Vera won't go out on foot," I say. I don't add that it might be better if they were out of the tent hunting for us.

As we get closer to the dry quarry and medical tent, we hear Reuben's truck coming. Through a screen of leaves, we watch it slide back and forth on the muddy track. Reuben is at the wheel.

Jack says, "See you at the tent," and sprints after the truck. He jumps into the back and waves to us before ducking down.

"Reuben has probably been drinking," Tom says in my ear as we wait for the truck to move out of sight.

"Does he drink?"

Tom nods. "A lot. He keeps a bottle in the truck. Says it's the only way he can live with the 'setup' on the island this summer."

"That means he knows what they're doing."

"I didn't ask him what he meant," Tom says bitterly. "If I had, I might have found out why my boys died."

We bend our heads into the wind and walk on.

* * *

Half an hour later we reach the road that leads down into the dry quarry. Tom points to a cluster of young pines and leans close to me. "Hide in there," he says. "I'll see who's in the tent."

"Wait, let's make a vow. 'Not one more death.'"

He looks into my eyes. "Not one more death."

Grateful for a chance to rest my leg, I squirm under the low limbs and sit on a pile of dead needles. Rain hits the entwined branches over my head, but few drops penetrate.

Soon I hear footsteps and voices. "Where is the truck, you drunken old fool?" asks Nurse Blunt.

"I parked it on the trail," says Reuben. "I wasn't fool enough to drive down this suicide track. And for the record, I haven't had a drink since Sunday last."

Peering through the low-hanging branches, I see the three nurses, Dr. Ritter, and Reuben, bringing up the rear. All of them wear black waterproof coats and hats, which makes them a lot better off than we are.

"The truck isn't there," whines one of the nurses.

Jack took it.

"Gone," Reuben says in a cheerful voice, "I reckon the wind blew it away."

"We can't walk in this rain," Dr. Ritter sputters. "I will lodge a

- 239 -

complaint with Miss Van."

"Honestly," says Nurse Blunt, "it's less than a half mile to the staff cottage. Stop complaining."

"I don't like this one bit," the whiny nurse says. "Miss Van and Dr. Jellicoe will come back for the patients like they promised to, won't they, Dr. Ritter?"

"That's not your concern, Nurse," he snaps.

Their footsteps squelch away from me.

Tom gives his owl call, and I crawl out of my hideaway.

"Jack has the truck," I say. "And Vera Van and Dr. Jellicoe aren't here, but they're coming back."

"You saw Jack?"

The wind gusts suddenly and pushes me into Tom. He steadies me. The roar of the wind drowns out his words. With a loud *craaack* another tall white pine falls in a cascade of branches and needles. This one blocks the way back to the cave.

As we start down into the quarry, I grab Tom's arm as my crutch slips on the wet granite chips. I lean against him, my heart beating so fast my teeth shake.

"Oh," he says and stops walking. "I knew the tide would come up in the quarry, but look."

Below us a shifting silver skin of water covers the quarry floor under dark scudding clouds. The tent is almost completely surrounded by water; its canvas sags and bulges as it strains against the ropes. Salt spray, blown by the wind, crusts my lips. With a shriek, a gust of wind slams rain into our faces. Tom pulls me along, and we run, slip, catch our balance, and run again until we reach the tent's front entrance. Gripping my crutch, I dive through the canvas flaps, driven by one thought, *Dorchy*.

The slatted floor is ankle-deep in icy salt water. I follow Tom down the dark hallway past the supply closet and curtained cubicle where I saw Dr. Jellicoe and Vera yesterday. Now shin-deep water pushes against my legs and crutch as we move toward the gray light in the back of the tent. Seaweed and salt drown the smells of medicine and wet canvas. As we get closer, the water rises higher and the wind shrieks louder. The back flaps of the tent are open to the flooding tide.

Tom stops, knee-deep in seawater. In the watery light I see only Dorchy and rejoice. *She's here. She's fine.*

But why is she sitting *in the rising water*? Posy is sitting in the water too.

I scream their names and wade toward them. Dorchy half stands, slips, and falls. Posy falls on top of her.

"Dorchy," I scream, as I fight my way forward. My crutch slips, but I catch myself. "Get up."

As if she heard me, Dorchy wobbles to her feet, coughing and spitting out water. She holds up her hands. They're tied together in front of her.

With a roar like a locomotive, the wind slams into the tent. Around us, the canvas billows and flattens, and the water trembles. Posy's scream is almost as loud as the wind.

I look for Tom; he's disappeared.

Dorchy leans toward me. "Get Posy."

Instead I grab Dorchy's hands and wrestle off the rubber tubing tied around them.

She rubs her wrists and grins at me. "I could have done that," she shouts.

"Sure you could, Houdini."

Another gust of wind and a loud crack. I look up. Overhead a tent pole hangs down surrounded by slabs of canvas that used to be the roof. I grab Posy's shoulder. She stares through me.

Dorchy gives me a look that says, *What do we do now?*

"Posy," I lean down and shout in her ear. "It's Rowan. Let me untie your hands."

She lunges at me, and I fall facedown in the water, mouth open. She collapses on top of me, holding me under. I swallow salt water but stay calm. It's like being caught by a big wave at the beach. I manage to shove her off me but lose my crutch. Choking, I try to stand but can't. Dorchy lifts me and hands me my crutch. Then she drags Posy upright.

Posy is docile now and lets me untie her hands. Then Dorchy guides her down the hallway to the front of the tent. I follow them, and Tom appears supporting Lester and Christophe. All of us are shaking with cold. Overhead, the wind shreds more canvas. Tent poles groan. Tom yells, "Hurry up. We have to get out of here. We'll be trapped."

"Wait." I stop by the supply closet. "Tom, grab some blankets."

He looks as if he might argue, then ducks inside and comes back with three blankets.

"Where are the twins and Elsa?" I ask Dorchy as we leave the tent, with Posy, now wrapped in a blanket, between us.

"Vera took the twins," Dorchy pants, "when the water started coming into the tent. That's when Jellicoe tied our hands. He said they'd be back."

"But we didn't believe him," Posy says. "Vera and him ran out like the fires of hell, beg pardon, were at their heels."

"And," Dorchy says, taking a deep breath, "Elsa died. Dr. Jellicoe was taking her body out when Vera brought me in this morning."

"I'm sorry," I say. "We should have found you first."

"You found me now." She smiles at me. "Besides I got to ride on

Viking. Vera slung me over the saddle like a dead deer. I'd like to think I gave that horse a shock he'll never forget."

"We heard you yell," I say, "and Jack told us about the jump."

"You'd have done the same," she says. "Now let's get away from here."

Tom has an arm around Lester on one side and Christophe on the other. We look up the steep road and catch our breaths. Water foams around our feet.

As we climb out of the quarry, the wind dies down and it's possible to hear each other speak.

"The boys are really sick," Dorchy says.

"What about you?"

"I'm fine, even though they gave me their stupid inoculation."

My heart sinks. "But you had the flu."

Dorchy makes a face. "That was a white lie I told Miss Latigue so I could come here with you."

Oh, Dorchy. The ground drops out from under me. *Not you.*

"You *told* them you never had the flu?"

"Yes. I didn't think they'd do anything. I reminded them that we're agents of the Council. But that witch Vera said, 'Do it.' Dr. Ritter said, 'There'll be hell to pay.' And even Jellicoe hesitated. So Vera grabbed the needle and said, 'She's an orphan,' and jabbed me. I punched her. But I'll be fine. I'm a carny, remember?"

A carny who can con almost anyone and climb anything. I squeeze her hand, ignoring the fear clawing at me.

CHAPTER 42

Posy can walk by herself, so Dorchy helps Lester up the hill while Tom half carries Christophe. The truck is idling at the top.

"They've come back." Posy grabs my hand.

"It's only me," yells Jack, "but it's too slippery to drive down."

He helps Tom and Dorchy get the boys into the back of the truck. It's open to the rain, so they rig a shelter out of blankets. Jack and Posy ride with the boys to keep them covered.

Dorchy climbs in the front with Tom. I look back at the quarry before I get in. In the dying light, white-capped waves close in on the tent, now sagging with its center pole broken and its roof in shreds. The ocean and the wind have destroyed it. Good riddance.

Inside the truck, Dorchy and I share a damp blanket as Tom starts down the track toward the cave. He's forgotten the tree that crashed across the road, and we stop just in time.

"Why did you stop?" Dorchy says, teeth chattering. "We have to get the boys to the gym or the house. We all need dry clothes."

The truck rocks in the wind, and rain thunders on the roof. Tom says, "Snout and Magdalena are still in the cave."

Dorchy jabs me in the ribs. "Do something."

"Tom," I say, "Jack can walk to the cave and tell Magdalena and Snout what's happened. Take the rest of us to the house." When he doesn't move, I add, "There's plenty of food and water at the cave. As soon as the storm is over, we can get them."

Tom seems to consider this, then shakes his head. "Vera and Jellicoe could be at the house," he says through tight lips. "They'll take back their patients."

"Cecily won't let anything happen to us at her house. She hates Vera." I concentrate on making him believe me. "Even if Vera is there, Cecily will do the right thing. Anyway I'll go in first. Please."

"All right," he says finally. "I'll tell Jack." He gets out of the truck, holding the door so it doesn't rip off in the wind.

Dorchy grabs my arm. "We have to signal for help." Her voice rises. "Vera and Jellicoe will never let us get away from here now. As soon as the storm is over, they'll round us up. I don't want that." She shivers violently, and I put my arm around her. "First we have to get warm," she says. "Then we have to get help."

Tom climbs in and turns the truck around. We head for the house.

"The lighthouse," Dorchy says. "We have to light the lamp and signal the mainland." She sounds defiant, as if we had already objected.

"You're right," Tom says. "Even if Reuben is against them, he's in no shape to protect us. And we can't wait for the ferry. It has to be tonight, as soon as the storm moves out."

"But you're scared of heights, Tom," I object. "And Dorchy's half drowned. Jack might have done it, but..."

"*I'll* do it," Dorchy says. "A good climb is just what I need. Get me dry clothes, though. These wet ones weigh a ton."

I imagine the flimsy lighthouse, as full of holes as Swiss cheese, rocking in the wind. "It's not safe. The wind will blow the light out, and anyway no one on shore will see it."

"We have to get help." Dorchy is adamant. "We have sick boys and maybe Posy and me. I don't know yet."

"Dorchy's right. They won't give up." Tom says this as if it's a new idea. "As soon as the storm is over, they'll come after us again. Even if the tent is washed away. I know you think Cecily will protect us, Rowan, but you're the only one they won't touch. What was it Ratty overheard?"

"'No one leaves the island alive.'" It comes out in a whisper.

"So there you have it." Dorchy sounds impatient. "We *have* to send a signal."

"We can't." Tom sounds defeated. "Reuben said the stairs have collapsed. He wanted to fix them and Vera said no."

"I climbed it Wednesday night," Dorchy says, "all the way to the top walkway. The kerosene is there; the matches are there. I can do it."

Tom gives a low whistle. "Well, that cinches it." He sounds impressed.

"The house first," I say.

"Right," Tom says. "Then I'm going to the lighthouse with Dorchy."

I snap back, "So am I!"

* * *

As I squelch up to Cecily's door, I imagine Dr. Jellicoe opening it, needle in hand, ready to stab me. But the thought of Dorchy shivering in the truck pushes me forward.

The door is locked. I hammer my knuckles raw before Louise opens it and pulls me inside.

I stay close to the door, ready to run, and look around in the dim light. "Is Vera here?"

"No." Louise doesn't smile. "Don't know where she and the doc have got to. Don't care either." She looks me up and down. "Where are the others?"

"Outside in the truck. They need to be in here. Vera and Jellicoe left them tied up in the tent as it flooded. There are three more hiding in the woods." I stop for a breath, and she says, "Well, bring the ones outside in here right now. Mrs. Van Giesen is in no state to complain."

As I turn to go back to the truck, she adds, "I locked her in her room."

She couldn't have surprised me more if she'd sprouted wings and hovered over my head.

"You did?" My voice squeaks.

"I did. And if Vera shows up, I'll lock *her* in the cellar. Now get those kids in here."

I go back to the truck, and Posy climbs out of the back, shaking with cold.

Tom and Dorchy help Christophe into the house. Posy helps Lester.

The electricity is out. Louise thinks a tree fell on the generator shed. By lamplight she provides dry clothes and lanterns for us to use getting to the lighthouse, even though she doesn't approve. "You say that girl is going to light the lamp?" she asks, handing me a waterproof bag of matches.

"Dorchy, yes. What about her?"

"She's sick." Louise avoids my eyes. "Fact is, she ought to be in a warm bed."

I refuse to believe her. "She's fine, but without knowing where Vera and the doctor are, we have to call for help."

"They won't come back here to the house," Louise says. "Vera came by and took a bag. She didn't ask for her mother, and I didn't tell her I'd locked her up. I would've locked Vera up too, if she'd stayed around."

"Well, no one can get off the island," I say, "so we're signaling for help. The storm is letting up."

She hangs a shopping bag on my arm. "Get that boy Tom to carry the lanterns. You take this thermos of hot cocoa and some sugar cookies. Give that poor girl a drink before she goes up that thing. Better'n medicine."

"Thanks, Louise."

"Stay here," Posy begs me. "You're the only one of us who's been here before."

"I'll be back." I hurry out to the truck.

"He wanted to go without you," Dorchy says when I get in. "But I made him wait." Like me, she has on dry clothes and an oilskin coat and hat. Tom is still in his wet clothes but covered now with a waterproof coat and hat that Louise said belonged to Vera's father "when he was alive."

Telling us this, Tom adds, "Well, they wouldn't have been much use to him when he was dead."

* * *

The wind pushes the truck sideways on the cliff track, and Tom fights the wheel.

"The sky is clearing," Dorchy says. I feel her body heat through the waterproof coat. She is as tight as a coiled spring.

"Nervous?" I ask her.

"No. I did it before, didn't I?"

Yes, on a mild evening with light in the sky and no wind.

"After this storm the lighthouse could be a pile of timbers on the rocks," Tom says.

"It isn't." Dorchy points. There it is, a dark shape silhouetted against the clearing sky. "They didn't plan for this," she says with satisfaction. "They didn't dream anyone would ever light that lamp again."

"Reuben did." Tom brakes, and we slide across the muddy track and come to a stop on the edge of the cliff. "He wanted to fix it."

"Quit stalling," Dorchy says. "Spend your breath praying for somebody to see the light"—she coughs, a deep, wet sound—"know what it is"—a harsh gasp—"and come to help us before Vera and Jellicoe hunt us down."

"Wait. Louise wanted you to drink this." I dig out the thermos, unscrew the top, and pour a capful, offering it first to Tom and then to Dorchy.

"You think I'm contagious?" Dorchy laughs. "Never felt better."

Tom lights the two lanterns. Dorchy leads the way with one, followed by Tom and me sharing the other.

Stars wink in the gaps between shifting clouds. The rain is a soft drizzle, and the smell of salt is thick on the light wind. Dorchy turns around. "It's clearing. They'll see it on the mainland and they'll come." Her harsh laugh has a sob behind it.

"Dorchy?" Suddenly I'm drowning in regret. Why didn't we stay on Cape Cod or go to New York when we had the chance? We'd be safe now, with nothing to be afraid of but the Ogilvies. *What would they say if they saw us now?*

Dorchy stops suddenly, and we stare at the dark, sodden mass of the lighthouse. "I'll take one lantern up the stairs as far as I can go one-handed," she says. "Then I'll go by feel."

Tom gives her the package of waterproof matches. "These will work," he says. "We don't know if the ones up there still do."

"How will you get the lamp open to light it?" I ask.

"I'll get it open."

"I should be the one going up," Tom says in a strangled voice.

"You'd break the ladder," Dorchy says. "I can climb it because I'm lighter than you are." She sounds excited, like the Dorchy I know.

"I'll be at the foot of the ladder," Tom says. He sounds very tense, and I realize he doesn't know what a powerful climber Dorchy is.

"Be careful," I call after them, hating how useless that sounds. "I'll wait for you, Dorchy." I add quietly, "Till hell freezes over."

She's not sick. She's fine.

The wind shifts and the lighthouse creaks. *I want my leg back.* The words ring in my mind. I grip the crutch. I won't sit down while Tom and Dorchy are in danger. I brace for the sound of tearing wood and a scream, but all I hear is the pounding surf.

When two small lights shine through the gaping hole in the side of the building, I let out a breath I didn't know I was holding.

One light moves into a higher window and disappears. The second one follows. Then both lights appear even higher. Tom must have both lanterns at the foot of the broken ladder while Dorchy climbs.

I count to a hundred, promising myself that I'll see the lighthouse lamp shining before I finish. I do that five times. Then Tom runs out of the lighthouse, swinging a lantern and calling, "Rowan." The fear in his voice pierces me. Joy and courage drain away.

Dorchy.

I walk toward Tom's voice, not even feeling the ground under my feet. The sky has cleared enough for me to steer my way through the rocks and vines. Then Tom is in front of me. In the lantern light his face looks haggard.

"What happened?"

Dorchy coughs. The thick and agonizing sound comes from the top of the lighthouse. I clutch at my own throat. *No, Dorchy's fine. She must be fine; she has to be fine; she climbed up there. She'll save us all.*

The coughing stops abruptly. Tom turns away from me and yells, "Dorchy, are you all right?"

I trip on a vine and my hand hits a small, sharp rock. I jump up, cradling my hand. "Don't talk, Dorchy," I yell. "I'm coming up."

Tom swings around. "How?" he says in a low voice. "The ladder. Your leg."

"One of us has to go up there," I say, loud enough for Dorchy to hear. "It's going to be me. I'll help you down, Dorchy. You'll be fine once we get back to the house."

To Tom, I say, "I'm not talking about her as if she can't hear us." A vein of anger stirs inside me. My weak leg will *not* stop me. "*You* can't climb the ladder," I tell Tom. "So you can help me do it."

At that moment I feel strong enough to climb three lighthouses. "Hold the ladder and boost me up. I'll get her on the ladder. You get her off."

Tom holds up the lantern. A muscle twitches in his cheek. "You'll have to light the lamp," he says in a low voice. "She had trouble with it before she started…"

"I'll do it," I say. Maybe if we don't say the word *coughing*, she'll stop. I concentrate on getting into the lighthouse.

Tom shifts the fallen beam in front of the door so it's easier for me to get in. Then he helps me climb over the pile of wreckage at the foot of the stairs.

"Stay to the right on the stairs," he says. "I'll follow you up with the lantern. But I'll have to put it down to hold the ladder. Up top the only light is from the sky."

"Until I light the lamp," I say. Then I yell up the stairs, "I'm on my way."

From above comes a small voice, barely recognizable as Dorchy's. "Use your arms to pull yourself up the ladder."

The higher we climb, the more the building narrows. The walls seem to be embracing us.

My legs ache with the effort of climbing the stairs. Twice I stop to rest.

At the foot of the ladder Tom puts his lantern down. Now I just have to get up ten rungs, light the lamp, help Dorchy get down, and get down myself.

I can't wells up inside me. The words drain my strength. I fight a sudden sting of tears.

"You coming up or not?" Dorchy asks in her familiar voice. "The view is great."

Inside me, midway lights snap on, banks of them, spinning, flashing, spelling out *I can.* "Hold your horses," I say.

Tom holds up the lantern, and Dorchy's face beams in the opening above us.

The ladder dangles sideways on the wall.

"I'll use this board to brace it," Tom says, demonstrating. "Go slowly, no sudden moves. If the bolt gives way, we'll both fall." I look behind him down the stairs to the lower landing and shudder.

"Coming up," I say.

"Remember, pull with your arms," Dorchy says. Her face is close, only a few feet above me.

I step on the first rung with my right foot and Tom positions my left. Then he braces the ladder in a vertical position. I use my arms to pull myself up, as Dorchy ordered. Tom helps me as far as rung four. There are six more. The ladder sways every time I pull on it, dragging my left leg up. Half the time my left foot isn't even on the rung. Once both feet slip off, and the ladder lurches to the side. My full weight hangs from my arms until I get my right foot in position again.

Tom says, "You're fine."

This is so far from the truth that I choke back a laugh that is half a sob.

My arms start trembling. I use my right leg to push off the rung I'm on, and my hands slip again.

"Take a rest," Dorchy says. "What's the rush?"

"Don't make me laugh," I gasp.

"Two more," Dorchy says. "Piece of..." She starts to cough.

Somehow I manage the next two rungs and crawl out onto the floor. My eyes adjust to the starlight filling the round, windowed room. Dorchy crouches by the lamp, head hanging down. Blood drips on her sweater. "We have to light the lamp," she says, standing up, all business. "I figured out what to do." She takes a ragged breath. "Unscrew this cap." She points to the base of the lamp.

I try but it doesn't budge. "Open," I command and twist the cap again. Nothing. I try again. My hand slips.

"What are you doing?" Tom calls from the landing.

"Opening the lamp," I say. This time when I twist the cap it opens. I feel a rush of pure joy.

"Now the kerosene," Dorchy says. "Here's the funnel." I fit the funnel in the hole in the lamp and open the kerosene can. It's almost empty, and the sharp fumes sting my eyes and make Dorchy cough.

I pour the kerosene in, cap it, and remove the funnel. Then I cap the lamp.

Dorchy wipes her mouth. "Matches," she says and hands me a long match.

"Where do I light it?"

"The wick. It's just a big oil lamp," Dorchy says. "Easy as pie."

I can see the huge wick under the glass lamp with its hundreds of faceted pieces.

"How do we get this off?" I tap the glass.

Tom calls up the stairs. "There's a handle. Reuben's father invented it to raise the glass to light the wick. His motto was, 'Easy enough for a child.'"

"Well, this child needs to know where it is."

Dorchy sits on the floor, head resting on her knees. "Help me, Dorchy," I say finally. "I found the handle. I need you to hold it while I light the wick."

She comes over and takes the handle, moving so slowly that my breath catches in my throat. I strike the match and hold it close to the wick. Nothing happens. The match burns almost to my fingers.

"Any ideas about lighting the wick, Tom?" I say.

"It's dried out," he says. "Wind it down into the kerosene."

I try that. Then I light a new match and hold my breath until the wick starts to burn. The flame trembles in the wind from the opening to the walkway.

I take the handle from Dorchy and lower the glass over the wick. Rich golden light, magnified by hundreds of angled pieces of glass, sends our message out across the rough waves. It's the most beautiful light I've ever seen.

I clap my hands and yell, "We did it, Dorchy. Bravo!" Then I say,

"Please, please, please let people on the mainland see the light and come to help us."

Dorchy covers her eyes. "Bright," she says and starts coughing again.

When she stops and says, "Now help me climb down," she sounds almost like herself. The light—warm, golden, all-encompassing—will heal her.

"You have to kneel at the top of the ladder and hold my hands," she goes on, "while I get my feet on the rungs. It's only three rungs until Tom can catch me."

But miraculously, once her feet are on the ladder, she tells me she can hold on.

"I didn't think I could do it, but I can," she says. "After all, *you* did."

While Tom makes her comfortable on the landing, I take a minute to go out on the walkway. The wind is still blowing, but the storm has moved on. The light behind me is so bright I can't see the stars, but I can tell the sky is clear. Looking down the path of light reflected in the ocean, I almost miss a curve of white sail, moving fast, away from the island, across the white-topped waves. Vera's sailboat. Cecily said Vera could sail anything in any weather from the time she was ten. Well, there she goes. And with her the doctor and the twins probably. I'm glad the adults are gone, but how will Lolly and Dolly, sick as they were on the ferry, survive in a sailboat tonight?

Tom calls my name and steadies the ladder for me. Going down takes longer than climbing up. My arms give out just before the bottom rung, and I fall in a heap. Tom helps Dorchy down the stairs. She does some of it on her own, but when we reach the bottom, she sags against him.

He carries her out of the lighthouse and all the way to the truck.

When I get there, I hug Dorchy. "You're so brave," I say.

She shakes me off. "*You* climbed up there with one leg."

We look back at the lighthouse sending our golden message over eight miles of ocean.

Dorchy says what I'm thinking, gasping after each word. "They'll see the light, won't they?"

Tom starts the truck. "They'll see it and they'll come."

"But the storm," she says.

"Lobstermen go out in all weather," he says. "This is nothing to them."

"I saw a sailboat from the walkway," I say, "before I came down. It had to be Vera's. Heading southwest like a bat out of hell."

"No one else sails," Tom says. "Maybe the doctor is with her."

"They took the twins, I bet," Dorchy says.

Tom lets out a long breath. "Reuben will be on our side now that Vera and the doctor are gone. He knows who butters his bread."

"And which way the wind blows," I say.

Dorchy manages a laugh. She rests her head on my shoulder as Tom drives to the house. When we get out, she takes hold of my free arm for support.

By the time we reach the door, my heart has turned from feather-light to stone.

CHAPTER 43

Tom drives off, heading for the cave by another trail. Louise opens the door. She puts her arm around Dorchy's shoulder, keeping her upright. In the lamplight, I see the dark patches on Dorchy's cheeks. Her bloody nose. She sinks to the floor, head down.

And doesn't say a word.

I'm falling down a long shaft with no hope of landing. We got her back, but not in time. I failed my best friend.

I help Louise get Dorchy out of her oilskin coat and into the sitting room where an oil lamp glows on top of the bookcase. We spread sheets on the couch and prop Dorchy up with pillows. I tuck the blanket around her, and Louise puts a warm towel over her chest. Then she brings a steaming cup of herbal tea.

Dorchy tries to swallow the tea and chokes. More blood. I sit on an ottoman next to her and take her cold hands in mine.

"Here's what you taught me," I say. "Even away from the midway, a carny's a carny for life."

A soft pressure on my fingers, barely there.

I tell her then how she saved us today, not just by climbing the lighthouse or keeping Posy from drowning. I look into her eyes, "Thank you for dropping out of the tree in front of Vera."

Her lips stretch into a smile. She opens her eyes. "Almost got away," she whispers and coughs for a long time.

You saved us. I should have saved you.

We sit in silence for long minutes. My throat clogs with grief.

I smooth her damp hair, look into her eyes, and drink in her face. "Thank you for telling me the rowan is a magical tree."

I fall asleep and wake up with a start, ice-cold. Dorchy struggles to breathe, seconds passing between each ragged breath. Her hands claw the towel. Her ears and nose and lips are blue.

I hold her hands in mine. "I'll see you on the midway, Wave Rider," I say.

She makes the smallest sound. It might be good-bye. I let her have that last word.

Her fingers go slack.

I hold on.

A long time later Tom comes in. I shake my head.

"Her spirit is free now," Tom says. "Where will it go?"

"To the midway." I'm crying now. *To midways everywhere, forever.*

CHAPTER 44

I can't leave her. I sit there feeling as empty as I did onstage as Ruthie. Tom's eyes bore into mine. "Are you all right?"

I shake my head, and he puts his hands on my shoulders. "Those bastards got away with everything."

"They didn't get us." I take no joy in saying it.

He puts his hands over his face and stumbles out of the room.

* * *

A long time later I leave the sitting room so Tom and Louise can move Dorchy's body. I go to the kitchen, suddenly hungry. Louise comes back and dishes out a bowl of stew and a thick piece of bread and butter.

"What about Cecily?" I ask. And then, "Dorchy and I lit the lamp. People will come by boat tomorrow."

"Mrs. Van Giesen wants to talk to you, when you're ready," Louise says. "I explained what happened and that Vera's gone. She wants to stay up there. 'Let them who need it most have the run of the house,' she said. And, 'I bear you no malice for locking me in.'"

"I'll talk to her in the morning." I'm so sleepy I can't hold my head up.

Louise carries a candle to light my way upstairs to the bedroom Magdalena and I will share. She brings me a nightgown and slippers, another warm sweater.

"Where's Posy?"

Louise shakes her head. "Posy has to be quarantined with the three boys. They all have influenza."

"I was exposed to it. I could have it too."

"Stay here with Magdalena," Louise says. "She's had a shock. Snout died in the cave, and she spent hours with his body."

When I lie down, I rub my aching left leg. Five years ago in the hospital, Dr. Friedlander taught me how to massage the muscles. We sat together in the solarium at Bellevue. "Your fingers need to gently remind your leg it's alive and still useful," he said, sucking on a peppermint. "If you believe it, in time your leg will too."

Magdalena watches me work on my leg. "Tomorrow is better," she says finally. "The storm blows away."

CHAPTER 45

In the morning I go to see Posy. Her room is small and sunny. Someone gave her a flannel nightgown, and she looks much better than when we got her out of the tent yesterday.

She is sitting up in bed, her breakfast tray across her knees. Magdalena follows me in and takes the tray away. "I feel fine," Posy says. "I don't even have a fever."

I smile and speak to her from inside my ice cave.

"Dorchy had it bad," she says. "She told me she was going to die. I said, 'No, you aren't.'" She wipes away a tear.

"She died." I can't say anything more.

"I know." She plucks at the sheet. "What happened to the twins?"

She looks so worried that I tell her only part of the truth. "They aren't sick."

"I liked them," Posy says wistfully. She looks at me the way I used to look at Dorchy, searching for answers.

I squeeze her hand and tell her she'll be fine.

Next I go to see Cecily in her bedroom overlooking the ocean. Big swells but no whitecaps today.

"I'm so sorry about Dorchy," she says, holding out her hand to me. "But I must say, you girls brought this trouble down on yourselves."

I ball my fists and stand rigid.

"God is my witness," she says. "I was against it all from the first time Vera told me about it."

"Don't bother with excuses," I say. "I know all about 'blue.' I have the letter."

"I backed out right then," she says fervently. "Just as your father did. You have to believe me. But it was too late. Nothing could stop Vera. I tried to save as many as I could."

I feel like a visitor. I'm here, but I am also at home with Father, tearing down the house I grew up in. I feel the light from the window. I have stepped into a new place, a new body, a new strength.

"Then why did you lie to Miss Latigue?" My voice is calm. I am in the right and she is not. My friend was killed by her inaction, but I don't feel rage, just an intense curiosity. "You could have told her, and she would have 'saved' the ones who came here with me. All you had to do was tell her."

"I told her we had deaths." Cecily's voice shakes. "You know, I always admired your father's passion on this issue. You share it, I see."

"I share nothing of my father's," I say, still calm.

Cecily stands up and paces from her chair to the window and back. "I was a prisoner in this house long before Louise locked me in yesterday. I'm eager to help you prosecute Vera and Hiram Jellicoe. They should be locked up." She looks at me, appealing with her eyes. "Can't we be allies, Rowan? Let's work together to get justice for those who died."

I stare her down. "No. I'll get them justice on my own."

She holds out her hands to me. "I have documents, minutes from meetings. I have charts and photographs. Vera took very little with her, according to Louise. I'll open everything to the authorities. Will they come today?" She touches her hair. "I hope I'll have time to make myself presentable before they do."

"I don't know when anyone will come, but I'm sure the police will want to talk to you. I assume the ferry will be here tomorrow as scheduled."

She nods.

We stare at each other across a divide so deep it steals my breath.

Her face changes from soft and appealing to hard and sly. "It's not at all what it looks like, you know." She goes to her dresser and pulls out a leather notebook. "My journal," she says reverently. "Let me read you what I wrote in here last night. Louise, with your approval I'm sure, gave me an opportunity to reflect, but please listen objectively. I think I've earned that courtesy."

A part of my mind sits apart from this scene commenting drily. *Look how her true nature surfaces. Listen and learn. This is where Vera got her ideas. Not from that soft woman trying to save her own skin, but from this calculating one.*

"I'm listening," I say, forcing a polite note in my voice. Thinking, *Go ahead and hang yourself.*

Cecily remains standing, holding the journal. But instead of reading from it, she starts talking. "Sterilization is a stopgap, not a solution. Sterilization has its place—I know Julia and your father advocate it. But what we perfected here on Loup Island provides a fast, easy, and *permanent* solution to the burden of the unfit for the first time in history."

I keep my face blank.

"Rowan, look at what we've accomplished." Cecily smiles warmly.

I hear in her voice and see in the way she stands—relaxed, open, eager—that *this* is what she's been dying to say, and couldn't, in front of Miss Latigue.

"We give the unfit a chance to help society. Even you must admit that. Each inoculation adds to our understanding of influenza, the strain we call blue. That is a contribution to all of mankind."

I can't let this pass. "You cause terrible suffering," I say. "As does sterilization." I'm thinking of Minnie and Tom.

"No one suffers *here*!" Cecily laughs. "The medical experts on our board are unanimous that our solution to solving the problem of the unfit is quick and painless."

"Don't insult me!" I say coldly. "You inject people and they die. Slowly and painfully."

"It takes more than three days to understand our process," Mrs. Van Giesen says as she tucks the journal back in the dresser drawer.

"Do you inform the campers when you inoculate them? The unfit *are* human beings, despite what you believe."

Cecily snaps, "The unfit can't handle information like that. We're dealing with what our German colleagues Hoche and Binding call '*lebensunwerten Lebens.*'"

"'Life unworthy of life,'" I say. *Dorchy? Elsa? Ratty?*

She nods approvingly. "Your father taught you well. But you have to understand that our mission goes far beyond this summer, this island. When we perfect our methods, they will be embraced by every state."

"That will never happen," I say. "The police will have your files documenting the true number of deaths. We have the letter describing 'blue,' your 'solution.' These are murders. The killers will be prosecuted."

"No, my dear," Cecily says with a pitying look on her face. "The letter seems damning. But in court, it will be laughed at. There is nothing that says we ever used this plan.

"We merely inoculated the unfortunates who had been exposed to the flu before they came here. Sadly some died. You need a piece of paper that says, 'We, the undersigned, plan to do this, this, and this to kill the unfit.' You don't have that and never will. It doesn't exist."

"I'll testify to what you just told me." I can feel my face getting hot.

"And I'll deny it. Now who is more likely to be believed, hmm?"

"What about Father then? He was one of you, but he hated the 'solution.' He'll testify about your plans."

Cecily shakes her head. "No, he won't. He didn't approve of this project, but he never knew we put it in practice. And even if he did"—she leans toward me, triumph shining in her eyes—"he would take the long view and do what is good for the Betterment movement as a whole. He would not drag us through the mud."

I leave the room; I can't breathe. She has strangled me with her words.

The key is in the lock. I lock her in and give the key to Louise, saying, "The next time Cecily leaves that room will be with the police."

CHAPTER 46

Voices rise into the warm, sunny morning, carried on a light breeze. Pools of water in the road reflect the bright sky. Reuben is sawing the tree that fell on the generator. He gives me a wave. Tom and Jack stand a few feet away, deep in conversation.

I walk down the front steps and sit taking deep breaths of fresh salt air and feeling nothing.

"No, I said." Tom's voice is low and desperate. "I won't go back. I can't. Not now. Not after this."

"After what?" Jack says.

"Don't follow me."

"Stop," Jack yells. "Don't go."

I stand up. Tom is running along the narrow cliff path away from the house, toward the bay.

Fear, as sharp and urgent as a kick, sends me after him, walking as fast as I can.

That tone in Tom's voice scared me too. I have to catch up to him. The sun turns the ocean rippling far below to gold. Above, small white clouds sail across the deep blue of the sky. The storm has blown out to sea. But nothing distracts me. I'm being pulled straight to Tom.

The cliff path rises to a high point, and when I get up there, I find him. He sits on the edge of the cliff, legs dangling into nothingness. He doesn't seem surprised to see me. "Reuben told me about this place. He calls it the top of the island. It's as good as any."

I sit down. I study his handsome face, locked in a mask of pain. "Good for what?"

"I learned something here," he says.

After a long silence, I ask, "What?"

"How to help people." His voice has a bitter edge.

Far below, waves surge against shiny black rocks, dousing them in foam. "Yes." I say, "Dorchy and I saw it. You helped us." It is hard to say her name, but when I do, it feels good. As if she's here with us.

He looks at me with a lopsided grin. "You did the same for me. And Dorchy." He shakes his head, remembering. "Hands down she's the bravest person I ever met. She saved us by jumping out of that tree. To stop Vera and save us, she had to yell and jump in front of the horse at the same time."

"I'll never stop feeling guilty," I say.

"Me neither."

I hear the pain in his voice and say softly, "Now the police will go after all of them, especially Dr. Jellicoe and Vera. In my mind I can see their pictures on the front page of a newspaper. Walking into court, heads hanging low."

He spits out into space. "You have a lot to learn, if you think that."

"That letter I found in the file is evidence of what they did here,"

I say. Cecily dismissed it, but I want to give him hope. A gull swoops below us, screaming a warning.

"I know you believe that evildoers get punished," he says. "I used to. But nothing in my life or yours bears that out."

He stands up and moves back from the cliff edge, then bends to untie his boots. "It comes down to this." He kicks the boots off. "I let down the boys I was supposed to protect. I closed my eyes to what happened to them and to the ones who came after them."

I stand up next to him, my heart racing. "Come back to the house with me." I struggle to sound calm.

He grabs my hands and gives them a squeeze. "You mean well, Rowan, but you shouldn't have followed me up here. Go back. Now."

Desperation makes my voice tremble. "You aren't responsible for what happened to the boys. The killers are. Who will bring them to justice if not us?"

He shakes his head. "There's no justice for them. No one will believe us. We're just corks in a river headed for the falls." He takes a deep breath and abruptly moves to the cliff edge, dislodging loose stones. They cascade down through the blue air.

I follow him, begging now. "Move back, Tom. You're too close."

He gives his head and shoulders a shake and says without turning. "Go back, Rowan. Please."

"Tom, listen." He's so close to the edge. I have to keep him talking. "We stopped them. We got the boys, all except Ratty and Snout. We got Posy and Magdalena. Louise says all the sick ones will recover. That's something."

"But not my boys, Harry, Arthur, Bert, and Tommy. Or Ratty. Or Elsa. Or Dorchy." His voice breaks on her name. He turns to look at me and spits the words. "Not the twins. And the worst criminals got clean away."

"They won't win." I will him to believe this, even though, after listening to Cecily, I'm not sure.

He says nothing. Turns back to face the ocean. A breath. A heartbeat.

I grab his hand, keeping my crutch close to my side.

"No." He tries to pull away.

I lean back and hang on. "If you jump, you'll take me with you." My heart, mind, and body connect in the words I fling out: "I lost her; I won't lose you."

In front of us, a gull dives straight down the face of the cliff, an arrow into the waves.

"Let go," he says, and starts prying my fingers back. The loose rocks under our feet start to slide. I shift my weight to keep my footing, stabbing at the ground with my crutch, loosening more stones. The ground starts to give way.

He yanks me back so hard I fall, dragging him down onto the path with me. Safe. Still holding hands.

Staring up at the sky, I say, "We have to live to remember the ones who died. They don't have anyone else."

He doesn't say anything, but after we stand up, he squeezes my hand.

When we get to the house he says, "Thanks. I'm all right now."

"Promise?" I try to read his expression.

"You won't lose me, Rowan. I promise."

CHAPTER 47

Later that morning three lobster boats arrive. In one is a police constable, in another one an undertaker, and in the third a newspaper reporter. The lobstermen have wind-toughened faces and reddened hands. Everyone else looks seasick. Tom and Reuben meet the boats at the dock and bring the constable and undertaker first to the cave to collect Snout's body and then to Cecily's house. The reporter is left with no one to talk to except Dr. Ritter and the nurses at the staff cottage.

I go into the sitting room to say a final good-bye to Dorchy before the undertaker comes. Her body is covered with a white sheet. But everything that was Dorchy has escaped this small, sad room. I leave the way I would depart a station waiting room, eager to be on my way. On my way out, a moth—small, plain, light brown—brushes my cheek.

The constable takes Cecily, Dr. Ritter, and the nurses to the mainland where Miss Latigue will join them. Cecily's lawyer will meet all of them at the dock.

Louise asks for help nursing the sick boys and Posy until the ferry comes tomorrow, bringing Louise's sister, a nurse. Tom and Jack help with the boys, while Magdalena and I amuse Posy. Tom, Jack, Magdalena, and I will leave on the ferry.

* * *

Reuben is staying at the house while Cecily is gone. No one has seen or heard of Vera and Dr. Jellicoe. Maybe they drowned, as Tom seems to think.

The rest of that day and night I feel pulled in so many different directions that it's hard to know what to feel.

Posy asks me about Dorchy's body, and if she'll have a funeral. That's up to Miss Latigue, I say. I expect she'll try to find Dorchy's uncle, a carny at Coney Island in New York. Otherwise the Council will take care of a burial.

I tell Posy about the moth and the feeling that Dorchy wasn't there anymore.

"The moth was her spirit," Posy says. When I protest, she says, "Don't argue. I believe it. And someday you will too."

When the ferry arrives on Sunday, I'm ready to go. I have a plan, and I have the rest of the money Dorchy took from Mr. Ogilvie and the twenty dollars Miss Latigue gave Dorchy and me. I know Dorchy wouldn't mind me using her share. I give Mr. Ogilvie's watch to Tom.

Tom surprises me on Sunday. As we walk to the ferry, he tells me that before Cecily left, Reuben asked her if he could hire Tom to stay on the island to work and she said yes.

"I'll be earning money," he tells me with pride in his voice. "I'd like to save up and get an education, maybe even be a teacher someday."

"But Reuben helped Vera and Dr. Jellicoe," I say. "How can you trust him?"

Tom says, "I can't explain it. He could have led them to the cave, but he didn't. And he refused to hunt down Ratty. Besides, his loyalty isn't to them anymore. We're going to rebuild the lighthouse in Dorchy's memory. And Cecily has agreed to put in a radio, so there will be direct contact with the mainland."

At the ferry he says, "Be happy, Rowan."

And I say, "Good-bye, Tom."

He stands waving on the dock for as long as I can see him.

CHAPTER 48

On the ferry I write a letter to Miss Latigue, promising to give her a full report soon. I mail it in Rockland and catch the train to Boston. It's late when I arrive, so I go to the Parker House Hotel, where Father often stayed before the war.

I have enough money to pay for a room for two nights. I ask the desk clerk to help me call Dr. Friedlander at the Children's Hospital right away.

"It's Sunday, miss," he says gently.

"All right," I say, "first thing tomorrow, please."

Then I send a telegram to Julia in New York: *Staying at Parker House Hotel. Home Tuesday. Rowan.*

At noon on Monday Dr. Friedlander and his wife come to the hotel restaurant where I've asked them to meet me. Dr. Friedlander looks the same, tall and quiet with a twinkle in his eye. He introduces me to his short, bubbly wife, Annie, who is also a doctor. "Call me Dr. Annie," she says. "Two Dr. Friedlanders in one conversation can be very confusing." Over lunch, they disagree about almost everything, but in a lighthearted way. I bask in their banter and tell the story of riding the waves on Cape Cod. Climbing the lighthouse is too hard to talk about right now.

Before lunch is over, I get to the point. "Dr. Friedlander," I say, "I have left the Boston Home for good. Now I would like to work with you as a ward assistant with polio patients. And enter nursing school next year."

"I'd be delighted," he says, smiling. "But I need to hear in your own words why you want to do this now."

"Because from the very beginning, you believed that I would walk again. You made *me* believe it. And now that I'm walking and climbing and riding the waves, I know I can help other patients believe in themselves."

He smiles. "I support your plan. But what do your father and sister say about it?"

"I wanted to ask you first," I say. "I'm on my way to New York to discuss it with them. But since it is the only thing in the world that I want, I believe they will be very happy to support me in this." *Do I really believe this? Or did I just lie to Dr. Friedlander?* "To be honest," I go on, "I'm *trying* to believe they will support me."

"Tell your father and sister you'll be living with us at the start," says Dr. Annie, patting my hand. "That may ease their fears about a young girl living in a strange city. And maybe I'll convince you to study for a medical degree. You never know."

"Thank you." Tears well up. I brush them away.

As we say good-bye, Dr. Friedlander hugs me. "If I thought you wanted this just to get back at your father and sister, I would discourage it," he says. "But your reasons are very gratifying. You will be an enormous help to my young patients. Bravo."

He promises to write a letter to Father, explaining about the job at the hospital, my studies and their cost, and his offer to provide me with a place to live. He'll mail the letter to the hotel so I can take it to Father.

When I go back to my room, I have a message from Julia. She's in Boston and will meet me here at five o'clock. If she expects me to go back to the Home and Dr. Pynchon, she's in for a surprise.

CHAPTER 49

Julia appears at the door of my hotel room in a beautiful summer suit of paisley silk, pale yellow gloves, and a pretty straw hat. She takes one look at me and sinks down on the bed.

"What's happened to you? You're thin as a rail. Those horrible clothes. And that crutch. Father paid good money for *two* crutches, and here you are three months later looking like an orphan."

I feel like one.

She doesn't wait for me to answer but just goes on. "What possessed you to get involved with the Van Giesens? They are out of control, always have been. That's why Father broke with them years ago."

I stare at her, not knowing where to begin. She's turned me into a speechless ten-year-old.

Julia unpins her hat and lays it on the bed. Then she strips off her gloves and jumps up to study her face in the mirror. "The train is a disaster for one's skin," she says. "Don't you agree?" She takes out a pretty gold compact and powders her nose. "Now tell me everything that happened. It's been in the papers that children died there." She turns around expectantly.

"Another time, Julia." A huge weariness sweeps over me. "Ask Miss Latigue."

"Well, you'll be glad to hear you're coming home with me."

Home. Not the Boston Home. Just home. How happy those words would have made me in June.

"Dr. Pynchon has been informed in no uncertain terms that what she did was completely unacceptable. Your things are being shipped to New York at her expense," Julia says. "That woman betrayed our trust and hired you out as a freak in a sideshow run by the New England Council." She shudders. "Those awful carnival people you were forced to rub shoulders with."

How dare she?

"My best friend is a carny," I begin, but she rides over me as always.

I stop listening. She'll never know what I accomplished this summer. She'll never know me.

But her next words drag me back to the conversation. "Father gave me a camera to use in Europe this summer," she says. "We've spent the past few days in the darkroom. Father thinks I can be quite a good photographer with more training. So, guess what? He's sending me to the Art Students League to study photography in the fall. Whatever happened to your little Brownie?"

I shrug and fight back tears.

"Now let's talk about us. We'll spend a couple of days in Boston," she says, "enjoying ourselves and"—she looks critically at my clothes—"shopping." She takes my hand and bows her head. "I'm sorry I broke my promise to come on your birthday," she says.

"Father asked me to do something for him, and I couldn't say no. I'll make it up to you when we get to New York. Just tell me how."

Father asked me…I couldn't say no. Does she ever think for herself?

I explain my plan to return to Boston as a ward assistant living with the Friedlanders until I enter nursing school. She looks relieved. "You'll need Father's permission and money for expenses. I'll help you get both."

Later, as we're getting ready for dinner in the hotel restaurant, I ask her the question that has tortured me all summer. "Dr. Pynchon showed me a letter with your signature on it, permitting me to go to the Unfit Family show. Did she forge your name?"

"No, I signed it, but I can explain," Julia says, tears running down her face. "Dr. Pynchon wrote to Father about 'a five-week sterilization-education project,' and because we were going to Europe, it sounded perfect. You'd be away from the Home and learning something useful. Father told me to give permission. I apologize for not standing up to him and asking more questions."

Her tears make me feel better. I don't mention that without the Unfit Family show I would not have met Dorchy, the best thing that ever happened to me.

The restaurant food tastes rich and unfamiliar; I nibble at it. Julia goes on and on about her trip to Europe with Father. She's afraid to be silent for one second in case I tell her about my horrible summer. She doesn't really want to know.

"Julia, stop." I interrupt her description of Father's lecture on sterilization in Paris at the European Academy of Science and Society. "You have to think for yourself now."

Julia snorts, or maybe it's a choked-back sob. She looks very pale. I stop, wondering if I've gone too far.

She folds her linen napkin, pressing on the creases. "But Father needs me. You know that."

"You say you're afraid of the ocean," I say. "But you liked it once. I saw the photographs Mother took when you were little. You can like it again. And you can have your own ideas, not Father's."

She leans forward. "I never envied you as much as that day you rode a wave," she says. "But that was the day you got polio." She sits back. "I never envied you after that."

"Not even now?"

She waves away the dessert menu, telling the waiter, "*Mousse au chocolat* for two, please."

Then she looks at me. "You seem very sure of yourself. I think you'll do as well in life as your condition allows. Father and I truly hope so."

As well in life as your condition allows. I can almost hear Dr. Friedlander laughing about this halfhearted compliment. I wish Julia had seen me dancing on one leg before my treatment had even begun. Or climbing the lighthouse ladder. Lighting the lamp. But it's too late—she will not, cannot change.

"I do need new clothes," I tell her, spooning into my chocolate mousse. "You'll be a big help with that."

* * *

Father looks up from his newspaper when we walk into his study two days later. I go straight to his desk with the brass inlays and say, "Hello, Father."

Julia hangs back. This is my moment.

He sucks in a ragged breath and struggles to stand up, the newspaper clutched in his hand. I read: *Eugenics Group Accused of Mass Murder on Island; Bodies Uncovered in Shallow Graves; Maine Attorney General Promises "Swift Justice."*

"Rowan." His voice is a croak. His pale face is deeply lined and his hair entirely gray, but he still has the same piercing blue eyes. "I had no idea about this Loup Island business. I hope you believe me."

"You broke with them in 1917." It's not a question.

He lays the newspaper down and steps from behind the desk. "Yes, I did. I thought they were horribly misguided. I honestly believed they had dropped the nonsensical idea when the war started. To my shame, I was wrong." His voice fades.

Julia's skirt rustles behind me as she takes a step forward, but he shakes his head and raises his hand. "I want Rowan to know everything." He smiles at me. "Your sister warned me about them when she heard rumors last spring. I refused to listen."

"Oh, Father," Julia wails. "It's not your fault."

"Julia," I say, "let me talk to him alone." The door clicks behind her.

The house, which I once longed to see again, is affecting me—odors of new plaster, old leather, and Father's pipe tobacco. Mother's portrait, still beautiful. Through the tall, screened windows come familiar sounds of traffic from the street, and in the lulls, even more familiar birdsong from Gramercy Park.

I sit down on a cracked leather hassock and smooth my new pleated skirt over my knees. After a few seconds, Father lowers himself back down in his chair.

"I'm going to live in Boston to study and work at Boston Children's Hospital."

He nods. Then, in a voice as cold and bleak as November rain, he says, "I have reviewed the chronology of your illness. I admit that when you were first diagnosed with polio, the war provided an easy escape for me. An escape I embraced without looking back. I did not, could not accept a cripple for a daughter. For that I am sorry."

I frown as a vise tightens around my heart. "I needed you here, Father."

He goes on as if I hadn't spoken. "I was horrified that despite my preventive measures you were infected with polio. Quite unfairly, I blamed your illness on an inherited weakness." His voice cracks. The first sign of emotion. "But I left Julia in charge, knowing she would carry out my wishes. I see now that was cowardly."

That was cowardly? No, you were *cowardly.* "What were your 'wishes,' Father? To shut me away forever in that Boston Home with other people labeled 'cripples'? To hire me out to the Unfit Family show where I almost burned to death? To have me almost killed on Loup Island?"

"No," he roars back. "Never! Julia found the Boston Home when I was in France. She said it had a good reputation. I had heard of Dr. Pynchon so I agreed." He draws a deep breath and shakes his head. "But I cannot blame Julia. It was all done in my name."

"Well, I blame you both," I say coldly. "She, on your behalf, sent me to two hells—one in Massachusetts and one in Maine."

He looks down, avoiding my eyes. "She reported on your progress. I authorized an operation."

"It was successful." *Stay firm,* I tell myself, *don't soften your heart because he looks so broken and unhappy.* "You and Julia did that one thing right. Well, that and one other. You told Dr. Pynchon that I was not to be sterilized. She wanted me to agree to it, but I refused. So your genes will survive in another generation. When the time comes."

He lowers his head into his hands. "In some cases, sterilization is the answer." His voice becomes a sob. "But not for you. Never for you." He wipes his eyes with a handkerchief. "I'm sorry, Rowan." I'm not sure whether he's apologizing for crying or for what happened to me, or both.

This is exactly what I wanted. To tell Father what he didn't know and force him to learn the truth about me and my five years away. Part of me wants to embrace him, feel his strong arms, accept his apology, and come home to live. *Study in New York*, the voice says. *Be a Collier again.*

I force myself to go on. "I wanted to see you, Father," I say, opening the leather briefcase Julia bought for me, "for your approval on this." I hand him the letter from Dr. Friedlander offering to be my guardian in Boston while I work in the polio ward as an assistant and later enter nursing school.

Father reads it and looks at me. His eyes are dry; he is back to business. "And this is what you want? You have discussed these… opportunities in Boston with the doctor?"

"I have. And I plan to earn my tuition, Father, but for a few months I will need an allowance."

He takes out a notebook. "I'll send Dr. Friedlander a telegram with my approval. And I'll make arrangements with the bank in Boston for your allowance."

Free of the vise, my heart soars. I see myself flying down the marble steps and into my new life.

"Wait. I want you to have this." Father walks over to Mother's framed photograph of bird tracks in the sand and lifts it down. "It will fit in your briefcase," he says. "Please."

I open the briefcase.

"And this," he says, handing me Mother's camera. "I kept it for you."

My throat closes and tears sting my eyes, but I manage to say, "Thank you, Father."

Last of all he hands me a roll of banknotes. I thank him again and walk out. Across the hall and down the stairs. No good-bye. Out the front door and away from the house forever.

The hot, dusty afternoon clings to me like sweat. I breathe deeply the smells of coal smoke and cooking, exhaust fumes from automobiles and trucks and buses—and over all the others, the sour smell from the brewery on the East River.

I swing along on my crutch, holding my briefcase, feeling so light and strong that I could run all the way to Boston. Or at least to Pennsylvania Station where my luggage is waiting. But I need to do something first.

On the Staten Island Ferry I stand by the rail, enjoying the sea breeze on my face, the taste of salt on my tongue. Halfway across New York Harbor, I open the briefcase and pull out narrow strips of paper. They flutter in my clenched hand.

Last night in Boston, I wrote a name on each strip. Before I started, I wasn't sure it made sense. But as soon as I wrote "Ratty," my heart began to beat faster. I wrote "Snout" and "Elsa," and "LollyandDolly" as one name. We don't know what happened to them, but I want to honor them and they belong together. I wrote the names of the four boys Tom brought to the island.

The final name was the hardest to write: "Wave Rider."

I lean over the railing. The churning green water reflects the afternoon sun.

I open my hand. As the wind catches the names, I whisper, "I'll remember you."

Wave Rider joins the others, fluttering, spiraling, and drifting down to the water's surface. The tide will pull them out into the Atlantic and, after that, to all the waters of the world.

EPILOGUE

Boston Children's Hospital
Friday, December 1, 1922

As I leave the children's polio ward after my shift, Head Nurse hands me a letter—pale-blue linen stock, brown ink, Julia's handwriting.

November 28, 1922

Dear Rowan,
I thought you'd be interested in the latest developments in the case against Cicely Van Giesen, Dr. Ritter, and the others. All charges have been dropped for lack of evidence. The prosecutor feels the explanation offered by the defendants clears them all. The flu was brought to camp by one unfortunate orphan who infected others. The affected orphans were removed to the medical tent for quarantine, and those who died were buried on the island. Doctors at the camp responded by inoculating each new batch of campers with an experimental

vaccine. Some campers reacted negatively and some of those died. However, many others were spared the disease. The tragedy could not have been avoided, case closed.

However, thanks to Miss Latigue, the camp run by the New England Betterment Council will no longer be held on Loup Island.

Your loving sister,
Julia

P.S. Just as I was getting ready to mail this, the International Journal of Betterment arrived and I leafed through it. Lo and behold, in the "News" section I saw this: "American Researchers Join Faculty: Professor Vera Van Giesen and Hiram Jellicoe, MD, have joined the medical faculty at the University of Dusseldorf in Germany. Their particular research interest is diseases in twins."

AUTHOR'S NOTE

In 1916, when she was four years old, one of my relatives contracted polio in an epidemic that swept the northeastern United States. While most of her family was supportive and caring, her father never saw her in the same way after her illness. Years later she told me that on her tenth birthday her father said to her, "I never wanted a crippled daughter."

At one point in her young life, my relative was wheelchair-bound. By the time she was a teenager, she could walk unassisted, though with a slight limp. She credited her transformation to the Boston doctor who operated on her leg and provided years of further treatment at Boston Children's Hospital. The fictional Dr. Friedlander in *Of Better Blood* is modeled on the forward-thinking doctors who revolutionized treatment of polio victims after the 1916 polio epidemic.

Eugenics was a popular pseudoscience in the United States from the early 1900s to the late 1930s. The double aim of eugenics was (1) to keep Americans with a "strong" heredity (family background) having children, and (2) to prevent those with a "weak" heredity from having children. (The definitions of "strong" and "weak" were defined by the people who naturally counted themselves among the "strong.")

The popular method of preventing reproduction among the unfit was to sterilize men and women. This made it impossible for them to have children. A majority of states passed laws stating that people in prisons and mental hospitals (among others) could be forced to undergo sterilization. This shocking violation of human rights resulted in sixty-five thousand people in thirty-three states suffering compulsory sterilization between 1897 and the 1970s.

In *Of Better Blood,* Rowan is called a "cripple," a category of people who, in the 1920s, were believed to be happiest warehoused among their own kind. One of the boys at the Loup Island camp is labeled "incorrigible." Hard as it is to believe, that fuzzy category was grounds for compulsory sterilization under the laws of some states in the 1920s, laws that remained on the books for decades.

While the Unfit Family show and the New England Betterment Council are fiction, "Fitter Families" exhibits and contests were real. They were a popular feature at state fairs starting in 1920 and had their origins in "Better Babies" contests at fairs in the early 1900s. The Fitter Families contests were sponsored by the American Eugenics Society as part of an education program promoting the reproduction of the "fit," and the contests' detailed questionnaires were used for eugenics research.

In "Eugenics Buildings" at the fairs, thousands of people voluntarily answered questions about their own and their family's physical and mental health, educational and musical achievements, and social involvement (from churchgoing to hobbies). Those found to be "Fitter Families" were awarded medals. In each state, a variety of groups supported the Fitter Family campaign—among them women's clubs and charitable and public health organizations.

Many white supporters of eugenics believed in their racial superiority and developed racist policies that led, directly or indirectly, to decades of systematic abuse of African Americans, including lynching, segregation, sterilization, medical experimentation, and laws banning interracial marriage.

Some African Americans also believed that it was possible and desirable to select positive genetic characteristics to improve their race. In the 1920s the National Association for the Advancement of Colored People held baby contests that have been described as working for "racial uplift." W. E. B. DuBois, one of the founders of the NAACP, wrote eloquently and influentially about racial equality. At the same time he publicized the idea that fit and unfit individuals existed in every race.

Eugenics research was funded by the Carnegie and Rockefeller foundations. Respected public figures—such as Margaret Sanger, an advocate for family planning; Alexander Graham Bell; Thomas Edison; and President Theodore Roosevelt—were advocates of eugenics and made it seem respectable. Respectability did not, however, make it science. Eugenics was subjective. It fit the prejudices of the elite and ignored the rights of those labeled "different." Behavior such as vagrancy was called hereditary, although it is not. Imprecise labels such as "feebleminded" or "incorrigible" were used as an excuse to sterilize people. Beliefs were substituted for facts and became public policy.

American eugenics principles and laws regarding compulsory sterilization were adopted in other countries. Adolf Hitler praised American eugenics in his book *Mein Kampf*. In the 1930s, Nazi Germany expanded on eugenics ideas imported from the United States to carry out Hitler's aims for a master race. In Nazi Germany, sterilization was only the beginning. Euthanasia (the government-mandated killing of those labeled undesirable) was the Nazi regime's distortion and escalation of eugenics for political ends. The Holocaust was the final step in the Nazis' program to identify, imprison, and kill those "unworthy of life."

From the earliest days of eugenics in the United States, some people called for euthanasia as a way to eliminate the unfit permanently. The gist of their argument was this: why should the public pay to feed and care for the unfit when they could be eliminated? Some isolated examples of euthanasia were carried out by institutions and individuals in the name of eugenics. But in the United States, sterilization was overwhelmingly the more popular solution. In *Of Better Blood*, the experiment in euthanasia carried out on Loup Island on "unfit" teenage orphans is fiction.

By 1922, scientists had isolated the virus that caused the Spanish flu pandemic of 1918. But there was no flu vaccine. The 1918 flu mutated to a version I've called "blue," and the letter in the novel about "blue" is based on an actual letter from a doctor at Camp Devens, a military base in Massachusetts, describing the disease's dramatic progress through the camp in the fall of 1918. But neither "blue" nor any other variant of the Spanish flu was ever successfully transmitted to a human being by injection.

I wrote *Of Better Blood* to emphasize the danger of policies in which people are categorized, isolated, and eliminated for political ends.

In researching and writing my book *Teaching the Diary of Anne Frank*, I was horrified to learn what can happen when ordinary people turn a blind eye, tell themselves they have no choice, and allow evil to take root. Out of inertia or self-interest or fear, millions of ordinary people allowed the Holocaust to happen. Other ordinary people showed extraordinary courage in resisting that evil and helping others.

We are the ordinary people of our time. It is up to us to be informed, to face facts, and to recognize and resist policies based on hatred and ignorance.

ACKNOWLEDGMENTS

Thanks to my family and friends—story lovers all—you are my blue water and safe harbor.

Thanks, Kate McKean, agent extraordinaire, for seeing the promise in this novel, nurturing it brilliantly, and finding it a home.

Thanks to Wendy McClure, my awesome, sure-handed editor at Albert Whitman for guiding this book to new heights and to the Albert Whitman team, Kristin Zelazko, Andrea Hall, Diane Dannenfeldt, Jordan Kost, and Kyle Letendre, for bringing it to life.

Thanks to my amazing critique group, Mary Bargteil, Jon Coile, Wendy Sand Eckel, Denny Kleppick, Terese Schlachter, Greg Gadson, Vicki Meade, and Joe Nold for never letting me settle for an imprecise word or image and doing it with humor turned up to 11. Thanks to the other wonderful writers in my life: Ben Moger Williams, Patricia Moger, Sid Reischer, Toby Ball, Mariya Hutto, Ed and Teri Sparks, Kirby Posey, Marilyn Recknor, Esther Geil, Becky Shiles, Charles Ota Heller, Ren Klein, and Penny Henderson.

My writing students' dedication and talent are a continuing inspiration to me.

I am grateful to the Maryland State Arts Council for an Individual Artist Award in Fiction, and to Susan A. Cohen, whose beautiful personal essay, "Littoral Drifter," sparked my imagination at a crucial moment.

Finally, thanks to Ted Armour—husband, cat whisperer, lover of words—for believing in me.